"We both went through a lot, Darcy. Some people don't recover from things like that." Nora sighed. "I can't stand the thought of hurting you again . . . or me being hurt either for that matter. It took me a long time to get over what happened. In some ways I've never gotten over it."

"Neither have I." Darcy sat up straighter in the chair. "Let me ask you something. We're all grown up now and we're not kids anymore. Between the two of us, I'm sure we have a lot more life experiences than most people our age. Are you at all curious about what things could be like with us now?"

"Curious?" Nora said. "Oh, I'm curious about a lot of things."

"Like what?"

Nora shrugged, feeling shy all of a sudden.

"Tell me something you're curious about."

Forcing herself not to think too much before speaking, Nora decided to dive in. "For one thing," she said, "I'd like to know if kissing you can still make me feel like swooning."

Visit

Bella Books

at

BellaBooks.com

or call our toll-free number

1-800-729-4992

Shelter from the STORM

PEGGY J. HERRING

Bella
BOOKS
2006

Bella Books, Inc.
P.O. Box 10543
Tallahassee, FL 32302

Printed in the United States of America on acid-free paper
First Edition

Editor: Anna Chinappi
Cover designer: LA Callaghan

ISBN 1-59493-067-8

For Stormy

Acknowledgments

Thanks to Frankie J. Jones, always my first reader. I depend on your insight and attention to detail.

Thanks to Deborah H. Scantlin for her enthusiastic support. I'm glad we've found each other again.

A special thanks to Dr. Sean T. O'Mara, MD. You've always been eager and ready to answer my endless string of questions. I couldn't do it without you!

Also, I'd like to thank Laverne R. Bell for the love and laughter you've brought to my life. You're an inspiration and a joy.

About the Author

Peggy J. Herring lives on seven acres of mesquite in south Texas with her cockatiel, hermit crabs and two wooden cats. When she isn't writing, Peggy enjoys camping, fishing and traveling. She is a recipient of the Alice B Award and the author of *Once More With Feeing*, *Love's Harvest*, *Hot Check*, *A Moment's Indiscretion*, *Those Who Wait* and *To Have and to Hold* from Naiad Press; and *Calm Before the Storm*, *The Comfort of Strangers*, *Beyond All Reason*, *Distant Thunder*, *White Lace and Promises* and *Midnight Rain* for Bella Books. Peggy is currently working on a new romance titled *All That Glitters* to be released in 2007 by Bella Books. You can contact Peggy through Bella Books at www.Bellabooks.com, or directly at FishstickRancher@aol.com.

Chapter One

Nora Fleming heard the alarm go off again and punched the snooze button. *Just ten more minutes*, she thought as she rolled over and wadded up her pillow to stuff it under her head. As if those precious few extra winks just weren't meant to be, not even thirty seconds could have passed before she heard the telephone ringing. It startled her awake as she peeled one eyelid open to peek at the clock.

Even though the phone was disruptive, Nora didn't feel like answering it. After the third ring she heard her own voice on the answering machine in the living room say, "Hi. I can't pick up the phone right now. I'm out changing some things in my life. If I don't call you back, then you're probably one of them." A nanosecond later there was a beep just before she heard her brother's voice.

"Pick up. I know you're there," Greg said.

Nora reached for the phone and rolled over on her back.

"Good morning," she mumbled.

"It's four in the afternoon."

"It's still morning to me. I'm working a string of nights this week."

"And that message on your answering machine is *sooo* not funny," he said with a chuckle. "If Holly hears it, I'm sure it'll be on both phones at the house in no time."

She stretched and muffled a yawn. "I'll change it once Dr. Ortega hears it and leaves me a message," Nora said, referring to the calls she'd been getting from her ex lately. They had agreed to start seeing other people over a month ago, but Sally Ortega kept finding excuses to call or see Nora at work.

"I thought all of that was *finito*," Greg said.

"Yeah, so did I." Nora threw the covers off and sat up on the side of the bed. "So what's up?"

"Holly and I went to see Mom over the weekend like you suggested."

Nora rubbed her left eye and stretched again. She needed to get up now so she could take a good nap later that evening before leaving for work. "How is she?"

There was silence on the other end of the phone. After a moment, Nora heard a little alarm go off in her head when he didn't answer right away.

"Greg?"

More uneasy silence followed. In the back of Nora's mind she already knew what this call was about. She had been to see her mother a few weeks ago and didn't feel right about what she had seen while visiting the Fleming farm.

"Greg? Are you there?"

"Uh . . ."

"What's the matter? Is something wrong with Mom?"

"I . . . uh . . ."

She waited a moment then said, "You what?"

Just then the alarm clock on the nightstand buzzed, scaring the bejesus out of her. Nora dropped the phone and reached over to

2

turn it off. Picking up the phone again, she said, "Is Mom all right?"

"She's . . ." Greg started. Nora could hear the emotion in his baritone voice. "She's old, Nora."

"Old?" Nora repeated. "Of course she's old. She's been old for a while now."

"But I really noticed it this time. There were weevils in the flour and piss ants in the sugar bowl on the table. You know how Mom is about her kitchen and her house. I guess she just can't see that well anymore. There's no telling how long she's been stirring ants into her coffee every morning."

Nora took a deep breath and lay back down on her stack of pillows. The ants in the sugar bowl were new. She hadn't seen anything like that during her last visit.

"She's going to be seventy-five," Greg said. "That shouldn't be old these days. The closer I get to fifty, the younger sixty sounds, you know?"

Nora smiled. "Yes. I know."

"It hit me this time. I saw more things going on with her that I didn't like."

"A lot of it's the lupus. Medication controls most of her pain, but the disease itself takes a toll on the body."

"With what I saw this weekend, I think it's time, Nora. I don't like the thought of her living alone anymore. If she fell or something . . ." His voice trailed off, leaving that thought hanging in the air between them.

Nora closed her eyes and nodded. She had been aware this day would arrive at some point, and after her last visit, she knew it was closer than ever before. Nora had hoped, however, that they would have more time before having to take any action or make a decision.

"Okay," she said quietly.

"We can go down there together and you can see firsthand what—"

"I've been there already," she said. "I didn't like what I saw when I was there either. I'll give my two weeks' notice tonight and make arrangements to put some stuff in storage."

"It wasn't an easy thing to see," Greg said, "and this wasn't an easy call to make. Are you sure this is what you want to do?"

"She won't let a stranger come in and help her," Nora reminded him. "They have those types of services available where she's at, but I've heard her opinion of that kind of thing before. She's got a stubborn streak and won't let us get away with anything. It'll be tricky pulling this off."

"Mom still has a lot of spunk left. Seeing all those bugs in her kitchen sort of freaked me out. That's not her."

Nora heard her brother sniff. Sometimes the depth of his sensitivity and compassion surprised her, but it also made her love him even that much more.

"You should've seen Mom and Holly together," Greg said. "There was so much potential for Mom to be mortally embarrassed about the condition things were in, but Holly helped get rid of the old buggy food and they almost made a game of it. Even though the kitchen was spotless and had that fresh lemony smell I always remembered it having, there were some serious problems. They must've thrown out two whole garbage bags full of cereal boxes, flour and sugar. If it wasn't in a can, then out it went."

Nora was only half listening now. The other half of her was already visualizing packing things up and hauling some of it off. She looked around her bedroom to see what could go with her and what would either have to be sold, given away or put in storage. She was suddenly grateful not to be a collector of "stuff." Her needs had always been simple and she was surprisingly ready for a change, even though it would be a lot of work.

"Anyway," Greg said with a sigh, "are you sure this is what you want to do?"

"I'm sure," Nora said. "I've just been waiting for the right time to make a change and it looks like it's here. You know I can't just move in with her. She won't stand for that if she thinks I'm doing it because she's sick or can't take care of herself."

"Yeah, I know."

"We need to present this to her in a certain way," Nora said, "otherwise it's not gonna fly."

"Got any suggestions?"

"I'll drive down for a brief visit and tell her I have some issues I need to sort through. Let's try something like that. If she thinks I'm coming home because it's something I need, she'll go for that a little quicker."

"Issues," he repeated with a laugh. "Hey, even your issues have issues, kiddo."

Nora got out of bed and stretched again. "Gee, thanks."

"Use this Dr. Ortega breakup thing to your advantage. Tell her you've got girlfriend problems again."

"Excellent idea since it's true."

"You know," Greg said, "Mom's not an invalid. She gets around okay even though she has a few bad days here and there. You could probably work part time if you wanted to get out of the house some once you get settled in."

"Let's see how's she's doing first. Finding a few piss ants in the sugar bowl isn't the end of the world and it doesn't mean she can't take care of herself any longer. It might just mean she needs new glasses and an exterminator."

"If that's all it is—"

"It doesn't really matter if that's all it is," Nora said. "I'll eventually end up there on the farm anyway. I might as well make the move now while the time is right for me. This could work out to be the best thing for both of us right now. Sally keeps sending me mixed messages here. I need a change before I get sucked back up into all of that again."

"Well, I plan to do my part."

Nora smiled. "I'll make sure you do."

"I feel better already," Greg said. "It was awful seeing her that way. It was the first time I noticed my mother getting old. It made me sad." His voice broke again and a lump formed in Nora's throat.

"She could still outlive both of us," Nora reminded him. "I'll let you know how it goes when I see her again in a few days."

Nora knocked on the door of the head nurse's office. It surprised her a little that she didn't feel uneasy with the changes she was about to make. Nora reasoned that in a way she had been preparing herself for this new phase of her life for several months now. Over the years she had purposely kept things uncomplicated in several ways, one of which was resisting the urge to buy her own home. Each time she had thought about it, Nora reminded herself that at some point she would eventually have to sell it and move back home to care for her mother. She and Greg had decided a long time ago that bringing their mother to live with either one of them in the city would never be an option. Opal Fleming had been born and raised in Prescott, Texas and had lived on the Fleming Farm for nearly sixty years. She wanted to die there just like her husband had and taking that away from her was something neither of them wanted to do. That sense of family and respect of one's parents and elders had been instilled in Nora and Greg since they were born. Nora even saw a trace of that Fleming spirit in her niece Holly. It was a part of their heritage and what had set them apart from their peers when they were younger. Growing up, Nora and her brother liked spending time with their parents. Family came first and Nora was glad to do whatever had to be done in order to give her mother the best quality of life possible for as long as they had her.

"Nora," Silvie Garza said. "Good to see you! Come in. Have a seat."

Silvie had the best smelling office in the emergency department. Nora spotted one of those plug-in deodorizers in the corner and inhaled the fresh peach scent that drifted through the air.

"What can I do for you? Are you ready to give me your vacation schedule for the rest of the year?"

"No," Nora said. "Actually I'm here to give you my notice."

Silvie's eyes widened. "What? Are you serious?"

"I'm serious."

"Has something happened? I thought things were going well here. I'm not aware of any problems."

"It's personal."

"Is it the money? Did you get offered—"

"No," Nora said. "It's not about money. It's personal."

Silvie dropped her pen on the desk and sat back in her chair. "Does this have anything to do with Dr. Ortega?"

Nora tried to hide a crooked smile, but knew she wasn't very successful. "It's not quite that personal." As they sat across from each other it occurred to Nora that she might not get out of there without offering a good explanation. Apparently saying, "It's personal," wasn't enough.

"You're my best ER nurse," Silvie said. "I just want to make sure there's nothing I can say or do to keep you."

"It has nothing to do with the job. I love working here. It's my mother. She needs me now and I want to spend time with her."

Silvie's expression didn't change, but she nodded and picked up her pen again. "I remember you mentioning she has lupus."

"There's that and the fact none of us are getting any younger. Someone should be with her now. There's just me and my brother, and he's raising a teenager. It's just easier for me to be the one to make the move."

"I hate to lose you, but I understand."

Nora stood up to leave. "Is there a way to keep my departure sort of low key? I'd prefer to just leave with no fanfare."

"I understand. That can be arranged."

Nora was relieved that Silvie would do what she could to keep Nora's plans a secret for as long as possible. The less Dr. Ortega knew, the easier it would be for Nora to leave town without a scene.

Chapter Two

With the gas prices so high and time working against her, Nora found it easier to fly to San Antonio and rent a car for her visit to the Fleming Farm than driving there from Dallas. In addition to seeing her mother and using her nurse's eye to judge how she was doing, Nora also wanted to get an idea about how much of her furniture and personal items she would be able to bring with her when she moved.

Nora turned down the gravel road and looked in the rearview mirror. She could tell that it had been a while since it had rained— a cloud of dust followed her. She slowed down beside the mailbox and got her mother's mail. The cattle guard at the Fleming Farm entrance was one of the last things her father had installed before he died ten years ago. They had all spent too many years having to get out of vehicles during bad weather to open and close the gate. Having a cattle guard helped keep the cows in and the humans dry. It was a convenience Nora still appreciated ten years later.

Opal Fleming was out on the wraparound porch by the front door when Nora pulled up in the yard. Opal had steel-gray hair that she kept in a loose bun on top of her head. She wore a light blue floral print housedress that hit well past her knees. Her matching blue sneakers seemed so out of place on a seventy-four-year-old woman, but Nora thought they were cute on her. *Why shouldn't she be wearing comfortable shoes?* Nora thought. She remembered last summer when her niece Holly had talked her grandmother into trying on a pair of sneakers during a trip to the local Wal-Mart. They fit her perfectly, were outrageously comfortable and Opal had been wearing them ever since.

Nora got out of the car with her overnight bag. Her mother looked the same—still plump and a little stooped, but she appeared to be in excellent health and having a good day for someone with lupus. She was glad to see Nora and in return, Nora had been looking forward to spending a few days with her mother. There were things about the Fleming Farm that tugged at Nora's heart and other things that she had never really missed about leaving home. But overall, coming back here made Nora happy to have such a warm, safe place in her life. The farm would always be home to her.

"Just in time to help me clean out the henhouse," Opal called.

Nora laughed. Her mother knew how much she disliked that chore. As a child Nora had loved helping her mother tend to the chickens and collect the eggs, but the fun stopped when she got older and reached into a nest one day only to find a snake with a whole egg in its mouth. After that, the egg business became a new source of teenage nightmares. The same thing had happened to her brother once and introduced an intense dislike for snakes.

Opal Fleming had been gathering eggs daily from her chickens for over fifty years now and delivering them to customers in the surrounding area. At a dollar a dozen, she made weekly trips to her customers, all of whom she considered to be friends. Opal drove up to twenty miles to make the deliveries and she enjoyed every moment of it. Her friends received fresh eggs and in return, Opal got an opportunity to visit, drink coffee, sample pastries and exchange stories before heading back home. She often claimed her chickens—fondly referred to as "the girls"—were what kept her young. Her egg business had helped supplement the family's income over the years, but these days Opal didn't do it for the money. Her son Greg kept a nice amount in her checking account in addition to what she made with social security. Opal's egg business was a labor of love. She adored her chickens and as a result, they blessed her with a bucket full of eggs every day. And from those eggs came a social life that anyone would envy.

"Gimme a hug," Opal said, opening her arms.

Nora set her overnight bag down on the porch and gave her mother a long hug.

"I'm still cleaning up the eggs I gathered earlier. Come on into the kitchen with me."

Nora followed her mother into the house and set her bag by the sofa. Everything was exactly as she remembered it. The mantel over the fireplace held pictures of her, Greg and Holly that had been taken during special events throughout their lives. Everything was always in its place. Opal was meticulous in her housekeeping rituals. Nora had maintained most of those good habits over the years, but had been known to leave mail lying around and magazines here and there on occasion. When she moved in with her mother, Nora realized she'd have to be a bit neater than she was lately.

"Any new chicken baubles since I was here last?" Nora asked.

"Someone gave me another set of chicken salt and pepper shakers."

Over the years, friends, customers and relatives had given Opal everything chicken-ish that they could find. She had a chicken crossing sign in the yard, enough different hen and rooster salt and pepper shakers to supply a chain of restaurants, aprons, gloves, plates, cups, saucers, mugs, tumblers, whirly-gigs for the yard and chicken T-shirts for egg gathering. Opal used all of it and dusted her chicken knickknacks when they needed it. The Fleming farmhouse was more like a chicken trinket museum than anything else. Nora knew exactly where her aversion for "stuff collecting" had come from. All that dusting had never appealed to her.

"Your brother was just here over the weekend," Opal said. "My goodness what a delight that Holly is. She reminds me so much of you when you were that age."

"You mean because she's so smart?" Nora teased.

"That's only part of it."

Once they were in the kitchen, Nora saw a few fresh eggs lined up on a huge beach towel on the table. All the eggs there were speckled with chicken poop and had to be cleaned off before being sold. Nora rolled up her sleeves and washed her hands in the sink. Having a mother-daughter chat during an egg-cleaning session would bring back another nice set of memories for her.

They sat down across the table from each other. Nora reached for an empty egg carton and tore a paper towel off the roll on the table. She dunked part of the paper towel in a bowl of water and selected her first egg.

"Is that a new car?" Opal asked.

"It's a rental I got in San Antonio. I flew down."

"I could've picked you up."

Nora smiled. "But wasn't this easier?"

"Maybe for me. Not for you."

"It's okay. I'm not complaining. It was a short flight and a nice drive out here. When was the last time you had any rain?"

"Just a sprinkle about three days ago," her mother said. "The hay out back needed it." Opal was faster at cleaning the eggs, but Nora was getting the hang of it again. The kitchen was cool with the open windows and the back door causing a nice cross breeze.

"Once we finish up here," Opal said, "I want to take a drive out to the creek to see how it's doing."

Nora nodded. "I thought you haven't had much rain."

"They've had some real frog-drowners just north of here. Sometimes that's all it takes to fill up the creek. Might have to move the cows to another pasture."

A ride to the creek will be fun, Nora thought. She had spent a good part of her childhood either swimming or fishing there when it had water in it. During droughts they could find arrowheads along the dry creek bed. It had been years since she had been that far back on the farm property.

"Did Greg tell you about my little weevil incident?"

Nora tried concentrating on the egg she was cleaning. "He mentioned it," she said nonchalantly.

"I wasn't sure he was gonna let me cook for him after that."

"Nah. He loves your cooking."

"He was sure different while Holly and I took care of things. She made him go watch TV while we went through everything."

"Greg eats out all the time," Nora said. "He has no idea what can go on in a real kitchen or pantry." She reached for the last egg on the table and didn't want her mother to know how freaked out Greg had been about the weevils and ants. "You could've very well bought all of those products with the critters in them already."

"I thought about that, too," Opal said. "I look things over a lot closer now before I put anything in my shopping cart these days."

She watched her mother slowly get up from the table and pick up the metal bucket on the kitchen counter by the sink. Opal came back to the table with a bucket full of eggs. Nora rolled her eyes.

"And here I thought we were about finished!"

"After this bucket we will be."

Just as they were about halfway finished cleaning the last of the fresh eggs, Opal turned on the radio perched on the window sill over the sink.

"Time for the Hometown News," Opal said. "One of my customers mentioned the donkey basketball game was coming to town, but she didn't know the date."

"Donkey basketball," Nora said. "They still have that? I thought PETA would've shut them down by now."

"None of those PETA people know anything about Prescott, Texas."

Nora nodded. "True."

"Ever wonder where all that PETA money goes? They collect a lot of it, but what do they spend it on?"

"I never thought about it."

"They get millions in the name of saving animals," Opal said. "They mail out some flyers and pay a few picketers. How many of those PETA people are vegetarians?" she asked. "It's all a bunch of hooey if you ask me."

Nora smiled. "Hooey" was about as close as her mother ever got to cussing. Nora was also proud of how in touch with the real world her mother seemed to be. The Hometown News wasn't the only source she depended on to keep her informed. Opal read the paper every morning and watched the news on TV in the evening. After dinner sometimes she would turn the TV off once the news was over and then turn on the police scanner to see what was going on in town.

"How long can you stay?" her mother asked.

"Just two days. I have to be back at work on Friday."

"Interested in going with me in the morning to deliver eggs?"

"Sure."

"You gotta get up early."

"I know."

Nora wanted to get the "moving back home" discussion out of the way while their only distraction was cleaning up chicken poop. She went to wash her hands again and then pulled off a fresh paper towel when she got back to the table. Nora also kept a close lookout for ants in the kitchen. It wouldn't take long for them to be out of control again.

"I was wondering, Mom," Nora started. "Would it be possible for me to move back home for a while?"

"Back here?"

"Yeah. Back here."

"Why on earth would you want to do that?"

"I have a few reasons," Nora stated simply.

"Is one of those reasons a woman?"

Nora tried to keep her smile in check, but it wasn't working. "Oh, you think you're so smart."

"Not really. I just know you. So what else would send you fleeing home?"

Nora shrugged. "All I do is work and sleep. I need to do some other things with my life while I still can. I need a break from what I'm doing now."

"Sounds like you just need a vacation."

"So is that a no? I can't come home for a while?"

"You and your brother both know you can always come home. I would love to have you here."

Nora let go of a huge sigh. "Thanks."

"When do you think you'll be moving back?"

"In about two weeks or so."

"That soon?"

Nora told her about putting most of her things in storage.

"There's room in the barn for it if you don't mind it getting a little mousey."

The mouse factor didn't appeal to Nora at all.

"That's okay. I'll find a local storage unit for my things."

"Sure," Opal said. "No mice ever get into a local storage unit."

Nora smiled. It was common knowledge that in the country, mice got into everything. They continued cleaning the last of the eggs while listening to the Hometown News. As the announcer named local people who had died recently, Nora couldn't help but be impressed by how different life in a small town would be. Lucky for her the Fleming Farm was on the outskirts of town where you could scratch your butt and not have a neighbor tell everyone about it. But it was still easy to fall under the microscope if you screwed up somewhere. Nora used to shudder at the thought of how easily it would have been for her and Darcy Tate to be the opening story on the Hometown News while they were still in high school. They had been very lucky that none of it had gone any further than the principal's office. Leaking stories like that was common in a small town, and what seemed like the end of the world in those days was finally something she could look back on without the pain and humiliation of a teenager.

"Here comes Hilda after some eggs," Opal said as she looked out the front kitchen window. "Can you put on some coffee for us?"

Nora glanced out the window to see an old truck coming up the driveway. Hilda Romero was a neighbor who had been stopping by for eggs once a week for well over thirty years. Opal got up and washed her hands while Nora tended to the coffee. It was nice being someplace where things were so predictable. Nora was looking forward to a slower pace and some low-key familiarity.

Chapter Three

"Am I interrupting anything?" Hilda asked.

Nora could hear them out on the porch as she reached for the can of coffee in the freezer. Her mother made the best coffee, always strong and flavorful, so Nora was a little nervous about fixing it for her.

"Not at all. Nora's here for a few days. Come on in."

"I didn't recognize the car."

They came into the kitchen just as the coffee brewed. It had been years since Nora had seen any of the Romero family, but her mother kept her posted on what the neighbors were up to. Nora gave the woman a hug and asked how many grandchildren she had now.

"Fifteen!" Hilda said proudly. "Opal's way behind me with the grandchildren!"

Hilda's husband was hard of hearing and refused to get checked for it, so Hilda tended to talk loud no matter where she was or what she was saying. Nora found it annoying, but figured she'd eventually get used to it when she moved back home.

"I made a poppy seed cake this morning," Opal said. "We can have some with our coffee."

Hilda took a seat at the far end of the table and away from the egg-cleaning area. "I saw a flyer at Junior Mart this morning when I stopped to get gas," Hilda said. "Old man Rucker died. Have they announced it on the Hometown News yet?"

"No!" Opal said. "Lordy. We can't be missing that. When did it happen?"

"Is that *the* old man Rucker?" Nora asked as she picked up another egg to clean.

"That's him," her mother confirmed.

"Wow," Nora mumbled. "He was older than dirt when I was a kid."

"He was older than dirt when *we* were kids," Hilda admitted with a laugh. "I wonder who's the oldest in the county now?"

"The Hometown News will probably tell us," Opal announced.

With a shake of her head, Hilda said, "Poor man outlived most of his children. I'd never want that. I hope the good Lord sees fit to take me first."

"Amen to that."

Nora poured three cups of coffee—two of the cups had chickens on them while the other was shaped like a chicken. Opal sliced the poppy seed cake that was still warm. Nora listened to their chatter and finished cleaning the eggs. When she had tended to the last one, she took the full egg cartons to the other refrigerator out in the sunroom where her mother kept all her outside potted plants in the winter. The refrigerator was full of egg cartons stacked just right so they would all fit. They were ready to be delivered the next day.

After putting the fresh eggs away and cleaning off the table while her mother and Hilda continued to talk, Nora excused herself and went out on the front porch to sit in the swing and sip the rest of her coffee. The porch was another one of her favorite places on the farm. She felt at peace there and had so many good memories of her parents sitting in the swing in the evening, while she and Greg sat on the front steps. There was always a breeze and plenty to talk about.

When Nora left home to go to college, the closeness she had shared with her family was one of the things she had missed the most about being away. Her new friends at school thought it was strange, but Nora didn't care. Her homesickness and attachment to her family were totally foreign to them. She had spent most of her young life feeling confident in who she was and what she wanted. Being out of sync with her peers wasn't anything new for her. In a way it was just one of many things that set her apart.

Nora woke up to voices on the porch. She barely remembered stretching out on the swing with every intention of just laying there and enjoying what was left of a quiet morning. The breeze had been perfect and the smell of honeysuckle at the side of the house had helped lull her to sleep.

"Well, there you are," Opal said. "We were wondering where you disappeared to."

Nora sat up, careful not to hit her coffee cup setting on the porch at her feet.

"Wow. I forgot how comfortable this swing is," Nora said. "Remind me to never sit here when I have things to do."

"I need to get back home and start thinking about dinner," Hilda said. "Nice seeing you again, Nora."

Hilda carried a carton of eggs to her truck. She got in and drove off, waving one last time as she sped away.

Dinner, Nora thought. *How long was I asleep?!* She glanced at her watch and saw that it was only eleven. "Oh, yeah," she said. "It's breakfast, dinner, and supper here. Not breakfast, lunch, and dinner like it is everywhere else in the world."

Opal sat down in the swing beside her.

"So you thought you'd slept all afternoon?" her mother asked with a chuckle.

"It was just a little brain fart, Mom. I'll catch on to the lingo again."

Giving her daughter's knee a pat, Opal said, "Ready to go check out the creek?"

"Sure. Let's go."

Nora climbed into her mother's 1968 Ford pickup and closed the door. She rolled down the window and rested her elbow there.

"Why don't you let us get you a new truck?" Nora asked.

"Don't need one."

"This old thing doesn't have AC. Does the heater even work?"

"The heater works, the defroster works, I've got new windshield wipers and tires, and it starts when I need for it to. That's all that matters to me."

"A new truck would have all of that, too," Nora reminded her. "Plus AC."

"You kids save your money. I've got what I need."

The truck started up right away and off they went around the back of the house and down a worn road that ran beside the fence to one of the pastures. The ride was bumpy and brought back another rush of warm memories for her. Nora had learned to drive in the old pickup. When the weather had been too bad for her and Greg to wait for the bus at the end of the driveway, the three of them would get in and their father would let one of them drive down to the gate to wait for the school bus. Nora remembered how exciting it was to wake up to the sound of rain on a school day. Even on rainy mornings when it was Greg's turn to drive, it was still a great reason to jump out of bed and throw some school clothes on.

As they bounced along the washed-out road, Nora was suddenly glad her mother still had the old pickup. It had character and was the perfect vehicle for her mother's vocation as the county egg lady during the winter, but in the summer there was a lot to be said for an air-conditioned vehicle.

They finally came to the back gate and Nora got out of the

19

truck and opened it. Once Opal drove the pickup through, Nora closed the gate and got back in the truck again.

"Looks like I need to move the cows down here," Opal said. "The grass is a little higher than I like it to be."

Opal drove slowly along the bumpy road until they reached a clearing near an old cypress tree. Nora saw the concrete picnic table right where it had always been. The table had a collection of branches and debris on top of it from an earlier flood.

"None of that's new," Opal said as she shut the truck off and opened her door. "The table had all that on it the last time I was here a few months ago."

Together they cleaned the table off, pitching the branches further up the bank and away from the creek. They brushed the leaves and twigs off the top of the table as best they could, then sat down and listened to the birds and the rushing water.

Leaning back on her elbows, Nora said, "It's beautiful out here."

"Your father loved this part of the farm."

Nora stood up and walked closer to the water. The creek was clear enough to see fish at the bottom. The water was deeper than she remembered it being as a kid.

"Are you up to helping me move the cows down here?" Opal asked.

"Today?"

"Yes, today. Right now, in fact."

Nora wasn't convinced the two of them could do it, but her mother seemed to be, so that was good enough for her. Most things that had to do with the larger animals were handled by Jack who lived next door. *But if you're coming back to live on a farm,* Nora reasoned with herself, *you better be willing to help out with farm chores.*

"Then let's do it," Nora said.

"Okay. In a minute. Let's enjoy this a little longer first. I forgot how nice it is down here."

Nora smiled and leaned back on her elbows again, feeling relieved they didn't have to jump up and move cows right away.

"It'll be good having you home again."

Nora smiled and filled her lungs with clean country air. "It'll be good to be home again."

Most of the cows were cooperative, but the bull seemed to have a mind of his own. Opal had been able to herd nearly all of them across the pasture with the truck and get them through the gate leading to the creek, but the bull wasn't having any part of it.

"Let's see if I can get around him," Opal said.

Nora climbed up into the bed of the pickup and waved her arms when they got close to the bull again.

"Come on, big fella," Nora heard her mother say. "We've got all your women down by the creek. Get on down there after 'em."

Opal honked the horn and the bull took his sweet time strolling toward the gate. Nora jumped out of the truck and locked the gate once he moseyed on through it. She could see that the cows were already down by the creek getting a drink.

"While we're out here," Opal said, "I need to check out a few more pastures. Your cousin Jack planted some corn in one of them."

"Does he still have your tractor?"

"Yep. He keeps it tuned up and running, so I let it stay at his place." Opal gave the dashboard a pat. "He does the same for my truck, too. All it costs me is a dozen eggs a week."

At home, Nora thought, *a dozen eggs would last me at least two months.*

"He's a good boy," Opal said. "We had a bad storm a while back and as soon as it was over, Jack came by to see how I was doing."

Jack Fleming was Nora's favorite cousin. He had inherited the adjoining two hundred acres from his parents and was the only member of the family to continue on in the farming business. All three of his siblings lived in the surrounding counties, but no one else had an interest in farming. Nora remembered her father's disappointment when her brother Greg never showed any interest in farming. As a teenager, they were more likely to find Nora out on a tractor than her brother.

"If Jack plants corn out here," Nora said as they bounced along through the pasture, "what's in it for you?"

"Depends on how much he plants," Opal said. "But he'll give me a nice cut of the profits."

They came to another gate and Nora got out to open it. Sticking her head out the truck window, Opal said, "Shouldn't be any cattle back here. You can leave it open."

Nora got back in the truck and was surprised at how much she was enjoying this little adventure with her mother. The terrain and landscape were foreign to her now. The property was the same—a six-hundred-acre spread, but it looked nothing like it had when she was a kid. There were pastures now where there had been nothing but crops before when her father worked the land.

"How often do you come out here?" Nora asked. This particular pasture was about ten acres and had more trees, wild mustang grape vines, scrub oaks and mesquite trees than anywhere else on the farm. Like the other pastures and fenced-in areas, it was so overgrown that Nora didn't recognize it. As a youngster, she and her brother knew every square inch of the farm, but this particular pasture didn't look like anything she remembered.

"Once a year or so," Opal said. They slowly drove along for a few more minutes and finally reached another gate. Nora got out to open it and startled a flock of wild turkeys by a bushy area. Her heart was pounding so hard that she wasn't sure who had been the most surprised—her or the turkeys. She could hear her mother snickering in the truck.

"That wasn't funny at all," Nora said when she got back in the pickup. They laughed all the way to the next fenced-off pasture.

❧

"Well, fiddle," Opal said a while later.

Nora looked around, but didn't see anything other than tall grass and brush along the fence line. The word "fiddle" was another cuss word to her mother, so Nora knew something was up.

"What's the matter?"

"That bad storm we had a few weeks ago damaged the windmill."

Nora spotted the old wooden windmill off to the right. A blade had broken off and it wasn't turning in the breeze.

Opal drove the truck closer so they could get a better look at it. "I can't move the cows back here after the corn harvest if the windmill isn't working," Opal said. "That's their only water source."

"Where's the creek from here?"

"It's fenced off over there. That back fence is the end of the property line. No creek access this way." Opal gave the old windmill a long look and made a little smacking sound with her lips. "Your father loved this windmill. He said it had the sweetest water in the county."

Nora smiled. "I remember Greg climbed on it once and bumped a hornet's nest. He squealed like a girl and scrambled down like he was on fire."

"Was that the time his face got so swollen he looked like a catcher's mitt?" Opal asked.

"That was it!" Nora confirmed.

"What was he doing up there anyway?" Opal asked as she turned the truck around.

"A neighbor's bull chased him up there," Nora said. "Pop had planted corn back here and you sent us out to pick some for supper. I had the corn in a sack and was heading back to the house when the bull came out of nowhere. He'd been hiding and feasting in the stalks where we couldn't see him. The bull headed straight for Greg and up the windmill ladder Greg went." Nora started chuckling again. "So when the hornets got after him he had to make a quick decision—get chased some more by a bull, or stick it out up there with the hornets."

They were both laughing now.

"If I remember correctly," Opal said, "the thing that saved him was the hornets chasing him *and* the bull."

"That's right," Nora said. "Both Greg and the bull headed back home in opposite directions. At record-breaking speeds." She got out of the truck to lock the gate and could still hear her mother chuckling. When Nora got in the truck again, she said, "Remember what Pop said when we got back to the house?"

"No. I was busy tending to supper and taking care of Greg."

"Pop said, 'Well, did you get that bull outta my corn?!'" There was another round of chuckles. "By then one of Greg's eyes had swollen shut. Once Pop saw that, he felt bad."

"You kids sure had your share of mishaps."

Nora shrugged. "All kids do. No matter where they live."

"I have to admit," Opal said with a chuckle, "I've never had this much fun checking the place out before. Thanks for riding along with me."

Nora smiled. "I wouldn't have missed this for anything."

Chapter Four

It seemed to get darker a lot earlier in the country, but Nora attributed that to the absence of all those city lights. Darkness took on a whole new meaning when it was accompanied by a canopy of stars. The evenings were cooler too.

Opal made pork chops, sliced tomatoes and fresh green beans from the garden for supper. She had brewed a pot of tea earlier in the day and it was ice cold when Nora took the pitcher with brown chickens painted on it out of the refrigerator.

"Do you need help moving?" Opal asked once they sat down to eat.

"Greg and Holly will help me. I have a few things to get rid of and I need to find a place to store some of my stuff. Maybe we can look at storage facilities tomorrow after we're finished delivering eggs."

"There's still the barn out back."

Nora smiled and cut into her pork chop. "You mean Opal's mice-r-us storage? No thanks."

Her mother's laughter made Nora laugh too. After supper they watched the early news and then went out on the front porch to relax in the swing. The police scanner was sitting on the windowsill in the living room and the porch swing was right next to the window. They could hear the scanner each time the dispatcher or someone in a patrol car said something. The scanner didn't come on often enough for Nora to get used to hearing it, so each time a name or license plate number crackled out into the evening air it made her jump.

"Don't forget about the bathroom light," Opal said. "We had a fitful time sleeping when Greg was here."

Nora leaned her head back and closed her eyes to listen to the crickets in the yard. "Which one of them couldn't remember to keep the light off?" she asked.

"Your brother."

Nora chuckled. "I knew it."

The one and only bathroom was on the north side of the house facing the chicken coop near one of the barns. Each time the bathroom light was switched on after dark, the young rooster thought he was seeing the crack of dawn and would begin to crow. It usually took him about an hour to settle down again, but in the meantime, no one got any sleep while he continued to announce the false arrival of a new day.

"Heavy curtains on the window don't work?" Nora suggested.

"Nope. Probably nothing short of boarding it up would work."

"Gets too hot in the summer for that."

The easy laughter she shared with her mother was no surprise to Nora. Growing up on the Fleming Farm had been a blessing for her and her brother in many ways. It wasn't until they moved away and embraced life in the big city that either of them realized it though, but Nora and Greg had never ventured very far from their roots.

Opal yawned and put her hands on her knees. "I'm ready to turn in. Let's put some clean sheets on your bed."

They went inside and Nora followed her mother down a hall-way toward the bedrooms, stopping at the linen closet along the way. It was nowhere near time for Nora to be sleepy yet. As if reading her mind, Opal said, "Holly left a small TV here last weekend. You can put it in your room if you like."

"I should've brought something to read. That usually makes me sleepy."

They changed the linens on the bed and Opal gave her daughter a hug.

"Don't forget about the bathroom light if you get up in the middle of the night," Opal reminded her again.

"I won't. Have you ever thought of maybe blindfolding him after dark?"

"My thoughts have been more along the line of throwing him in a pressure cooker after dark, but you can't cook your friends and my chickens are my friends."

Nora nodded. "That's good advice, I think. Don't eat your friends."

"I'll see you in the morning. You know where I'll be if you need anything . . . or . . . on second thought, you know where everything is. Just get it yourself."

It was five in the morning the first time Nora heard the rooster crow. The next time she heard him, it was daylight. She got out of bed and met her mother in the hallway. Opal was already dressed for the day. No telling how long she had been up already.

"You sure you want to go with me on my egg run this morning?"

"Of course I'm sure," Nora said, stifling a yawn as she shuffled down the hallway to the bathroom. "Wouldn't miss it."

More awake after a shower, Nora could smell bacon frying on her way to the kitchen. Never much of a breakfast eater, she was nevertheless surprised at how her stomach grumbled.

"If I don't eat something first thing in the morning," Opal said, "my medicine makes me sick."

Nora poured herself some coffee in a red rooster mug and sat down at the table. Just before settling in to get comfortable, she asked her mother if she needed help with anything.

"Check the biscuits in the oven."

"Mmm. Biscuits!" Nora opened the oven for a peek and decided they needed a few more minutes to brown. She was a little disappointed to have missed watching her mother make them. Opal never used a recipe and just put things in a mixing bowl as if by habit instead of know-how. A pinch of this and a cup of that and before long Opal had the biscuits in a pan and popped them in the oven. Nora's father had liked biscuits for breakfast and cornbread for supper. Nora hadn't realized until then that the "cornbread for supper" ritual had disappeared. There hadn't been any cornbread on the table last night.

"Do you make biscuits every morning?" Nora asked.

"If I'm feeling good I do."

"Ah. Okay." Nora checked the biscuits again and took them out of the oven.

"How'd you sleep?" Opal asked. She brought two plates with four strips of bacon on each, then set a bowl of scrambled eggs on the table.

"I slept great. I heard the rooster once when it was still dark."

"That's because I turned the bathroom light on," Opal said as she sat down at the table. "Sometimes I just like messing with him."

Nora shook her head and smiled. *Moving home might be more fun than I thought,* she mused.

Nora helped her mother load all the egg cartons into the three huge ice chests in the back of the truck. Opal had sheets of ice on the bottom of each ice chest to keep the eggs cool during transport.

"Are we ready?" Nora asked as she raised the tailgate on the pickup.

"I just need to get a fresh bonnet and lock the doors."

The bonnet was part of Opal's "Egg Lady" costume. She never left home without a fancy one. During an ordinary day she had her favorite "piddling around" bonnets that she wore for tending to her garden, gathering eggs or feeding the barnyard animals. Once both women were in the truck, Opal switched on the radio to listen to the Hometown News program.

"Where's our first stop?" Nora asked.

"Your cousin Jack's place down the road."

Jack Fleming hadn't changed any since Nora had seen him last at Christmas. He looked enough like her brother Greg for them to be twins, except Jack had a farmer's tan and bigger muscles.

"Good to see you, Nora," Jack said. His sandy hair was neatly trimmed. He wore his usual short-sleeved blue denim shirt, jeans, worn tan boots and a straw cowboy hat.

"I have some coffee if you ladies would like some," he said.

Nora smiled as she caught the faint scent of Old Spice in a breeze. Whenever she smelled that particular cologne on a patient it always reminded her of her cousin Jack. He'd worn it ever since he was a teenager.

"We just finished breakfast," Opal said.

"How long you staying, Nora?"

"Just a few days this trip."

"Why don't you two come over for supper this evenin'? I'll throw some steaks on the grill."

Nora caught the look her mother gave her—the "it's okay with me if it's okay with you" look. Nora nodded at him and said, "What a nice idea. We'd like that, right, Mom?"

"What time?" Opal asked as she handed him a carton of eggs.

"Six. It'll give me something to look forward to later after workin' in the field all day."

"We'll bring dessert."

They got back in the truck and waved. Opal slowly drove down

Jack's bumpy crushed limestone-base driveway, careful not to upset the delicate cargo in the ice chests.

"That boy gets lonely," Opal said. "He hasn't been the same since his wife left him."

"Are they divorced yet?"

"He won't give her a divorce. He keeps thinking she'll come back to him."

"It's not easy being a farmer's wife," Nora said, "but I don't need to tell you that."

"She knew he was a farmer when she married him."

"Any chance she'll go back to him?" Nora asked.

"Not likely. Nothing's changed there, and he's working harder than ever to keep his mind off things. He's a good boy. Once he gets over her he'll find someone else." Opal reached for the radio knob to turn up the Hometown News. "In the meantime, don't eat any of that poppy seed cake I made yesterday. We're taking the rest of it for dessert this evening."

By the time they had delivered the first ten cartons of eggs, they had been offered ten cups of coffee along with a various assortment of snacks and services. At Darla's Curl Up and Dye hair salon they were both offered a free haircut while eggs and money exchanged hands, and at the Lube Works in Scribner, another of Nora's cousins wanted to change the oil in his Aunt Opal's truck while they chatted with his wife. Nora let her mother handle all the free offers and enjoyed seeing her in action. It warmed Nora's heart to know so many people truly adored her mother not only for what she did, but for the nice person she was.

Back in the truck again, they waved and set off for their next stop. The Hometown News program was over, so there was no need for the radio to be on. Nora was just along for the ride and resisted the urge to reach over and assume control of the airwaves.

"How do you remember who all these customers are?" Nora asked after a while.

"Same way a paperboy knows which house to throw a paper to. It's a business. I've been doing it forever."

"Have you taken on any new customers?"

"Nope. I'd have to get more hens. Right now they lay just enough. Me and the girls got what we can handle."

Nora nodded. Depending on how things went when she moved in with her mother, Nora hoped to be able to help her enough so she could have more time to relax and take care of herself better.

"This next stop is one of my favorites," Opal said. "She makes the best apple cobbler and always has some ready for me. It's a nice bathroom break, too."

It was after two when they finally returned home. Nora was tired and couldn't imagine why her mother wasn't exhausted. The constant in-and-out of the truck and the handshaking, hugging and small talk was a bit overwhelming, but Opal seemed to thrive on it.

"I'll bring in the empty egg cartons and the ice chests," Nora said.

"Thank you, dear. If you take care of that, then I can go spend time with the girls."

Nora watched her mother climb the front steps to the porch. When she came out again, Opal had changed her clothes and her bonnet.

"Drive the truck around back and dump the ice in the garden."

After that I'm taking a nap, Nora thought as she got in the pickup. *Being the Egg Lady's helper wore me out today!*

Chapter Five

On their way over to Nora's cousin's house later that day, Nora held the plate with the rest of the poppy seed cake on it. As they were getting ready to leave earlier, Opal had instructed her to put the cake on a platter or something that had chickens on it.

"That way he'll know it's mine and I'll get it back."

Nora remembered looking in the cupboard and thinking, *Is there anything in this kitchen that* doesn't *have a chicken on it?!*

"Jack's actually a good cook," Opal said as they turned into his driveway. Jack's house was identical to Opal's. The Fleming family had built them both at the same time in the late Forties.

"He could sure stand to spend a few bucks on getting this driveway fixed," Opal said. She slowed down to dodge the immediate effect of several potholes. "You could shake your liver out if you weren't paying attention."

"Interesting visual there, Mom," Nora said. She held onto the poppy seed cake as if her life depended on it.

Jack was there to greet them and to help his Aunt Opal out of the truck. He appeared to be a bit more relaxed and casual than he had been earlier in the day—at least he had less starch in his clothes now. He wore his usual Wrangler jeans and tan boots, but his baby blue T-shirt and Fleming Feed and Seed cap made him seem less like a farmer and more like the rest of the good-old-boys in the area.

"The fire's just about ready to throw the steaks on," Jack said. "Come in. I'm so glad you're both here."

They went inside and Nora was immediately struck by the simple arrangement of antique furniture and the overall neatness of the living room. It was strange seeing what looked like her mother's home, only without all the clutter of chicken trinkets.

He offered them something to drink and they followed him into the kitchen—it finally looked like where an average male lived. Dishes were piled in the sink and an assortment of fresh vegetables from the garden were lined up on the counter.

"How long you been saving these?" Opal asked as she took dirty dishes out of the sink and ran some hot water.

"Oh, those," Jack said under his breath.

Opal looked at Nora with a glint of fondness in her expression. "Sometimes he tries to hide them from me out on the back porch."

Jack shook his head as he filled two tumblers with ice. His flushed face made him seem even younger.

"Maybe he likes them that way, Mom," Nora suggested. She couldn't imagine going into someone else's kitchen and doing their dirty dishes. She didn't like doing her *own* dishes much less someone else's. After a moment, Nora noticed them both looking at her.

"Why would anyone like having dirty dishes?" Opal asked.

Nora shrugged. "Perhaps it gives him an excuse to invite you over."

Once again Nora noticed them both looking at her. Then Jack tossed his head back and laughed.

"Oh, you're on to me now, Nora," he said. "I have family over all the time so I can get my kitchen cleaned." He popped the top

33

on two soft drink cans and poured the contents into the tumblers. "Actually," he said, "those dishes are the ones I'd forgotten about on the back porch. They're probably still warm from the sun. No telling how long they've been out there."

"See?" Opal said to Nora. "I told you."

He handed them their drinks. "I washed, dried and put away the other dishes before you got here. I brought those in a while ago thinking I could get them taken care of before you arrived." Jack shook his head again. "Now I'll never hear the end of it."

"We'll let 'em soak for a bit," Opal said. "What are we having tonight?"

"T-bones, corn on the cob and fresh grilled veggie shish-ka-bobs." Jack pulled out a chair for Opal at the huge kitchen table. All three of them sat down with their drinks. "I learned how to make those shish-ka-bob things one evening when I lost the remote to the TV and was too tired to get up and change the channel. It was on some cooking show."

"Did you ever find the remote?" Nora asked.

Jack grinned. "Eventually. I was sitting on it."

Opal and Jack continued on with talk about the local economy and the ongoing success of the family's feed and seed business which was owned by one of Nora and Jack's uncles. Jack spoke of hoping to pay off his seed bill with the watermelon crop he had in the field.

"Should be some left over to put in the bank," he said. "If the corn crop in the back makes it, that'll be enough to more than break even on it. If we don't get the rain we need, I'll just collect the insurance and turn the cows out and let them have it."

Nora cut into her steak and was happy to see how tender it was. She hadn't had a steak that good in years and told him so. It had been a long time since she had sat down to a meal where the topic of conversation was corn prices and weather trends. Looking over at her mother, Nora watched as Opal stood her corn cob on end and easily sliced the kernels right off.

"This is the only way corn agrees with my dentures," Opal explained as she spread the neat pile of kernels around on her plate. "And these veggie shish-ka-bobs are delicious. You should lose that remote more often."

After supper Jack got out a box of pictures and wanted Opal to identify some of the relatives in the photos and write the information on the back of each one.

"You two tend to that while I do the dishes," Nora said. She stood up and collected their plates.

"Leave those," Jack said, indicating the plates and silverware she was stacking up. "I'll do them later."

"Or I'll do them the next time he invites me over for supper," Opal said, teasing him and they all laughed.

Nora continued what she was doing while her mother and cousin pored over the box of pictures. Watching her mother squint at each photo then take her glasses off and then put them back on again to try and see better prompted her to make a mental note to take her in for an eye exam soon. If she couldn't see relatives in a photo, then she probably wouldn't have been able to see ants in a sugar bowl either. Nora was beginning to see how her brother's assessment of their mother's physical and mental state could have been influenced by the condition her kitchen had been in. *Mom's far from feeble*, Nora thought, *but the lupus deserves our respect in its efforts to zap her energy on any given day. Me moving back home is a good idea now. It's the right time to do it.*

As she gathered all the silverware from their meal and what was already in the sink soaking, Nora just happened to see an ashtray by a row of canisters on the counter. She leaned closer to get a better look and saw a joint in the ashtray. She raised an eyebrow and looked back over her shoulder at Jack. *Hmm*, she thought. *He's always seemed so law-abiding and—boring. He never wanted to smoke pot when the rest of us were experimenting with it! A late bloomer? Or is this how he copes with his wife leaving him?*

By the time she got the dishes washed, dried and put away as best she could, Nora was ready to leave, but joined them at the table instead. Jack and Opal were only halfway through the pictures in the old boot box. Nora sat down and picked up a small stack of pictures they had already gone through. She recognized a young Felix Fleming standing behind a plow and a mule. It was her grandfather. Nora smiled as a string of fond memories of him came back to her. He loved his grandchildren and always had time to tell them stories and to take them down to the local grocery store for candy.

"Remember grandpa's old car, Jack?" Nora asked.

"I sure do."

"All of you kids loved that car," Opal said.

"I was just thinking about him always taking us to Chapa's in that car," Jack said. He set a few more pictures down in another stack. "In the backseat, parts of the floorboard were rusted out and we could see the road through the holes in it."

Nora set the photo down and picked up another one of her grandfather throwing feed to the chickens.

"I remember how Chapa's store used to smell," Nora said. "The wooden floors and the ripe fruit. We each got our own bag full of penny candy."

"Whatever happened to that old car?" Jack asked.

"Used to be down by the creek," Opal said. "Brush and no telling what else has covered it up by now."

Nora sifted through the photographs laid out on the table and occasionally turned one over to read what her mother had written on the back.

"Don't forget we brought poppy seed cake for dessert," Opal said.

"That means more dirty dishes," Nora reminded them.

"I'll be doin' my own dishes from now on," Jack said. He got up from the table to get three small plates and three clean forks. "I won't be making *that* mistake again."

Chapter Six

Darcy Tate made sure her father had taken all of his medication before he settled down for the evening to watch TV in his wheelchair. She had a little accounting paperwork to do on the computer later, but promised herself she would do it after getting him in bed for the night.

"See if that Matlock fella is on yet," Skip Tate said.

Darcy clicked to the channel that played his favorite TV shows and hoped there was something showing that would keep him occupied for awhile. Seeing Andy Griffith in Matlock's trademark white suit made Darcy let go with a sigh of relief. Now she would be able to get some work done as long as her father was engrossed in the program.

Darcy had been too busy that week to post the sales receipts or even go to the bank to deposit the stack of checks she had collected from customers. She had been a part of her father's windmill repair business for only three months and still didn't have a handle on all the intricacies of the never-ending paperwork. If she couldn't get the books set up on the computer the way she wanted to, then her next step would be to hire an accountant. Darcy knew her father wouldn't be happy with that suggestion, so she was trying her best to do as much as she could on her own without him knowing about it. He'd done things the same way for over forty-five years, so changing his mind on anything to do with the business wouldn't be easy. It wasn't enough that she had to spend so much time brushing up on how to repair windmills, now she had to sort through years of her father's bad bookkeeping habits. If the business were to ever be audited, there would be some serious explaining to do. Hopefully, Darcy would be able to get things recorded in a more simple and user-friendly way.

Having spent the last twenty-two years of her life in the Army, Darcy was still taking her time getting used to retirement. As was her usual habit while in the service, she got up early on her own each morning without the help of an alarm clock and was glad to have something to occupy her time each day.

Skip Tate's stroke four months earlier had cut short Darcy's military career and hastened her retirement. She got out of the Army and came home to care for him and try to keep the windmill business he loved running. The one thing keeping his spirits alive was the hope that someday he would be well enough again to start back to work. Darcy didn't see that in the future, but they both spoke of his recovery as if it were something that would eventually happen.

After high school and before she joined the Army, Darcy had helped her Uncle Calvin and Aunt Winnie in north Texas with their very successful windmill repair business. She had learned a lot and was surprised at how much was coming back to her with each new call she went out on. After "the incident" occurred during her junior year in high school, Darcy was sent to Denton, Texas to live with her aunt and uncle where she eventually learned to love old windmills as much as the rest of her family did. Repairing them was more than a way for the Tate family to make a living. It was a genetic passion they all shared.

As a child she had helped her father do simple things around his workshop, but she was never allowed to get too dirty or ask the string of questions she always had. Her father wasn't a patient man and didn't have time or take the time to mold her curiosity. Darcy's aunt and uncle, however, had enjoyed showing her things and sharing what they knew about windmills and the business in general. It was unfortunate that Darcy's need for independence alienated her from her family forever once she graduated from high school, but a simple future in repairing windmills in Denton, Texas wasn't what she had wanted at the time. "The incident" had given her a taste of what life could be like, a mere sample of what could possibly lay ahead for her, and joining the military seemed to be the answer to many of her problems and questions.

The incident, Darcy thought as she set the remote down on the end table next to the lamp. She glanced over at her father in his wheelchair and saw that he was content for at least the next hour or so. *The incident changed my life*, she thought. *What little fools we were. So young and absolutely crazy about each other.*

Darcy shook her head and picked up the shoebox she kept the weekly receipts in. She found a bank deposit slip and logged the checks, promising herself that making deposits every weekday morning would be an important part of her business day.

Over the last twenty-two years, Darcy had often thought it would be too weird to return to Prescott, Texas to live after she retired, but so far things had worked out well. She had expected most people in the small town to still remember "the incident" and point and stare at her, but she felt lucky enough lately to think that maybe most of those involved had either moved on, died or forgotten about it. After she was forced to move away, each time she spoke to her mother on the phone, she never failed to mention the humiliation and disgrace the Prescott townspeople continued to express over what happened. Darcy would get physically ill after a conversation with her mother. The devastation was so complete and debilitating that after a while Darcy's aunt intercepted the calls from home and made excuses for her niece not to have to talk to either of her parents. Darcy was still trying to get used to Prescott after all these years. The stares and looks of disgust from strangers on the street weren't there the way she had always imagined they would be. Farmers and ranchers with broken windmills shook her hand and looked her in the eye with respect and gratitude at what she could do for them. Only now after living here for three months did Darcy believe she could have a normal life. She had spent a long time avoiding her hometown, thinking it wouldn't welcome her back, when in fact her father was here and there were scores of windmills that needed her attention.

Darcy watched Matlock in the TV courtroom, but her mind was somewhere else. She thought back to that summer she had given swimming lessons with the Red Cross at the Prescott city pool. Darcy had known Nora Fleming since the first grade, but they had never been friends until their junior year in high school. Nora had also volunteered that summer to help teach younger kids to swim.

Darcy remembered those first two weeks at the pool as the most confusing time of her life. All she could think about was Nora Fleming in a bathing suit, her skin going from pink to red then finally a nice tan by the time the lessons were over. Darcy always got to the pool early each morning and couldn't wait to see Nora's reaction to the cold water every day. Nora would let out a little squeal and inch her way down the steps into the pool. Darcy, on the other hand, couldn't get in the water that way. She would always go down to the deeper end and dive in to get that initial shock of cold water over with. From there she would pop up to the surface and look for Nora.

During those two weeks of swimming instruction, Darcy and Nora got to know each other better and slowly became friends. By the third week into June, Darcy was certain she was in love with her. Those new butterfly feelings kept her in a constant state of confusion and shyness. *Why her?* Darcy kept asking herself over and over again. *Why not her brother? He's cute and smart!*

The summer before, Darcy had worked hard to get her lifeguard certification, but didn't get a job in Prescott until the following year. After those two weeks of volunteer work at the pool, Darcy didn't see that much of Nora until later in the summer. Then one day in late July, Nora, her brother Greg and several of their cousins came to the pool for the day. Nora's presence was such a distraction for Darcy that she was worried about possibly missing something and putting other swimmers at risk. She was being paid to keep the pool safe, and all she could think about was Nora Fleming in a bathing suit! If there had been someone available to replace her that first day, Darcy would have told the pool manager she was sick and had to go home, but they barely had enough lifeguards to cover their shifts as it was. No one could be off without making someone else have to work even that much harder.

Several boys from school were there as well and Darcy had to watch them sitting on the side of the pool talking to Nora. Greg and Nora were popular and always seemed to be in the company of an array of what Darcy liked referring to as watermelon royalty. Since Prescott was the watermelon capital of Texas, there was the annual Watermelon Jubilee each year where several teenagers from the area were voted for various titles and offices during the festivities. Each year the same last names were chosen to reign over the Jubilee and ride the floats during the parade. For years now there had been a Fleming voted as either a Watermelon King or Queen, and Darcy had always considered the Fleming family as watermelon royalty along with a few other local names. But what Darcy hadn't expected was how nice and down-to-earth the Flemings were. Nora, her brother and several of their cousins were just average kids. They were polite to strangers, helpful and all did well in school. They didn't fit the watermelon royalty role at all, but it was still difficult for Darcy not to want to put that label on them.

Another thing Darcy thought was weird about the Fleming kids was how well they seemed to get along with their older family members. She remembered going to the Rialto Theater downtown one Saturday night several months before in early spring.

41

Darcy and two of her friends were going to see "War Games." When they arrived and went to stand in line for tickets, there were about twelve Flemings of various ages already in line ahead of them. What struck Darcy as strange was how the younger Flemings seemed to enjoy talking to the older ones—not just their parents, but aunts and uncles too. Those in the older group took an interest in each of the teenagers, and the laughter and chatter was just short of amazing. Darcy also found it unusual that the younger Flemings didn't seem to be the least bit embarrassed to be there with the family that way, whereas Darcy would not have even gone to a movie with her parents and neither would her two friends. Not only that, but most of the older people Darcy knew, especially her parents, weren't moviegoers anyway, even if Darcy had wanted them to be. It was just strange to her how the Flemings related to each other. In a way, Darcy had always been a little jealous of their closeness as a family. She often liked to think that the dynamics of her own family life would have been a lot different if she hadn't been an only child.

Darcy finished logging the checks on the deposit slip and glanced over at her father again. He was enthralled with Matlock. Pulling a small calculator out of the shoebox, she totaled up the deposit slip and made another annotation.

Darcy had only thought about Nora once since moving home to help her father. Her first day back in town she drove by the high school where "the incident" had taken place. Most of the horror and humiliation had long since passed, but a twinge of embarrassment lingered. That morning, Darcy had gone into town to get feed for the guineas when the name "Fleming" jumped out at her as she stopped at Fleming's Feed and Seed store. She had forgotten that one of Nora's uncles owned the place. Now she couldn't get Nora and "the incident" out of her mind.

The incident, Darcy thought again with another shake of her head. Nora's courage that night was still astounding to Darcy even after nearly twenty-three years. Having the high school principal catch them kissing in the school parking lot wasn't something either of them would have ever recommended.

Outside of "the incident," the biggest surprise of Darcy's life happened one day in August that same summer at the pool. Once again, Nora, her brother and several of their cousins were there enjoying a break from the heat. As always, Darcy had trouble concentrating on work when Nora was anywhere near, but the interesting thing this time was that Nora seemed to be just as interested in Darcy. At the pool, the person with the whistle sitting in the lifeguard stand was the one in charge. There were always two lifeguards on duty and they constantly blew the whistle when the pool was full. Rambunctious teenagers and yelling children took time and energy to control. Darcy stayed busy and kept the peace on her end of the pool, and each time she scanned the water looking for Nora, she would find Nora looking back at her. All during the day, even with Nora surrounded by family, friends and a gaggle of testosterone-spiked teenage boys—each time Darcy spotted her, their eyes would meet and Nora would smile at her.

This realization immediately set off the butterflies in Darcy's stomach again while at the same time she could feel her breathing become shallow at the thought of having Nora's attention. Darcy concentrated hard on doing her job with the same dedication and attention to detail that was expected of her as a lifeguard, but she also made sure to keep an eye on what was going on with Nora during her stay at the pool.

Then at closing time, Darcy and the other lifeguard cleared the pool—Nora and her cousins were most times the last to leave. Darcy had to gather up all the things lying around at poolside— the goggles, ear plugs, eye glasses, tanning lotion, sun glasses, towels, shoes and an armload of other items forgotten during the course of the day. Both lifeguards were also responsible for cleaning the locker rooms where more items could be found. The facility had to be ready to open first thing every day, so tidying up was part of the job description.

An hour later, Darcy and the other lifeguard had finally gotten their evening chores done. When Darcy went out to her car in the parking lot, she saw five of the younger Flemings standing around a white pickup talking.

43

Nora waved at her and then walked toward Darcy's car. Darcy remembered how her heart pounded just as that butterfly feeling returned to the pit of her stomach.

"I wanted to ask you a few questions about being a lifeguard," Nora said. "Do you have time to talk?"

Darcy nodded, not trusting her voice at the moment.

"Can you take me home?" Nora asked. "We can talk on the way. My cousins are going for ice cream and I didn't want to go."

"Sure," Darcy managed to say. *Ohmigod!* she thought. *Nora Fleming will be riding in my car and it's a mess inside!*

Nora waved to her brother and cousins and the young Flemings all got into the pickup.

"Let me get some of this stuff out of the way," Darcy said as she pitched things in the backseat. Once they were in the car, Nora asked her what all was involved in becoming a lifeguard. Finally, Darcy was relieved to be talking instead of concentrating on who was sitting beside her in the car.

"I got my certification through the Red Cross," Darcy said. "I've been certified for over a year, but last summer they didn't have an opening for me at the Prescott pool, so I worked for a few weeks in San Antonio."

"Lifeguard classes fill up so quickly," Nora said. "I was too late last year and I missed the deadline again this year."

Darcy shrugged. "I like doing it."

"Well, it looks like fun," Nora said. "Have you ever had to save someone's life?"

"Not yet, thank goodness, but I know what to do if someone's in trouble."

"It looks like a huge responsibility and you end up with such a nice tan."

Darcy didn't know what to say. *Is she giving me a compliment? Or just making a general statement?*

"How much sunscreen do you use a week?" Nora asked.

"A lot. The pool provides it for us."

"You know where I live, right?"

"Yes," Darcy said. *I drive by there all the time now in hopes of getting a glimpse of you.*

"Maybe you could find out more about when the next classes are for lifeguard certification," Nora said. "It would be fun if we could work together next summer."

"I know the director. I'll see what I can find out for you."

"Thanks. I appreciate that. I'm a good swimmer and I did some volunteer work already."

"Will you be at the pool tomorrow?" Darcy asked.

"I probably will."

Darcy slowed down in front of the Dairy Queen and saw the white pickup parked on the side. *She gave up ice cream to talk to you,* Darcy thought, then couldn't stop smiling. *She could've called you on the phone for all this lifeguard information.*

"When does the pool close for the summer?" Nora asked.

"Labor Day."

"Then you've still got a job for a few more weeks."

Darcy slowed to turn down the dirt road that led to the Fleming farm. Suddenly, she didn't want this time with Nora to end. Darcy wanted to drive forever and keep her right there beside her. She slowed down even more, but before she knew it, they were in front of the gate.

"This is fine," Nora said. "I can walk the rest of the way."

"I don't mind driving you to the house."

"It's not that far. Thanks for the ride."

Nora got out of the car, opened the gate and locked it again. She stood there and waved, her smile meant only for Darcy. She was beautiful with her long blond hair tied back in a ponytail. Nora turned and headed for the house and Darcy backed the car up and drove toward town again.

That was the day Darcy knew for sure that she was different— that the things she felt for another girl her age were not as normal as they should be. But what she didn't know then was that Nora Fleming was beginning to feel the same way.

Chapter Seven

The next day at the pool, Nora was there again with her brother and a few cousins. The boys were showing off on the diving board while Nora and several other girls from school sat on the side of the pool dangling their feet in the water. Darcy noticed other boys who tried to get their attention, but Nora didn't seem interested. About twenty minutes before closing time, Nora came over to the lifeguard stand and asked Darcy if she would take her home again.

"Sure," Darcy said, making a valiant attempt not to sound too excited, "but I've got things to do here before we close up."

"Anything I can help you with?"

"Just cleaning and picking up after people. It's really boring."

"I have a brother," Nora said. "I'm used to picking up after people. I don't mind helping."

Darcy couldn't believe how happy she was to be spending more time with Nora. She hurried all the swimmers out of the pool the moment it was officially time to close. The rest of the Fleming kids had left already and Darcy let the other lifeguard go early so she could be alone with Nora. She had promised to get the pool ready to open the next day.

"Just collect anything you see laying around," Darcy instructed Nora. "Whatever's worth keeping goes in the lost and found."

"Does anyone ever claim this stuff?"

"Sometimes, but not very often."

As with every afternoon when the pool was closed, Darcy had an armload of things that pool patrons had left behind.

"What do they do with it if no one claims it?" Nora asked.

"I don't know. I never thought about it."

Darcy took all the items to the lost and found room, then went to her locker to put on a T-shirt and some shorts over her bathing suit. She hadn't been in the water that day, so she was still dry. Nora went to another part of the dressing room to change clothes.

Once she was dressed, Darcy tidied up the women's locker room. She made it a point to stay away from the area where Nora was changing, but just the mere thought of Nora being there with her was enough to make Darcy shift into high gear in order to get her lifeguard chores over with.

"I'll do the boy's side," Darcy called to her. "It's always a lot worse over there."

As expected, Darcy found the usual scenario in the boy's locker room—the abandoned underwear, swim trunks, candy wrappers, soda cans, stray socks and old sneakers strewn about everywhere. Most of it she threw away, but some things might be items someone would be looking for again.

"Yuck," Nora said, standing in the doorway with her hands on her hips. "So it's not just my brother who's a pig."

"I really hate picking up most of this stuff," Darcy admitted with a curled up nose.

"Let's get it over with."

Nora helped Darcy sweep and mop both dressing room floors. Darcy couldn't remember a time when she had enjoyed doing her lifeguard chores. When they were finished, Darcy locked up the offices and the entrance to the pool area.

"So you have access to the pool all the time?" Nora asked.

"In the summer I do. Now that you know a lifeguard also has to be a maid, do you still want to be one?"

"Oh, definitely," Nora said.

They got into Darcy's car and sat there for a moment with the air conditioner running.

"Have you ever been skinny dipping?" Nora asked.

"No," Darcy said, embarrassed by the question.

"You've got the keys to the pool. You should try it at least once."

"It might be a good way to get fired," Darcy said, "but it might also be worth it." She backed out of the parking lot and headed toward Nora's house. "Thanks for helping with my less glamorous lifeguard duties."

"It was fun," Nora said. "Why would someone leave their underwear in a place like that? You take them off, you put them in your gym bag and you put on your bathing suit. Or you keep your bathing suit on under other clothes before you go to the pool and leave your underwear at home. I don't get it."

"Me neither, but a lot of things get thrown away," Darcy said. "I don't even like having to touch some of that stuff to throw it away. I've thought about getting a pair of giant tongs to pick things up with, but eventually I probably wouldn't want to touch the tongs either."

They shared a laugh while speeding down the highway.

"On Saturday a bunch of us are going to see a movie," Nora said a while later. "You want to go with us?"

Darcy wanted to ask who was going, but she didn't. Just knowing that Nora would be there was reason enough not to care who else came along.

"Sure," Darcy said, "but I get off a little later on Saturday. I'll try and switch my schedule around some."

"Good. I'll let you know what time we'll be there."

On Saturday Darcy worked the early shift at the pool and got off at three. She went home and stressed over what to wear to the movies that night. Nora had left a message with Darcy's mother, so she knew what time to be there. After trying on three different outfits, she settled on white shorts and a bright yellow shirt—it would emphasize her tan.

She parked in front of the Rialto Theater early so she would be able to see everyone who came up to purchase tickets. When Darcy saw the white pickup pull in and park down the street with about eight young Fleming cousins getting out of the cab and the bed of the truck, she knew Nora had to be with them.

"Hi," Nora said as soon as she saw Darcy. "You got my message."

They stood in line together. All the other Flemings greeted her, too.

"Anybody know anything about this movie?" Greg asked everyone in line.

"Does it matter?" someone in front of the line said. "At least we're not home on a Saturday night!"

Once inside, they were all in line again waiting to get drinks and popcorn. The laughter, good-natured joking, and overall foolishness that went on between the cousins made Darcy feel unusually welcomed. As an only child she had often been accused of "not playing well with others." It was a total surprise to her that the Flemings weren't at all like she had imagined them to be. That realization made her begin to reevaluate her whole perception of her peers and the significance she had always placed on watermelon royalty in the first place.

Inside the theater they had to find enough seats for everyone, but they were early so that wasn't a problem. Darcy was glad that Nora wanted to sit beside her. The Fleming girls sat together at one end of the row while the boys were clumped together at the other end. Darcy had the last seat on the row and Nora sat beside her.

"Now you see why I insisted on having my own popcorn?" Nora said to one of her cousins. "Greg's all the way down there thinking I can share his."

"You could've shared mine," Darcy said.

"Well, thanks. Now you tell me! I'll never be able to eat all of this," Nora said pointing to her popcorn box.

Darcy felt giddy enough to just be sitting so close to her, but when the house lights eventually dimmed and the previews started, Darcy wasn't sure what to make of the way Nora's arm kept brushing up against hers. Darcy could feel the swoosh of a roller coaster in her stomach each time they would touch. She sat up straighter in her seat and kept her elbow and arm off the armrest they shared. Darcy even attempted to concentrate on the movie previews, but Nora seemed to be all over the place. After about two minutes of elbow tag, Darcy tried to relax and reclaim her part of the armrest again.

Nora gave her popcorn away to one of her cousins a few seats down and asked Darcy if she could have some of hers. Occasionally their fingers touched in the popcorn box and by the time the main feature started, Nora was holding Darcy's hand in the dark. Darcy was so glad she had been setting her soda cup on the floor beside her otherwise she might have dropped it from all the bubbling excitement zinging around through her body.

After that, Darcy had no idea what the movie was about or who was in it. All she could think of was holding Nora's hand and how this was exactly what she had wanted all along. She couldn't eat anymore of her popcorn either. Each kernel seemed to stick in her throat. During a funny part of the movie, they were the only two people in the theater who didn't laugh. It occurred to Darcy that perhaps Nora was as awestruck by what was happening between them as she was.

For Darcy, the movie seemed to end too quickly, causing Nora to let go of her hand. Everyone stood up to file out at the same time and in the crowded aisle, Nora put her hands on Darcy's waist for a moment. Feeling deliriously happy, Darcy moved through the crowd feeling like a new person. The Darcy Tate who had arrived at the Rialto Theater over two hours ago had been a lovesick shell of a person, but suddenly she felt alive.

Eventually they made it outside where the evening heat would have ordinarily given her a rude awakening, but nothing could have popped this euphoric bubble that surrounded her. Darcy didn't want any of this to end. How could she just go home so soon? She wanted to feel Nora's hand in hers again. She wanted their elbows touching on an armrest. Then as if Nora had been reading her mind, Darcy heard her tell her brother that she would get a ride home from Darcy.

"Meet us at the Dairy Queen," Greg called out as he opened the truck door. Two of their female cousins got in the cab with him while the rest of them piled in the back of the truck.

"No thanks," Nora said with a wave. "I'll see you later."

They got in Darcy's car and Nora immediately reached for Darcy's hand again. Nora's courage was just short of astounding to Darcy. No matter how much she had ever wanted to do such a thing, Darcy would have never been brave enough to make that kind of move. The fear of rejection or even worse far outweighed the benefits. When it came to expressing her feelings and taking a chance like that, Darcy was admittedly a coward, so it was just that much more incredible to her that someone like Nora had taken an interest in her.

"You okay with this?" Nora whispered.

Darcy swallowed the huge lump in her throat. "Yes," she croaked. "Very okay."

"Find a nice dark place where we can talk," Nora said.

Darcy was shaking so badly she wasn't sure she would be able to drive. "Got any suggestions?" She let go of Nora's hand long enough to start the car and turn on the air conditioner.

"The road out by the Catholic cemetery," Nora said, reclaiming Darcy's hand again. "No one ever goes there this time of night."

Darcy drove while her mind raced and her teenage hormones

did the happy dance all through her body. Once they were out of town, Nora asked, "What are you thinking?"

"I'm thinking this is the greatest night of my life," Darcy said. Her voice was low and serious. If she hadn't known for certain that the words had come out of her mouth, she would have never recognized them as her own.

Nora's contented sigh penetrated the darkness. "Those are my thoughts exactly. Turn in here," she said. "No one ever comes down this road at night either."

Darcy parked the car, but left it running. It was too hot to be without the air conditioner.

Nora shifted in the seat and leaned over to kiss her. The moment Darcy felt the softness of Nora's lips, she thought for sure she would faint from the fluttering in her stomach. There had never been anything else in her life that she could compare this moment to. Darcy felt as though she would explode from want, need and desire.

They must have continued kissing for an hour or more, with exploring tongues and wild, passionate embraces. Darcy couldn't get close enough to her and wanted to be swallowed up and swept away by Nora's mouth and arms. Her body ached for more, but their kisses were frantic, as if they both had only a short time left to make up for all the girl-kisses they had missed out on their entire lives.

"I feel like I'm on fire," Nora whispered just before she sucked Darcy's tongue into her mouth again.

Finally, just as Darcy noticed that her lips were beginning to get numb, Nora pulled away from her. "What time is it? I need to get home."

"Yeah, me too."

Even though their mutual need to respect a curfew was now out in the open, they continued kissing. Each time Nora's lips touched Darcy's neck or earlobe, Darcy could feel her entire body tremble. *I could never get tired of this*, she thought. *Never.*

"We really need to get going," Nora whispered in Darcy's ear before flicking her tongue against her earlobe.

They reluctantly pulled away from each other and Darcy drove to the Fleming Farm while Nora continued to kiss her neck and cheek. She didn't move back to her side of the seat until they drove down the dirt road that led to Nora's house. When they finally reached the gate to the farmhouse, they saw the white pickup, parked and headlights off.

"Uh-oh," Nora said. "If that's my pop, then I'm in trouble."

They both watched in fear as Nora's brother Greg got out of the truck. Nora's heavy sigh of relief made some of the tingling fear leave Darcy's body.

"Where have you been?" Greg barked out into the darkness. "I can't go home without you! Get in the truck."

"I'm sorry," Nora said to him. "We went for a ride." Lowering her voice, she whispered to Darcy, "I'll call you tomorrow. He's mad."

Nora got out of the car and hopped into the truck. Darcy expected to hear yelling, but she didn't hear anything else but the truck starting up. Things were fine. All the way home she felt lightheaded and giddy. Touching a fingertip to her slightly swollen lips made her smile. This was by far the best day of her life. She had just spent the evening making out with watermelon royalty!

That was a long time ago.

Chapter Eight

Darcy finally got her father settled in bed for the night. They both grew stronger since she had been home—he from the daily physical therapy Darcy had arranged for him and she from having to help him in and out of his wheelchair off and on during the day when she was home. It was also evident that working on the windmills had increased her stamina. For a forty year old woman, she was in remarkable shape. The physical requirements of her everyday life in the Army had kept her fit, but climbing up windmills and hanging on to them took a different type of conditioning that she was only beginning to get used to.

She sat down at the computer in the living room and waited for the bookkeeping program to load. The receipts for the last few days were in a stack ready for input, and she hoped to be able to record a few months of supply receipts and inventory before she got too tired.

She hadn't checked the phone messages for the day. Darcy got up from the computer desk and went through the kitchen and out the back door to the workshop area. The answering machine blinked furiously on the desk in the corner. She played the messages and wrote down the telephone numbers, once again surprised at how busy the windmill repair business was in this area. Darcy had to keep reminding herself that her father had the only business of this kind in south Texas and a lot of farms and ranches depended on windmills for their only water source.

She went back to the house and returned the calls, making sure to get good directions to where the windmills in question were located. Three callers wanted estimates and two others wanted outright repairs as soon as she could get to them.

Busy day tomorrow, she thought, hanging up the phone. She sat back down at the computer again to concentrate on debit and credit entries. *How did Dad keep up with all of this at his age?*

The stiffness in her neck let her know she had been sitting too long, then a glance at her watch revealed it was after eleven. She saved what she had been working on and sat down in the recliner to watch TV before going to bed. Her Army stint in Korea followed by eleven months in Iraq threw her out of the loop where American television was concerned. A lot of things on TV were new to her.

She flipped through several channels and stopped on a reality show. After only a few minutes of that, she surfed the channels again until she saw someone throwing a watermelon off a thirty-story building.

Watermelon royalty, Darcy thought with a smile as the old term popped into her head. *I bet this little podunk town still has all of that going on during the Watermelon Jubilee.*

She leaned her head back and stared at the TV, but Darcy was no longer interested in what happened to a watermelon once it was tossed off a building. Her thoughts went immediately back to Nora Fleming and those precious few months they had in high school.

Before "the incident," Darcy thought with a groan. *Before my life changed forever. If only I knew then what I know now.*

It had never occurred to her back then that Nora could be

wrong about anything. She was smart, beautiful, funny and incredibly personable. Darcy had followed her around like a little lost puppy. She was so enthralled with her that all common sense escaped Darcy when they were together. She had been mesmerized by Nora and without a doubt swept off her feet. When they were apart, Darcy always felt surprised that someone like Nora would find her interesting let alone desirable. Nora seemed to be so worldly about a lot of things, but when they were together it was incredible. Darcy could hear birds singing and children laughing. She could even imagine cartoon hearts hanging over her head when they were around other people, with those silly pulsating hearts giving her feelings away for all to see. Darcy felt corny and happy when Nora was close to her. It was no wonder "the incident" happened. They were young and careless—two things that never went well together when others might possibly disapprove of what was happening.

Once Darcy's parents had her safely tucked away in Denton, Texas with her aunt and uncle, she had more time to reflect on the mistakes she and Nora had made. How many times had they driven out to the Catholic cemetery with Nora nibbling on Darcy's neck, not giving another thought to the possibility that someone might see them or discover what they were doing? And then to think it would be a good idea to start kissing each other in Darcy's car in the school parking lot during a football game did nothing more than make Darcy cringe at the memory now. *What the hell were we thinking?* She shook her head. *We were young and stupid. Since when do teenagers think about anything or anyone but themselves?*

The look on Principal Szalwinski's face when he pulled them both out of the car was something Darcy would never forget. The only thing worse in her life had been the look on her father's face when the principal told her parents what he had found Darcy and Nora doing that night.

But everything had been leading up to that moment. By the end of September she and Nora had discovered the joy of fondling each other's breasts. By the middle of October they had worked their way up to getting blouses and bras off. They loved kissing and that was what they spent most of their time together doing. Only when they had an excuse to get away could they engage in more risky dalliances. However, those opportunities were not easy to come by. Nora had a hard time going anywhere without her brother and a string of cousins, so she and Nora just didn't have that many chances to be alone.

But that fateful night when the Prescott Dragons played the Harper Pirates at a rival football game, Nora and Darcy left the game in the third quarter and went back to Darcy's car. It was chilly that night and it wasn't long before the windows started to fog up. With Darcy's blouse unbuttoned and her bra hiked up over the top of her breasts, Nora feasted on her nipples with eager sucking and wild tongue flicking. They were both squirming in the front seat and oblivious to anything else except each other, until the first tapping on the driver's side window sent them both into a mad rush to fix their clothing.

"Who could that be?" Nora hissed.

"Everyone should be watching the game!" Darcy whispered.

When the flashlight beam hit them in the eyes, Darcy's blouse was unbuttoned and her bra was hiked up in an unflattering position.

"Open the door!" a booming male voice demanded.

Darcy didn't know what to do. The flashlight was blinding her, but she was finally able to snatch her bra back into the right place.

"Open the door!" the man said again while tapping on the window with the flashlight.

"How much do you think he saw?" Nora asked hysterically.

"My everything is still hanging out," Darcy said, fumbling with the buttons on her shirt.

"Both of you get out of the car!" the man hollered even louder this time.

"We're hosed now," Nora said. "If we try and make a run for it, they'll probably get the cops after us!"

"Open this door!"

Darcy finished buttoning her shirt and got out of the car, shutting the door quickly behind her.

"Who's in there with you?" Mr. Szalwinski demanded. The principal towered over Darcy by a good six inches.

"This was my idea, Sir. I'm very sorry."

He yanked on the door handle, but Darcy had pushed the lock down before getting out. He tried pulling on the back door, but it was locked as well.

"You there in the car!" he bellowed. "Come out now!"

"We promise to go back to the game," Darcy said. She could feel her knees knocking together, and at that particular moment she wasn't sure if she would be sick or not.

"I don't think so, young lady." He tapped on the window again with the flashlight and pointed the rude beam into the front seat. "You in there! Come out immediately!"

After a moment, Darcy heard the other door open and Nora got out of the car. Mr. Szalwinski looked from one to the other then slowly shook his head.

"Both of you come with me to my office."

Darcy had walked across the parking lot as if she were on her way to a firing squad. The humiliation of knowing this man had seen her breasts was almost unbearable, but the mere thought of him possibly seeing what Nora had been doing with Darcy's breasts was even worse. She willed herself not to cry, but wasn't sure how successful she would be. The urge to throw up was even stronger now than it had been a few minutes earlier.

Mr. Szalwinski unlocked the front door to the school and let them both in. He locked the door behind them and used the flashlight to find his office. The school looked eerie and foreign in the darkness. Darcy knew every inch of this hallway and had never before felt so unwelcome or afraid there.

"Sit down," he said in his deep, gruff voice once they were in his office. "Are either of your parents at the game?"

"Mine aren't," Darcy said quietly. *My parents! Ohmigod! We can't tell any of this to my parents! They'll kill me!*

Mr. Szalwinski looked at Nora. "Your brother is playing tonight, so I assume your parents are still in the stands."

"This has nothing to do with our parents," Nora said defiantly. To Darcy, Nora's spunk and anger seemed out of place at the moment. Darcy considered falling on her knees and begging this man to let them go and forget about what happened.

"This has everything to do with your parents," he said. "I'm sure they'll be very interested in knowing what you've both been up to."

From that moment on, Darcy must've zoned out because she didn't remember much of anything else that happened after that. All she remembered now, twenty-three years later, was being cold and shaking uncontrollably. She had no idea how long she and Nora were in Mr. Szalwinski's office before Darcy's parents arrived or how many times her father had slapped her that night in the principal's office or again once they got home. By the next morning her clothes had been packed for her and she was on a bus to Denton, Texas to live with her aunt and uncle. Darcy finished high school there a year and a half later then joined the Army. She never heard from Nora Fleming again.

Chapter Nine

Nora claimed to be better at backing up a trailer than Greg, so he got out of the truck and let her do it. That was easier than arguing with her and attempting to defend his manhood.

"Let me know when I'm close enough," she said out the truck window.

This was the last load of her things to be put in storage. For Nora, it was a huge relief to have the move nearly completed. She had gotten rid of a lot of things and kept her best furniture pieces. She actually liked the bed in her old room at her mother's house better than the one she had been using in Dallas. She sold it to one of her neighbors in the apartment complex, which saved them from having to carry it down a flight of stairs to the U-Haul.

Without Greg and her niece Holly's help, the move would have cost Nora a nice chunk of money, so she appreciated their efforts. All three of them had put in a full day and were tired.

"I won't get to see you as much now," Holly said with a little pout. She was turned around in the seat of her grandmother's pickup looking out the back window as Nora maneuvered the trailer toward the storage unit behind them. They had already unloaded the U-Haul back at the farm and turned it in earlier. Now they had the bed of the pickup, as well as a 10 foot flat trailer, full of boxes that needed to be stored. Nora was certain the storage unit she had rented would hold everything.

"Then you and your dad will just have to come visit Grammie more often," Nora said. She tugged on the steering wheel to try and get the trailer lined up. It wasn't as easy as she thought it would be since the pickup didn't have power steering.

"I'm trying to talk him into letting me come down for the whole summer," Holly said, "but he wants me to go to science camp in July."

"I bet you'd like that," Nora said with a grunt.

"I'd rather be here with you and Grammie."

Nora gave up trying to turn the steering wheel enough to do what she needed the truck to do, so she pulled up a ways to straighten out the trailer and start all over again.

"Good job there, sis," Greg called, putting a finger and thumb together in the universal okay sign. While he was making fun of her abilities to back up the trailer, Nora gave him a universal one-finger sign of her own out the window.

"You didn't see that," Nora said to her niece as all three of them rolled with laughter. One of the first things she planned to do once she got settled in at the farm was get her mother a new truck. *One that doesn't take having arms and buns of steel to back it up*, she thought.

"Get it all in there?" Opal asked when the three of them returned to the farm.

"We did," Nora said. She and Holly got out of the truck while Greg drove it around back to put the trailer in one of the barns.

"Did you feed the girls yet, Grammie?" Holly asked.

"No. I waited for you."

"I'll get the feed bucket!"

Nora climbed the steps to the porch and sat down in the swing. She wasn't used to so much heavy lifting. Her back was tired and she wondered if she'd be able to even walk the next day.

"That recliner of yours looks good in the living room," Opal said. She had on a light blue cotton dress that hit her well below the knees and white sneakers that made her look much younger than her seventy-four years. The bonnet she had tied around her neck was one of her favorite "everyday" bonnets. Nora could tell that her mother felt good today.

"Have you tried it out yet?" Nora asked, referring to the recliner they had unloaded earlier and put in the living room. Just thinking about heaving it off the U-Haul so she and Greg could carry it in made Nora's back hurt all over again.

"I did. That thing's dangerous. I wasn't in it three minutes when I felt my eyes get heavy."

"Oh, I know exactly what you mean." Nora moved her neck around and could feel some soreness moving in there already, too. It had been a busy two days with all the packing and driving. "Did you find our friend yet?" she asked her mother quietly.

Earlier in the day while Nora had been putting a few things away in a closet in the hallway, she found a snakeskin on the floor. After her initial shock, she called her mother over and showed it to her. Opal discreetly removed it and just shook her head.

"It's been a while since I've seen one of these around here," Opal said.

"Uh . . . how often do you find them in the house now days?" Nora asked, looking all around her now. *Great*, she thought. *And I was worried about a few mice.*

"This is the first one in a while. I'm not sure how they get in. He'll show up eventually."

"What if it's a rattler?" Nora whispered.

"Nah. I haven't seen one of those around here in years."

Her mother's unruffled demeanor helped calm Nora's anxiety

about having a snake in the house, but Opal was right. When Nora and Greg were growing up, they occasionally found a snake in the house and never did find out how they were getting in. As a child, Nora just assumed everyone in the country had to put up with it until she asked her cousins one day what kind of snakes got into *their* houses. It was then and only then, that she realized it *didn't* happen to everyone. At the moment, she wasn't sure which was worse . . . finding the snakeskin and knowing one was there somewhere, or just outright finding a snake without having had a clue it might be inside the house at all.

"Let's just hope it doesn't show itself until after your brother leaves," Nora remembered her mother saying.

Nora chuckled and thought about that as she relaxed in the porch swing.

Holly came out of the house with a bucket of feed for the chickens. She wore her shoulder-length blond hair in a loose ponytail to keep it out of her face. She looked like Nora and all the other Fleming cousins at that age.

"Let's go, Grammie. The girls are waiting for us. They aren't as scared of me anymore."

Nora watched them walk down the steps on their way to the chicken coop. Opal took the steps slowly with Holly holding her by the arm. Seeing them together warmed Nora's heart. If she herself had ever had any children, Nora couldn't imagine loving them more than she loved her niece Holly. As her mother and niece followed the worn path to the chicken coop, Nora watched her brother drive the pickup around the house and park it out front. He got out and moved his shoulders around. It had been a long, busy day.

"So you're all moved in now," he said as he sat down on the porch steps. "I still love it out here, Nora. I envy you."

"There's plenty of room. You and Holly should think about moving back, too."

He leaned on his elbows and took a deep breath. "Nothing quite like the smell of cow manure on a warm spring day. Gotta love it." His hair had been cut recently and he needed a little more sun on his neck to make it seem less obvious. He was a handsome man and she considered him to be one of her best friends. She would miss having them so close in Dallas where they saw each other often. "She's got friends there and she's doing so well in school."

"Holly could make friends here too, and she'll be just as smart no matter where she is," Nora reasoned. "Maybe even do better academically in a place like this. Plenty of Fleming kids around to help her get involved in things and ease the transition."

Greg turned his head to look at her. "I have a job in Dallas that pays me an exorbitant amount of money."

"So check into a transfer," Nora said. She leaned forward in the swing and put her hands on her knees. "Your company has a branch in San Antonio. It's doable."

"Each time I come back here I think about it," Greg said seriously. "But it's the same thing for me whenever I go to the coast and experience the beach all over again. I always leave there wanting to live on the coast. Then I'll go to the mountains and breathe *that* fresh air and want a place in the mountains."

"You're a fickle thing, aren't you?" Nora said.

"Guess maybe I am."

"Sounds like perhaps the allure of that cow manure smell is still in your blood, though. You should seriously think about it, Greg. None of us are getting any younger."

Nora got up Sunday morning and shuffled to the bathroom. Her mother was up already and had the coffee going.

"How are you feeling today?" Nora asked her.

"Tired. I might perk up a little after breakfast."

"Why don't you go back to bed for a while?"

"Nope. I'm up to stay."

"Then let me fix breakfast this morning."

"You know how to make biscuits?"

"Uh . . ." Nora said. She had been thinking more along the lines of a nice tall stack of buttered toast from a toaster.

Opal shook her head. "The fixing breakfast part might be what helps to perk me up. You know how I like cooking for you kids."

Nora poured them both some coffee. "How long do they usually sleep when they're here?" she asked, referring to her brother and niece.

"Holly likes helping me feed the girls," Opal said, "so she'll be up soon. That young rooster won't let anyone sleep too long." She got a mixing bowl out of the cupboard and turned on the oven so it could warm up.

Nora heard a loud thud come from the back of the house and then a shrill string of cursing that sounded something like "holy-apple-crapping-son-of-a-bitch!"

Nora set her coffee cup down and jumped up from the table.

"Your brother's awake," Opal said.

"Holly!" Greg yelled from one of the rooms in the back, his voice still sounding remarkably high pitched for a man's. "Is this thing yours?! Come and get it out of here!"

"And I betcha he just found that snake," Nora said.

Chapter Ten

Later that afternoon Nora and Opal took Greg and Holly to the San Antonio airport to catch a flight back to Dallas. They had spent most of the day laughing about the snake incident, mostly at Greg's expense. Nora was relieved that it had been found.

"Remember that little chat we had on the porch yesterday afternoon?" Greg asked his sister once Holly had removed the snake from his room.

"The cow manure chat?" Nora asked.

"Yes. Exactly. The cow manure chat," Greg confirmed. "In that regard let me just say this about that. It's suddenly come back to me why I moved to the city in the first place. My memory has been miraculously restored. Snakes do not belong in the house. As long as I've lived in Dallas, I've never *ever* seen a snake there."

"That snake was just as afraid of you as you were of him," Opal said in a calm, amused tone of voice.

"Yeah, well," Greg said, "I'm sure that snake didn't leave a lump in his shorts when we saw each other either, very much unlike me."

With that declaration, Nora choked on her coffee and spurted it out her nose. But now as she eased the car into the light Sunday afternoon traffic, Nora was conscious of missing her brother and Holly and of the fact that it was just her and her mother now. Having Greg and Holly there had made things much easier and the weekend had been fun. She realized that her mother must have been having similar thoughts when Opal said, "It's sure hard to see them go sometimes."

"Yeah, I know."

"I'm glad you're here," Opal said. "How 'bout we go back home and I'll help you unpack?"

"Would we be doing that before or after a nap?" Nora asked. Napping was one of her favorite pastimes. It also ensured that her mother got enough rest during the day.

Opal laughed. "Both, I imagine. I saw how many boxes the three of you unloaded."

Nora's mornings consisted of a nice breakfast, strong hot coffee, tidying up the kitchen, dusting all the chicken trinkets in the living room, sweeping and mopping the wooden floors and then cleaning chicken droppings off fresh eggs while listening to the Hometown News on the radio. Having taken over the regular everyday housework, Nora hoped her mother would have more energy for other things. Within a week Nora had caught up on all the local gossip and found herself looking forward to Little League scores and birth announcements. She remembered many of the names she heard on the local radio programs from her childhood. Several of her high school classmates still lived in the area and already had grandchildren by now—a very unsettling thought. It made her feel old.

When Nora woke on Wednesday morning, her nose immediately identified coffee brewing and a cake baking. She loved how the house smelled each day when she first awoke. It reminded her of growing up there and how lucky she had been as a child. Things had been much simpler back then. They didn't have a lot, but they always had enough and were willing to share it with family and friends.

"What's cookin'?" Nora asked as she entered the kitchen.

"A lemon cake," Opal said. "Hilda should be over later to get her eggs."

"I was wondering, Mom. Does Hilda ever help you clean any eggs? Or does she just sit and talk and watch you do it?"

Opal smiled. "She watches. Why?"

"I don't know. It must seem kind of weird having someone watch you work once a week and not offer to help."

"Well, if the truth be known," Opal said as she bent over to take the cake pan out of the oven, "I don't want just anyone cleaning my eggs for me. I want it done a certain way. I taught you and Holly how to do it the way I like, so you're the only two I would let help me."

"I'm sure there was a compliment in that statement somewhere."

Opal nodded. "There was. Did you notice I didn't include your brother in any of that?"

Nora was pleased to have her mother's trust in such a bizarre way. The next time she talked to Holly, she would tell her about this conversation and how special they both were.

"If your brother was to think about what an egg was and where it came from long enough, he'd probably never eat another one, much less touch it to clean it."

Opal slid a pan of biscuits in the oven and closed the door. Nora's stomach growled over the aroma from the cake she'd placed on the counter.

"Sometimes I wonder how it was that I turned out to be the gay one," Nora said. "Greg has always had some of that foo-foo gene in him somewhere."

"He's a sensitive boy and there's nothing wrong with that," Opal said. She took a package of bacon out of the refrigerator. "Your cousin Jack is like that too on occasion. When it's time for us to send a cow off to the packing plant, he makes me choose which one gets to go in our freezers. He doesn't like to do it."

"But Greg squealed like a girl when he saw that snake," Nora reminded her. "I can't imagine Jack doing that."

Opal laughed and held onto the kitchen counter with one hand as she put her other hand over her mouth in an attempt to stifle her usual snorting.

"Well, you're right about that," Opal said once she caught her breath again.

"Then he had his fourteen-year-old daughter catch the snake and take it outside," Nora continued.

Opal shook her head. "That kid's not afraid of anything. She reminds me so much of you sometimes. She's a delight to have around. Not the least bit squeamish about anything."

Nora poured herself some coffee and took over the bacon-frying duties.

"Tell me again that thing you think Greg has?" Opal said. "A foo-foo what?"

"The foo-foo gene?"

Her mother put her hand up to her mouth to hide another snort. "That's it. A foo-foo gene."

About five minutes before the Hometown News came on, Hilda drove up and parked next to Opal's truck in the yard. Opal stopped cleaning eggs, washed her hands, and met her neighbor on the porch. Nora kept up with the egg-cleaning ritual and glanced over at the full basket of eggs still on the counter waiting for her. It made Nora feel better knowing she was helping her mother. They had a lot more free time in the evenings now. Off and on during the day, Nora prompted her mother to take a nap in hopes of relieving everyday ordinary stress and just making things easier for her. As long as Opal's lupus was in remission or adequately controlled with medication, she would be able to continue doing the things she loved.

"Nora, I hear you're all moved in," Hilda said. "We like knowing your mother's not here all by herself."

"She's been a big help to me," Opal said as she got her neighbor a cup of coffee.

Nora continued cleaning eggs while the two older women chatted. Once the Hometown News came on, the three of them were a quiet captive audience.

"I thought they gave the date for that donkey basketball game yesterday," Hilda said the first time the program went to a commercial, "but if they did, they only announced it once."

"Donkey basketball," Nora said with a chuckle. "Does the high school gym still fill up for that?"

"Oh my goodness yes," Opal said. "We'll have to get our tickets beforehand and then get there early that evening."

When she and Greg were kids, donkey basketball was an annual event that none of the Flemings would dream of missing, and now that she was an adult, Nora wondered if she would still find it as entertaining.

"We'll have to get a ticket for Jack, too," Opal said to Nora. "He wouldn't think of going to the game on his own."

Nora liked the way her mother looked after her cousin Jack. She seemed to think of him as one of her own.

By the end of the Hometown News program, they knew who had died, what new babies had arrived, the price of corn, what heifers were selling for, who had found a pig, who had lost a horse, where the closest garage sale could be located over the weekend and where one could purchase donkey basketball tickets.

All is well and life is good, Nora thought as she picked up another egg and dunked a fresh paper towel in the bowl of water. *It's official. I'm really home again.*

"You going with me on my egg run in the morning?" Opal asked her that evening. They had just finished supper, done the dishes, watched the evening news on TV and were now out on the porch swing listening to the police scanner.

"Wouldn't miss it," Nora said.

"We need to get those donkey basketball tickets while we're out tomorrow. The seed store is selling them. Maybe you'll get to see your uncle Felix while we're there."

"How's he doing these days?"

"Still feisty," Opal said. "He quit smoking, but now he's dipping snuff."

"Save a lung, but rot a lip?"

"Something like that."

"Does he still look like Pop?"

Opal shrugged. "Sometimes. Has all of his hair like your father did and he has that silly Fleming grin. I see it in you, Greg and Jack all the time. I think his daughter Wendy works at the store with him now. You might get to see her tomorrow, too."

Wendy Fleming, Nora thought. *Wow. It's been about ten years since I've seen any of my cousins besides Jack. Seems like we only get together for funerals nowadays, when as teenagers we did everything together.*

The scanner blurted out a license plate number and made Nora jump. What was even more irritating was hearing her mother chuckle each time it happened.

"Glad you find that so amusing," Nora grumbled.

"Your tush clears the swing whenever they say something."

"My tush isn't used to hearing license plate numbers announced out into thin air in such a rude way. What is it you get out of that thing?"

"I like knowing what's going on," Opal said. "Especially if there's bad weather on the way."

"I can see having it on during something like that."

"It's interesting to know about shoplifters at Wal-Mart or whose cows are loose," Opal said. "It never hurts to know what's going on around you." She gave her daughter's knee a pat. "Speaking of rudeness, I had another thought about that snake Greg found in his room. What if that wasn't the one the snakeskin belonged to?"

"What?!"

"You know what I mean."

"That's something I didn't need to hear, Mom."

"I've been all around this house looking for a way they can get in. Your father did the same thing after we found the first one years ago. He helped build this place. He knew how tight and well-constructed it was."

"When was the last time you found a snake in the house?"

"About four years ago."

"What did you do with it once you got it out of the house?"

"Threw it in the back of the truck and took it down the road. It was a rat snake. They do a lot of good. I didn't want to kill him, I just wanted him out of the house."

"Maybe it took him this long to find his way back."

Opal looked at her then shook her head. "I'm just telling you this so you'll keep your eyes open," Opal said. "That snake this morning looked a lot bigger than the snakeskin we found. So keep a lookout for other signs that we might not be alone in the house."

"I did *not* need to hear that, Mom." Nora let the shiver she was experiencing run its course through her body.

"You know what signs I'm talking about, right?"

"Snake droppings?" Nora offered.

"Yup. That's the most common."

"It's amazing to me how much country life revolves around some sort of poop—whether it's chicken, pig, cow, mice or snake."

"It's not just animals," Opal said, leaning back in the porch swing again. "When I was a tot, the shape your outhouse was in determined how poor you were. Only rich people had indoor plumbing."

Nora stretched out and crossed her feet at the ankles. "We've had some interesting conversations out here on this porch over the years."

"I love it here," Opal said. "I've never wanted to live anywhere else."

Other than a few snakes in the house, Nora thought, *I love this place, too.*

Chapter Eleven

Early on a Saturday evening, Jack came over for supper before they were to leave for the donkey basketball game. Opal fixed meatloaf, mashed potatoes, a salad of vine-ripened tomatoes and cucumbers and green beans right out of the garden. She also had an orange Jell-O cake for dessert if they had room for it later.

"That was delicious, Aunt Opal," Jack said before finishing off his iced tea. He'd had two helpings of everything and had shown his appreciation for an excellent meal by offering a string of compliments nearly each time his fork went in his mouth.

"Maybe we should get going if we're gonna find good seats," Opal suggested.

"Let me put this stuff away," Nora said, indicating the food that was left over. "I'll straighten up the kitchen when we get back."

They took Jack's truck into town. It was big enough for all three of them to sit comfortably in the front seat of the cab once they were able to get Opal in it. Nora liked the truck and made a mental note to talk to Greg about getting something new for their mother. *But she'll need one a lot smaller,* Nora thought. *Something we can both get in and out of without assistance.* If Opal was determined to keep selling eggs, then the least her children could do was get her a nice vehicle in which to do it. The South Texas heat in the summer and the lack of air conditioning in the old truck were all the reasons in the world they needed to move forward with this decision. Nora was ready to make it happen.

They arrived early at the Prescott High School gym, but there was still a long line for parking. Jack dropped them off as close to the gym as he could get, then drove off to find a place to park his truck. Nora and Opal met a slew of people they knew. Opal was the Egg Lady after all, and almost a local celebrity. Once they made their way to the front entrance of the gym, they found a group of Fleming relatives there waiting for other family members to arrive. Nora listened closely as her mother spoke to everyone and hugged nieces and nephews she hadn't seen in a while. Opal helped Nora get reacquainted with her relatives.

Two of her female cousins latched onto Nora almost immediately, each with a few small children tugging at them. The cousins knew Nora was a nurse and they had a list of medical complaints to ask her about. As more family members arrived, several of them left to go inside to find seats in the bleachers. Finally, Jack made his way through the crowd and offered his arm to his Aunt Opal to escort her inside.

What a gallant gesture, Nora thought as she followed them into the crowded gym where they found a cluster of chaos inside. The noise factor alone was beyond anything Nora had been around in a long time. She wasn't much for concerts or sporting events, other than attending one of Holly's volleyball games occasionally, so this wasn't something she would care to do on a regular basis.

Jack found them a place on the end of the third row of the bleachers away from the congestion at the door. Nora liked the way he tended to her mother by helping her out of the truck and offering his hand to pull her up into the bleachers. Since losing his own parents a few years earlier, Nora imagined it had to be a comfort to him to have his Aunt Opal living so close.

There were still more people who waved at them, men tipping their hats and little tow-headed children climbing up on the bleachers to give their Uncle Jack a hug. The first twenty minutes they were inside, her mother spent a vast majority of the time leaning over toward Nora and whispering things like, "That's your cousin Arlo's boy," or "That's Cyrus Fleming and his second wife. Remember? His first wife died in a tractor accident."

"Do we like his second wife?" Nora asked.

"We do. She was married to that Jonathan Blackburn you went to school with. He used to beat her all the time."

"Jonathan Blackburn?" Nora repeated with an arched brow. "The math whiz? The banker's son was a wife beater?"

"Sure was. Used to beat his kids, too. I heard it on the scanner a few times with some of those domestic violence calls the police go on. He's in jail now, but not for that. They caught him embezzling at the Prescott Bank his daddy ran. He got seven years. Heard that on the Hometown News."

"Well, I'll be," Nora said.

Her mother kept a steady stream of conversations going with Nora, the two little boys beside her, Jack, and the people in front and behind them. Nora just nodded and would occasionally make a comment, but she was on sensory overload. She knew it was important for her to try to make more of an effort to get to know her family again, but that wasn't going to be easy. To her, all the cousins looked too much alike. It would take her a while to identify some of them well enough to call someone by the correct name unless they were with a spouse she could readily identify or an older relative that she knew, but she was up for the challenge. They were all good people and she was looking forward to spending more time with them.

Nora leaned over toward her mother and whispered, "Don't leave me alone with any of these Fleming people, and always use their names when we're stuck in the middle of a group of them."

"Stuck?" Opal said. "This is your family. You don't 'get stuck' with them. You're *already* stuck with them."

"Yeah, I know, but hey . . . everyone looks the same to me. The kids all have blond hair and blue eyes, kind of like a sequel to 'Children of the Corn' or something. I'll catch on, but it might take a while."

Opal gave her daughter's knee a squeeze. "Maybe we should have some of them over for supper so you can get to know them again. They're all nice people and well thought of in the community."

"Yeah, maybe that's a good idea," Nora said.

After a while, the announcer encouraged everyone to find a seat so the game could begin, but that didn't speed up the mingling very much. There were still hundreds of people trying to get into the gym. The three of them scooted over on the bleachers as much as they could to make room for a few more of Jack's little nephews who wanted to sit with them. The anticipation of the donkeys' entrance along with the excitement of the crowd made Nora just as eager as everyone else to be entertained for the evening. *Welcome to Small Town, USA*, she thought as warm memories of her father and nights like this came back to her.

It wasn't a surprise to her that the donkey basketball game was as much fun as she remembered it being as a child. There were ten donkeys that were trained to let grown men and women ride them while the people tried to make a basket with a basketball. There was no dribbling involved, which made it somewhat easier in theory. The Prescott Police Department wore the red T-shirts and blue jeans while the Prescott High School faculty wore the blue T-shirts and black jeans.

Each team had a female player riding a gentle, more user-friendly donkey, and each team had at least one donkey that would have preferred not to have a rider on it at all and would usually try to throw a player off its back. To make things interesting, the meaner donkeys nipped at the nicer ones, causing most of the donkeys to run away from each other or stand still no matter what the rider wanted it to do. Things were pretty much even on the teams where the donkeys were concerned, however, each time an unfriendly donkey would try to buck or throw one of the police officers off its back, the crowd seemed to enjoy the game a lot more. One of the police officers was named Stick McBroom who was the only player to receive any boos from the crowd. He was extremely thin and at six foot eight he didn't have to even touch the donkey he was riding since his legs were so long. Officer McBroom just happened to have the mean donkey that tried to throw him off every thirty seconds or so, and the crowd rooted for the donkey. The laughter and applause was so loud that little kids stuck their fingers in their ears from the noise, but would still cheer whenever a team scored.

Well into the game the score was tied with baskets few and far between, but seeing the donkeys in action kept the audience in near hysterics. Nora loved seeing her mother have a good time. Nora was also surprised at how much fun she was having too even though it was so incredibly loud.

At halftime, the school faculty was ahead by four points, mostly because the Prescott Police force just couldn't get their donkeys at the right end of the court. The two football coaches who were part of the faculty's team kept feeding the ball to a young female English teacher riding the only donkey on their team that would do what it was supposed to do. The female English teacher was Kit Fleming, so that made Nora, Opal, and Jack cheer even louder for the high school faculty. The Police Department's team was without a doubt too macho to give the ball to the only female player on their side—the only person in a red T-shirt who rode a donkey that minded and liked going toward their basket. No one wanted the police officers to win anyway, but Nora found it interesting how stubborn those particular players were being.

"The red-shirted boys are a lot like those donkeys they're riding," Opal whispered to her at one point.

Nora had to agree with her. "You mean a bunch of asses riding on asses out there?"

Opal snorted and then covered her mouth. "Yeah. I guess that's what I mean."

During halftime, Nora ended up with one of the little boys in her lap as people mingled around and stretched their legs. Everyone on the edges of the gym floor let the game organizer take the donkeys out while the human participants talked to people in the crowd.

"Over there by that big ice chest," Opal said as she leaned closer to Nora so she could hear her better. "See that older gentleman in the wheelchair?"

Just as Nora looked toward where her mother was pointing, the people in the row in front of them stood up, blocking their view.

"Well, fiddle," Opal said. "Now I can't see a thing."

Nora's Uncle Felix was the oldest living relative she had and he wasn't in a wheelchair yet, so she had no idea who her mother was talking about or trying to show her.

"His daughter came back to help him with his business after he had a stroke," Opal went on to explain. "You might remember her from school."

The people in front of them finally got out of the way, so Nora moved around to try and see better.

"He's sure persistent," Opal said. "He's the one who bought the old home place outside of town several years ago. Now he wants the mineral rights for it, too. I finally had to tell him they weren't for sale hoping he'd stop bothering me about it."

"You mean Skip Tate?" Jack asked, overhearing the conversation.

"That's the one," Opal said.

"He started calling me too trying to get me to change your mind," Jack said. "I remember thinking, if my Aunt Opal doesn't want anything to do with you, then I'm sure I don't either."

"You never told me he called you!" Opal said.

"The best way to get rid of people like that is to ignore them," Jack advised.

"He wasn't taking no for an answer."

Nora tried to look in the direction her mother had pointed to earlier and finally saw part of a wheelchair, but there were too many people around him to see much of anything else.

"Who did you say he was?" Nora asked her mother.

"Skip Tate," Opal said. "Some folks call him the windmill man."

Skip Tate, Nora thought. *Skip Tate the windmill man? Darcy Tate's father was called that when we were kids!*

"What did you say happened to him?" Nora asked, craning her neck to see him better.

"He had a stroke a while back. His daughter had to come home and help take care of him."

Chapter Twelve

"Here," Nora said, handing over the little boy that had been in her lap. "Hold him for me." She stood up and climbed down from the bleachers. Like a salmon attempting to swim upstream, she was determined to get to the other side of the gym. With a continuous series of "pardon me" and "excuse me" apologies at the edge of the gym floor, Nora finally worked her way close enough to the man in the wheelchair to see for herself if it really was the windmill man.

The bastard, Nora thought. *Even a wheelchair is too good for him.* She would have known those mean, squinty eyes anywhere no matter how old he or she ever became.

Nora looked around at the women in the immediate area of the wheelchair, thinking that if Darcy was there, she would be some-where in close proximity to her father. Finally, she saw a tall, attractive woman with short salt and pepper hair talking with three men. The woman handed each of them a business card and slipped the rest of the small stack into her shorts pocket. *That has to be her,*

Nora thought with a smile. The woman was taller than Nora remembered, but still had that great posture so few tall women felt confident enough with. All Nora could do for a moment was look at her like she used to that summer when Darcy had been a lifeguard at the public pool.

"Darcy," Nora called. Just saying her name made Nora smile all over again. It had been a long time since she had allowed herself to think about her. The memories had been too painful to keep alive after a while. Some of that devastation had lessened over time, but the memories of that night in October over twenty-three years ago still made Nora's heart ache whenever she allowed her thoughts to go there.

The woman turned and looked for whoever might have said her name. She saw Nora and stopped talking to the three men in mid-sentence. They stared at each other for a moment before Darcy smiled. She said something to the men and then looked back at Nora again. There were several children as well as the wheelchair between them, so it wasn't easy getting close enough to each other to have a real conversation. Nora felt relieved to find Darcy looking so well. The last time she had seen her was the night in Principal Szalwinski's office when Darcy's father had slapped his daughter so hard that she nearly fell down. Nora remembered being horrified that anyone would intentionally hurt someone she cared about—and right there in front of her at that! She had never been a part of, or even witnessed, real physical violence of any kind before, so the shock of Mr. Tate's actions still reverberated through Nora's mind even to this day. Flemings never struck each other or anyone else for that matter, but Nora remembered jumping up from her chair that night and getting between them when the windmill man raised his hand up to strike Darcy again. Everything happened so quickly, but Nora wasn't about to let anyone physically hurt either one of them. Finally, Principal Szalwinski scrambled around his desk to separate the three of them just moments before Nora would have sunk her fingernails into Mr. Tate's eyeballs.

But Darcy seemed to be fine now—no visible scars on her face or arms like Nora imagined would be there. She actually seemed better than fine to Nora at that moment. Darcy Tate was everything Nora always used to look for in another woman—that tall, soft butch exterior and a reserved kindness that was unmistakable.

The horrible nightmares about the windmill man hurting and then killing his daughter and tossing her body in the river had given Nora many sleepless and restless nights over the years. She always thought that her feelings for Darcy Tate had been sealed and immortalized in Principal Szalwinski's office that awful night. Nora had often wondered if having Darcy in her life those precious few months was the main reason all her other relationships had never had a chance to grow and mature. There had been many women over the years, but no one had captured her heart like this one had. For years Nora had tried to find her again, but she never heard anything about her. It was a relief to finally see her looking so well.

"Is it really you, Nora?" Darcy asked. She was standing behind the wheelchair smiling down at her. Darcy still had those perfect white teeth and hazel eyes that reflected a bit of shyness and sincerity. She wore a brown sleeveless T-shirt, khaki shorts that hit her just above the knees and white sneakers. She still tanned easily and it was apparent that she spent a lot of time in the sun.

"It's me," Nora said in a hoarse whisper. "I just heard you were back in town."

"I can't believe you're here. Of all the places to run into you again. Uh . . . a donkey basketball game?"

Nora shrugged. "I'm here with my mother and a cousin."

"Ahh," Darcy said with a smile and a nod. "Still hanging out with the cousins, I see."

"Just one for now."

"Are you still married?"

Nora looked at her and was sure both of her eyebrows had shot up in some sort of comical Lucille Ball fashion.

"Married?" Nora repeated. The word sounded totally foreign to her all of a sudden. "I've never been married."

"What?"

"Why would you think I was married?"

"Everyone please take your seats," the announcer boomed over the sound system.

With that announcement, people started to move almost as a unit and before long Nora was being carried away with the crowd.

"Give me one of those business cards!" Nora yelled over the tops of heads. She reached out for the card Darcy was trying desperately to give to her and someone between them finally passed it over to her.

"I'll call you later!" Nora said, waving the card in the air.

Nora eventually made it back to the other end of the gym and her mother and Jack. Nora could see there were two other women sitting where Nora's place should have been in the bleachers. She recognized them as the two cousins with the medical questions from earlier in the evening, but she couldn't be sure exactly which ones they were or who in the family they belonged to.

A man behind Nora in the crowd said, "Ten donkeys can run all over that floor for a few hours, but we can't put a pair of hundred-dollar tennis shoes on it?"

Nora and about four other people around her had to chuckle at that.

"The donkeys have special stuff on their feet," someone explained.

"Their feet or their hooves?"

"What's the difference?" the second person asked. "It's all the same. Their feet or their hooves aren't touching the gym floor."

"So these are flying donkeys?" the first man asked. "Is that what you're telling me?"

Sporadic laughter went down the row.

"No," someone said. "They aren't flying donkeys."

"Well," the original voice grumbled, "you said their feet didn't touch the floor. Whatever those donkeys are wearing on their feet or their hooves can't cost any more than these tennis shoes I just paid ninety-eight dollars for!"

Nora climbed up to the third row and immediately looked over to where the windmill man's wheelchair had been parked earlier. There were still too many people milling around down there to see anything other than a swarm of people trying to get up into the bleachers.

"We'd better get back to our seats," one of her female cousins said. "Come on, boys."

Nora got out of the way so the two women and the little boys could step down.

"We'll see you later, Nora," one of the women said.

Down at the bottom of the bleachers was a man in his fifties reminding everyone to stay off the gym floor and only walk on the edge. Nora recognized him as one of the coaches who was on the faculty's team.

"You mean so those donkeys can run all over it instead?" a man on the second row yelled down to him. Nora knew that voice to belong to the man with the hundred-dollar tennis shoes earlier as chuckles went down the row.

"It's the donkeys' show tonight," the coach said.

"Yeah, well . . . my tax dollars helped pay for that gym floor. I should be able to walk on it."

With a smile and a wave, the coach said, "And we appreciate you paying those taxes, too, sir."

"Donkeys don't pay taxes!" the man said, continuing the good-natured banter between them.

The coach nodded and offered a hand to help Nora's two cousins down from the bleachers.

"Oh, I beg to differ with you on that one," the coach said. "I bet a *lot* of donkeys pay taxes."

The crowd around him laughed again and the heckler with the hundred-dollar sneakers was quiet after that. Nora sat down and looked at the business card in her hand.

"Where'd you go?" her mother asked.

"The windmill man's daughter was a good friend of mine in school. I went over there to see if I could find her."

84

"Did you?"

Nora held up the business card. "I did," she said, slipping the card in her shirt pocket.

"We've got a windmill that needs fixin' before summer."

"I'll get that taken care of, Aunt Opal," Jack promised. "I've been meaning to take a look at it. We can't turn the cows into that back pasture without it."

Nora couldn't keep her hands off the business card and took it out of her pocket again. The card had a picture of a windmill on it and the name of the business. Skip and Darcy Tate's names were there with an office number and a cell phone number. Nora reached for her cell phone at the waistband of her shorts and wanted to call the number just to hear Darcy's voice again, but her mother leaned closer and said, "I invited two of your cousins over for cake and coffee after the game."

"Tonight?" Nora asked.

"Sure. Why not? We shouldn't be eating all that cake by ourselves anyway. Besides, you said you wanted to get to know them again."

"I said that?"

Opal shrugged. "Well, one of us said it."

The crowd erupted in applause when the donkeys were led back in. It was entirely too loud to make a phone call or to even hear a cell phone ringing, so Nora abandoned that idea. She put her cell phone away and looked over in the direction where the wheelchair had been earlier. She saw the windmill man parked there at the end of the first row with Darcy sitting in the bleachers beside him.

Why would she think I had gotten married? Nora wondered. *I graduated here from high school and went off to college the next year right after that.* She kept her head turned toward where the wheelchair was, in hopes of getting a better look at Darcy, but Nora was too far away to see anything. Just knowing she had found Darcy again made a certain calmness ease through Nora's body. *But you know absolutely nothing about her now,* Nora thought. *Maybe she's the one who has gotten married and has a boatload of kids. There were children all around the windmill man's wheelchair when I was over there! What if all those kids belonged to Darcy? And what if one of those men she had been talking to was her husband instead of a local farmer or rancher with a broken windmill!?*

Nora felt confused by this train of thought. She took the business card out of her pocket again and looked at it more closely. It actually said "Skip and Darcy Tate" under the name of the business. *If Darcy was married, she wouldn't be calling herself a Tate,* she reasoned.

Okay, okay, she thought, letting the initial panic subside. *So maybe she's not married and doesn't have a soccer-mom van full of kids. That still doesn't mean she's a lesbian now. And what we had together when we were kids might not have meant the same thing to her as it did to me. And besides, if she is a lesbian, the possibility of her not having a girlfriend now are probably extremely remote.*

Nora shook her head in frustration. It hadn't occurred to her to look for other lesbians around where Darcy had been standing.

After the way her father treated her that night? Nora thought. *There's not much chance that she would have a partner with her now. Maybe what happened between us had just been a phase for her like it is for a lot of teenage girls. But damn she looks good! And to me she looks like a lesbian. Yeah, yeah, yeah, but how many times have you seen what looked like a butch in the local grocery store—with the wallet in the back pocket, cowboy boots on, a baseball cap and five kids calling her mommy? Not to mention a husband asking permission to put a box of Cap'n Crunch in the shopping cart. Let's face it,* Nora thought, *the rules you are used to going by no longer apply now.*

Chapter Thirteen

Nora agreed with her mother and Jack that it would be easier to just wait where they were until some of the crowd thinned out. The two female cousins that would be joining them later for cake were also waiting out the crowd on the other side of the gym floor where a group of children ran up and down the bleachers. As Nora watched the kids playing, she couldn't remember *ever* having that much energy.

Opal pointed to one of Nora's cousins and explained, "Freida is the one in the pink tank top. I think she was a few years younger than you."

"Then the other one has to be Tina," Nora said. "You're right. I'll catch on. They married the Olsen brothers, right?"

"They sure did," Opal said. "All their kids are double cousins."

Double cousins, Nora thought, smiling at the term. That had been the magic phrase as soon as both the Fleming sisters became engaged to the Olsen brothers. All of their children would be double cousins.

"I remember that now," Nora said. "So whatever happened to Britany and Tory? I don't even get a Christmas card from them. We used to go everywhere together."

"Britany lives in Scribner with her husband and five of their kids. I'm not sure how many grandkids they have now. I don't see Britany that often, so I've lost track of her since your Aunt Hertha died. Tory lives on a ranch outside of Appleton with her husband, their three kids, and about four grandkids now. They just keep adding on a new extension to the house every three or four years to make room for everyone. It's a big ranch and lots to do to keep them all busy. Reminds me of that show *Dallas* with grown men and women still living at home with their parents."

"You mean like me?"

"No!" Opal said. "You and your brother went off and made lives of your own. Not your cousin Tory's kids. It's like she's Miss Ellie on that *Dallas* show. She likes her fingers in the pie. No one does anything out there without asking her permission first."

"Maybe her kids tried to leave and she wouldn't let them," Nora said with a shake of her head. "I remember her being kind of bossy when we were younger."

"You're right about that. She barks and they all jump," Opal said, leaning her head closer to Nora's. "Tory might have a little problem with you and the lesbian thing," she whispered.

"Oh, really? What has she said about me?"

Opal shrugged. "She knows better than to say anything outright in front of me, but every time I see her she asks me if you're married yet."

"Well, it's common knowledge that women my age who've never been married are more than likely gay," Nora said, rolling her eyes. "She never could understand how important a career could be to some women. Finding a husband and popping out babies has been her goal in life ever since we were in junior high."

"Her problem with you might stem from the announcement you made to the whole family at her wedding reception, if you'll remember," Opal said. "Maybe she's never gotten over that."

Nora groaned and held her head in her hands. "One of the ushers kept putting his hand on my butt while we were dancing! I didn't mean for the entire VFW hall to hear me."

Jack's laughter was even louder than her mother's.

"I personally think Tory's mad at you because you're still single and not as miserable as she is," Opal said.

"We make our own misery," Nora chimed in philosophically.

"Nah," Jack said. "You stole her thunder at the wedding. That's all anyone could talk about for weeks afterward. 'I'm a lesbian, you moron. Keep your hands off my ass'," he whispered to them in a hushed, high-pitched voice. "Wasn't that what you said?"

Opal snorted and put a hand up to her mouth while Nora glowed from embarrassment at the reminder.

The bleachers thinned out, but there was still congestion at the door, so they stayed put a while longer. Nora had been watching the windmill man and Darcy on the other side of the gym as they continued talking to several men around them. There was no way pushing a wheelchair through such a swarm of people would have gotten them very far either, so there were a lot of people still waiting for the crowd to disperse.

Finally, Jack, Opal and Nora stood up and were able to walk to the end of their row in the bleachers while everyone else was slowly filing out the door from the gym floor. They sat down again once they reached the end of the row, but this time they were directly across from Darcy and her father.

Nora leaned over toward her mother and Jack and asked, "What have you two heard about Darcy Tate?"

"Hmm," Opal said. "She retired from the military the best I remember from listening to the Hometown News."

"The Army," Jack said. "I remember them doing a feature article on her in the local paper a few months ago. She was in Iraq for a while, too."

Iraq, Nora thought. *Wow!*

"Does she have a husband?" Nora asked. "Any kids?"

"I don't recall the article mentioning anything like that," Jack said. "She also does some metalsmithing and welding. Or some sort of artwork like that, I think. Or whatever you call it. Metal sculpturing maybe."

"I'm also remembering the windmill man being the person who keeps tabs on the river," Opal said. "He used to be one of those weather spotter people."

"A volunteer for the National Weather Service," Jack confirmed. "He used to provide daily rain reports to the weather service and he would watch the river to see if it crested over the flood stage. Alerts to evacuate the lower areas of the county would come from his reports when they got too much rain north of us."

Nora vaguely remembered Darcy and her family being involved in weather-related things now that Jack mentioned it. Darcy had done an oral report on it once in a speech class they had together.

"I wonder if his daughter does all of that for him now, too," Opal said.

"I don't know," Jack said, "but I sure hope *somebody's* watching the river when we get some of those gulley washers."

Even though they had waited a while, it was still crowded outside the gym. The donkeys had been loaded up into several huge horse trailers at the side of the gym and the majority of the kids who had been at the game were there to see them. Nora tried to hang back to see if she could talk to Darcy again, but Jack and her mother rushed right out of there as soon as they found an opening in the crowd. Since Nora didn't know where Jack had parked the truck, she had to keep up with them.

"They're probably waiting at the house for us," Opal said once they climbed into the pickup.

"I know those people," Jack said helping his Aunt Opal in. "They'll wait for a piece of your cake."

Nora reached in her shirt pocket to make sure Darcy's business card was still there. She was excited at the thought of talking to her again. They had a lot to catch up on.

"Remember the time we went over to Appleton to see if the zebra was out?" Freida asked.

Nora's cousins Tina and Freida and their husbands were sitting around Opal's kitchen table eating cake and drinking coffee. Jack had helped himself to more meatloaf and mashed potatoes and had a full plate of food slowly turning in the microwave.

"What zebra?" Opal asked.

"Over there at the old Anderson place," Freida said. "They had llamas and ostriches in one of the fields and someone told us there was a zebra too. Only it stayed in the barn a lot. So whenever Greg and Nora had the truck, we'd all go over to Appleton and look for the zebra."

"Then one time I guess old man Anderson got tired of us driving by," Tina said, "so he came out on his porch with a shotgun."

Everyone laughed.

"We weren't too interested in zebras after that," Freida said.

Nora was enjoying the visit and could tell that her mother was too. It was interesting seeing her cousins all grown up. The Olsen brothers had been friends of Greg's in high school where the three of them had played football together.

"Anyone want more cake?" Opal asked. Jack passed down a small empty plate.

"Remember that Easter we were over here and hid Easter eggs all day?" Freida asked Nora and Jack. "We had our nice Easter baskets with candy and little trinkets. I think Grandma had one made up for each of us."

"I remember Jack getting conked on the head with a yo-yo that day," Nora said. "Someone was swinging it around."

"Someone?" Tina said, nearly spewing coffee across the table. "It was *you!*" she said pointing at Nora.

With her cheeks glowing again for the second time that evening, Nora had hoped nobody remembered that part. "It was an accident," she said sheepishly.

"A pump knot the size of a goose egg came up right there," Jack said pointing to his forehead.

"A few days later all those eggs you kids didn't find started to stink around the house, too," Opal said. "That's my Easter memory."

"Then Greg and I had another Easter egg hunt on our own," Nora said. "That wasn't quite as much fun."

"Remember Grandpa's old car?" Tina asked. "He'd get all the grandkids in it and take us to town."

"Nora and I were talking about that just the other day," Jack said. "Aunt Opal thinks that old car's still down by the creek. I might go down there tomorrow and see if I can find it."

"What kind of car was it?" Pete Olsen asked.

"Old," the four cousins answered in unison. Everyone at the table erupted in laughter.

It was after eleven before everyone went home. Nora thought it was too late to call Darcy now, but she would make sure and do it tomorrow.

"That was fun," Opal said as she stood beside Nora on the porch.

Nora could see the taillights on Jack's truck at the end of the driveway. "Yes, it was," she had to agree. "What do the Olsen brothers do? I don't remember."

"One's a farmer and the other is a bus mechanic and works in San Antonio. He didn't care for farming."

They went to the porch swing and sat down.

"Jack did so good tonight," Opal said. "I'm proud of him."

"What did he do?" Nora asked. "Besides finish off your meat-loaf?"

Opal nodded with a smile. "That boy does love my cooking."

"So much for us having nice meatloaf sandwiches tomorrow."

"Now that you're here, maybe we can have him over for supper more often," Opal said. "It's easier to cook for three than it is for one."

"If I keep eating this way, I'll have to take up jogging again."

"You look fine. Just enjoy yourself and let your mother have some fun."

Nora liked sitting out on the porch with the evening breeze a nice reminder that spring had arrived. It was even nicer without the police scanner on.

"So what did Jack do tonight that was so good?" Nora asked.

"His ex was at the game with her new boyfriend."

"And you didn't point them out to me?!"

"It didn't seem like a good idea at the time. It's one thing sharing information when the people you're talking about are across the gym from you, but it's a lot different when it involves Jack. He was hurting inside, but he didn't say anything or make a fuss."

"Then how do you know he even saw them?"

"We both saw them at the same time. That's one of the reasons he doesn't go anywhere now days. She's always out at things like that. But Jack kept his temper and enjoyed the game anyway. At times like that he draws strength from a lot of things. Having his little nephews there was also a good thing."

"I had no idea any of that was going on. Have there been scenes out in public between them?"

"After she left him, Jack would go out to a few of the local places looking for her. We had a talk one night and I explained to him that maybe it was best that she had moved on if that's the way she was gonna act. He could do better."

"What did he say to that?"

"I'd never seen him cry before. At least not since he'd lost his mama."

"It's a sad thing when you love someone who doesn't love you back."

"Yes, it is. That night he and I talked was a real eye-opener for him. He kept saying he would take her back no matter what she had done. I told him he deserved better than that and he needed to have more respect for himself."

"Did he listen?"

"He did," Opal said. "Tonight when we saw them in the bleachers on the other side of the gym, Jack hugged his little nephew tight and I heard him say, 'I deserve better than that'."

Nora felt a thickness in her throat hearing the emotion in her mother's voice. Jack was lucky to have her in his life. *We're all lucky to have her,* Nora thought.

Chapter Fourteen

On Sunday morning Nora got up once she realized the young rooster had no intention of letting her sleep any longer. Some days he didn't bother her at all, and other days it was like he was crowing right there under her bed.

"Good morning," Nora said as she entered the kitchen. Her mother had just come in from feeding the girls.

"Good morning," Opal said.

"How are you feeling today?"

"Tired. I thought I would sleep better after going to bed so late."

"How about I make us some breakfast?"

"You know how to make biscuits yet?" Opal teased.

"What? It's not breakfast without a biscuit? Have a seat and drink your coffee. Let me show you what I can do."

"Don't be fixin' me any of those Coco Puff things your brother likes in the middle of the night."

"Believe me," Nora said. "A Coco Puff has never touched these lips." She made her mother sit down. Nora glanced at the basket of eggs on the counter and knew what the rest of her morning would consist of. *And not only that,* she thought, *it looks like I need to learn how to make biscuits.*

A few hours later, a truck drove up and parked out in front of the house. Jack and Pete Olsen were there. Nora and her mother waved to them from the porch.

"We're going down to the creek to see about Grandpa's old car," Jack said. "If that's all right with you."

"Sure," Opal said. "You know where it is?"

"I used to."

"Don't forget we've got cows down there."

Nora was proud of herself for recognizing which of the Olsen brothers was with Jack. She was getting better at knowing who was who. The men drove around the side of the house toward the creek.

"Probably a family of skunks living in that old car," Opal said.

"Or a nest of hornets."

"If they don't come back soon we'll go down there and see how they're doing."

Nora waited until she and her mother had finished cleaning all the eggs before she even allowed herself to think about calling Darcy. Connecting with her again made Nora feel anxious and excited at the same time. After having lived in Dallas all these years, it had been hard to keep in touch with any of her old friends from school. In many ways, her hometown and the people in it hadn't changed that much, but Nora had grown away from all of it and was now faced with trying to find her place there again. It was strange to her how fate worked and weaved the circumstances of people's lives. She wondered where she and Darcy would both be now if they hadn't been caught kissing in the school parking lot that night.

Nora put the clean eggs in the other refrigerator out on the sun porch in the back. When she returned to the kitchen, her mother was there with the keys to her truck in her hand. Opal asked, "You going down to the creek with me?"

"No. I've got a phone call to make. I might walk down there later."

Her mother picked up a jug of ice water and put a few plastic cups in a bag. "Those boys are probably thirsty by now."

As soon as she saw Opal start up her truck, Nora went outside on the front porch with her cell phone and Darcy's business card. She sat in the swing and looked at the card for a long time before finding the courage to dial the number. She had no idea what to expect and knew even less about what she wanted to say to her.

"Hello."

"Darcy?"

"Yes. Who's calling?"

"This is Nora. How are you today?"

There was a pause and then Nora heard Darcy say something to someone there with her.

"You're busy. Is this a bad time?"

"Unfortunately, I'm working today."

"I'm sorry," Nora said. "I can call back later."

"It'll be easier if I call you. Would that be okay?"

"Sure. I'll talk to you then."

Nora closed her cell phone and slipped it into her pocket. *Well,* she thought. *That didn't go anywhere near the way I was expecting it to.* She picked up the business card laying on the swing beside her and stared at it almost as long as she had at the game the night before. *Don't you dare get your hopes up over any of this,* she thought. *There are a lot of people in this town you can become friends with again. Darcy Tate doesn't have to be one of them.*

She rubbed her left temple with her fingertips and took a deep breath. *Get a grip,* Nora reminded herself. *How much of this weird-*

ness I'm feeling is really about finding an old friend? Back then it was puppy love. I was crazy about her and neither one of us knew what we were doing. There's also a good chance she won't call me back, so get ready to accept that too.

Just as Nora's spirits were about to plummet, she heard a truck coming around the side of the house. It was her mother.

"Those boys have chainsaws out and they're gettin' after it."

"Chainsaws? What do they need chainsaws for?"

"That car's surrounded by trees. Even has one growing out through a window." Opal stood there at the bottom of the porch steps with her bonnet on and her hands on her hips. "I'm gonna make some sandwiches and take 'em back down there. I enjoyed watching them work. Now I know what Hilda gets out of it when she's watching me clean the eggs."

Nora helped her mother make ham and cheese sandwiches and even tossed a few cold homemade dill pickles in a plastic bag for them. She carried the small ice chest to the truck and was caught up in her mother's enthusiasm about going back to the creek to see how they would get the car out. Even after having been down there recently, Nora couldn't remember seeing her grandpa's old car, so she was looking forward to watching them uncover a bit of her past.

"So what's Jack going to do once he gets that car out of the trees?" Nora asked as they bounced along in her mother's pickup.

"Who knows?"

"It was a pile of rust when we were kids! I can't imagine what he's thinking. How long has it been down there by the creek?"

"Your grandpa died about twenty years ago. It wasn't too long before he died that he drove that car down there one day to go fishing. It wouldn't start when he was done, so he just left it there and walked back to the house."

"Didn't anyone try and help him get it started?"

"He was mad at it after that," Opal explained. "He just stopped driving all together. He thought of the car not starting as a sign, I think. It wasn't long after that he kind of gave up on everything."

Nora held on as they hit bump after bump driving down the road. When they reached the gate that led to the creek area, Nora got out of the truck and opened it. She could hear the chainsaws buzzing to the right and down the hill. All the noise had scared the cows off for now, but Nora could tell where they had been eating near the brush. Another few weeks and the cows would have things cleared out down there.

Opal parked her truck next to the picnic table. "Watch where you step," she said. "I see fresh cow pies all over the place."

They got out and sat down at the table. It was early enough in the day to still be cool.

"They make handling those chainsaws look so easy," Opal said. "I tried just picking one up once and nearly threw my back out."

"Boys and their toys."

"Isn't that the truth. I gave Jack all your pop's power tools. I didn't figure Greg would want them."

"Not with that foo-foo gene of his," Nora added. "I imagine any project Greg had going on that needed power tools, he'd just as soon hire someone else to do it."

The chainsaws stopped and Jack and Pete pulled the saplings and limbs from larger trees out of the way.

"We brought some snacks!" Opal called.

Pete pitched a sapling off to the side away from the old car and walked toward the picnic table while Jack continued tugging at some loose brush. As Nora handed Pete a sandwich and a glass of water, her cell phone rang. She reached for it at the waistband of her shorts and saw that it was a call from her niece Holly.

"Hey, kiddo. What's up?"

"He's not budging about science camp, Aunt Nora. Nothing I say seems to be working this time."

Nora heard her mother laugh at something Pete said as Opal sat down at the table again. Jack decided to take a break too and came over to join them.

"When is science camp?" Nora asked. She stepped away from the table to try and get a better signal on her phone.

"The last two weeks in July," Holly said.

"That gives you all of June and most of August to come visit us for the summer."

"I think he's trying to find other things for me to do here then."

"What makes you say that?"

"He mentioned his office hiring kids to work during the summer."

Nora smiled and shook her head. She knew for a fact that Greg missed his daughter when Holly spent time in Prescott with her grandmother over the summer break. He came down nearly every weekend to see her.

"You wouldn't like to earn some money over the summer?" Nora asked. She looked up as more chuckling from the picnic table distracted her.

"When I need money, Dad gives it to me. Why should I work during my vacation?"

"I see."

"If he thinks I'm working *and* going to science camp this summer . . . well . . . I can go to science camp and still have a vacation."

"Then maybe that needs to be your strategy," Nora suggested. "Science camp and vacation."

"Okay," Holly said. "Thanks. I'll try that on him. Is Grammie there?"

"Sure. Just a minute." Nora held up her cell phone. "Your granddaughter wants to talk to you."

Greg's a smart man, she thought as she gave the phone to her mother. *He knew what would get that kid interested in science camp. All he had to do was suggest she get a summer job instead!*

Jack finished two sandwiches and the rest of the dill pickles. "I would've never imagined that car could look any worse," he said. "It's like a rusty old time capsule. The keys are still in it."

"Once you get all the trees out from around it, just drive it on up to the house," Opal suggested with a smile. She handed Nora her phone back to her.

"You should've seen Pete run when that packrat scurried out of there," Jack announced. "It was a lot less offensive than a regular rat, but I still didn't want it anywhere near me," Pete said.

Nora's cell phone rang again. She answered it and got up and walked to where she knew the signal would be better.

"Hello."

"Nora? This is Darcy Tate."

Nora felt relieved to hear Darcy's voice again even though in her mind she had prepared for the fact she might not hear from her again. "Ahh. So you're working today."

"Business has been unreal. I haven't had a day off in six weeks."

Nora didn't know what else to say. The silence that followed was a gentle reminder that they probably had nothing in common any longer. In the past Nora had always been the one to initiate conversation or suggest things for them to do together. In Nora's eyes, Darcy had been a painfully shy teenager and eager to follow wherever Nora was willing to lead her, but Nora was past all of that now. She liked being the one pursued these days. With most of her friends and lovers during the last fifteen years or so being in the medical field, work was what she had in common with them. Conversations never lagged and the laughter usually flowed easily, but now here she was attempting to make small talk with a virtual stranger. The subtle differences were a real eye-opener for her.

"Maybe we could have lunch sometime," Darcy said finally.

"Sure. I'd like that. Why don't you give me a call when you're free?"

"I'll do that."

"Nice talking to you." Nora closed her cell phone and walked back to the picnic table where her mother was sitting. Break was over. The men had already picked up their chainsaws again.

"Keep your feet up," Opal said. "I've seen about three mice shooting out of that old car so far."

"Oh, yuck."

"Who was that on the phone? You've got your sad face on."

"That was Darcy Tate," Nora said. She and her mother moved up to sit on the edge of the picnic table and put their feet on the concrete bench. "The first girl I ever kissed."

"You don't say!" Opal put her arm around Nora's waist and gave her a hug. "You and the windmill man's daughter. He always looked like a mean old cuss. Your dad and I would see him at the water board meetings every few months or so. I didn't care much for him."

"I didn't like him either," Nora said, remembering how hard he had slapped Darcy that night.

"So why the sad face?"

Nora shrugged. "Have you ever wished you could go back and do some things over again?"

"Oh, goodness yes," Opal said. "But you can soon make yourself crazy if you think that way for long."

"What things would you change if you could do them over?"

"I would have hugged your father more and told him how much I loved him. The day we lost him was just like any ordinary day," Opal said. "We got up together and I made us breakfast. We'd done that same thing each day for thirty years. I went to feed the girls and he left to get the tractor. After a while I realized I hadn't seen him leave the barn. He always drove by and waved to me on his way to the field."

Nora and her mother sat there watching Jack and Pete toss more saplings out of the way. Nora felt tears welling up in her eyes and then heard her mother sniff.

"It was just an ordinary day like all the others," Opal said with a trace of emotion in her voice. "If I had known it was gonna be our last one together, I would've said something more . . . or . . . done something more to let him know how loved and cherished he was."

Nora leaned her head close to her mom's and then slipped her arm around her waist.

"I'm sure he knew," Nora whispered.

"Life's too short to take such things for granted. We've all got a limited time here on this sweet earth and we need to make the most of it while we can."

"You're right."

The chainsaws stopped and Nora looked over to see what progress had been made on freeing the car. Jack got the driver's side door open and then leaned inside the front seat.

"Found Grandpa's fishing pole," he said, holding it up. He leaned into the rusty vehicle again and brought something else out. "Here's his thermos." Jack shook the dingy thermos and laughed. "It still has something in it."

"Well, bring it on over here," Opal joked. "I could use some hot coffee right about now."

Chapter Fifteen

Once Jack assured Nora that the chainsaws, along with opening and closing a few squeaky doors, had scared all the field mice away, she ventured a little closer to the car to get a better look.

"What do you plan on doing with it?" Nora asked him. Even though she had asked that question numerous times already, she didn't think anyone had given her a satisfactory answer yet.

"Right now?" Jack said. "Just getting it free from the trees and brush." He turned to Opal who came over to stand beside her daughter. "Didn't anyone offer to help Grandpa with this car when he couldn't get it started?"

"We all did," Opal said. "Your dad and Uncle Felix wanted to tow it up the hill, but your grandpa got really stubborn and washed his hands of the whole thing. He wanted it to stay right here."

"Hmm," Pete said. "If that's what the man wanted, then maybe we'd better leave it alone."

"The tires are all rotted off," Opal pointed out. "Where's it going with no tires?"

"Oh, I could get it out of here," Jack said with confidence, "but now I'm not sure it's such a good idea. If this is where Grandpa wanted it to stay, then we should probably leave it alone like Pete says."

"It's not hurting anything here," Pete said as he looked around the immediate area.

"Cows can't drive," Nora said, attempting to lighten the mood.

"I'll drain the gas out in case the creek gets up or there's a fire or something," Jack said. "That's probably seventy-five cent a gallon gas in the tank."

They got a chuckle out of that.

Nora handed the fishing pole to him. "Then here. Put this back where you found it."

"This too," Opal said handing over the thermos. "It's too late in the day for me to be having coffee anyway."

Once they all drove back up to the house, Opal parked the pickup and she and Nora waved to the other two as they drove off.

"That was kind of fun," Opal said to her daughter. "I can't remember the last time I spent the day at the creek. Not to mention we got it cleaned up a little out there too and didn't even have to break a sweat doing it."

"They sure went to a lot of trouble for nothing." Nora took her mother's arm and helped her up the steps to the porch.

"He just wanted to have another glimpse of his childhood, I think," Opal said. "You kids have some good memories of that car. Last night Jack probably had a rough time once he got home to his empty house after seeing that floozy out with her boyfriend. Sometimes it's good to go back to a place that's familiar and safe."

"He needs to stay busy," Nora said. She sat down next to her mother in the porch swing. "But all work and no play makes Jack a dull boy."

"He's forgotten how to play, I think."

"In a way maybe we all have."

Nora's cell phone rang. She didn't recognize the number on the tiny display screen as she answered it.

"Hello."

"Nora. This is Darcy. Are you at your mom's place?"

"Yes."

"I'm in the area. Are you busy right now? Would this be a bad time to stop by?"

"Not at all. Come on over."

Nora was more nervous than she thought she would be. Whatever disappointment she had experienced earlier in the day over her two conversations with Darcy was now being replaced by a mixture of excitement and anxiety at seeing her again.

"That was Darcy," Nora said. Surprised at how calm she sounded, Nora rubbed her arms and took a deep breath. "She's in the area and asked if she could come by."

"I take it her visit has nothing to do with our broken windmill?" Opal asked with a teasing smile.

"No. Well . . . not yet anyway."

Opal gave her daughter's knee a comforting pat. "How old were you when all of this happened with her?"

"Sixteen or so."

"Once you became a teenager you were such a girly young thing," Opal said. "Your hair had to be just right and you spent hours making sure your clothes looked a certain way. Your dad and I just knew some young farmer would come along and snatch you right up."

"The windmill man probably thought the same thing about Darcy," Nora said. "Little did he know that a farmer's daughter was trying hard to snatch her up instead."

As they were chuckling, they both heard a truck coming up the driveway. Nora turned to see if it was a vehicle she recognized.

"Holy crap," she said. "I bet that's her."

Opal gave Nora's knee another squeeze. "Time for me to go take a nap."

"Oh, no! You're staying right here with me."

Suddenly, Nora wished she had never seen Darcy at the donkey basketball game or called her earlier. What had at one time been excitement and anxiety skirting through her head had now escalated to panic.

"You're always suggesting that I take more naps."

"Let's see how this goes first," Nora said. "You can nap later."

The truck pulled in next to Opal's pickup and the driver waited a while before opening the door. Darcy got out of the truck wearing boots, jeans, a long-sleeved blue denim shirt, dark sunglasses and a Tate Windmill Repair cap. As she came up the sidewalk, Darcy took her sunglasses off and put them in her shirt pocket. She seemed relaxed and confident. To Nora she looked stunning.

"Good afternoon," she said as she climbed the steps.

"Hi there," Nora said. "This is my mother."

"Darcy Tate," Darcy said and extended her hand to Opal.

"Opal Fleming," Opal said. She stood up to shake Darcy's hand. "Nice to meet you. I was sorry to hear about your father's illness. How's he doing?"

"He's much better. Thank you."

"Well," Opal said. "I'll go check on my girls and give them a few treats. Here. Have a seat," she said, indicating her place in the swing.

Nora gave her mother the evil eye at being left alone with Darcy so soon.

"The girls?" Darcy asked.

"Her chickens," Nora explained. "I swear, Mom. Every time you say something like that around a stranger it sounds like you're a madam with a brothel out back."

"Oh, fiddle," Opal said as she waved a hand at her daughter and went into the house chuckling.

"What a delightful woman," Darcy said. "I hear she still sells eggs."

Nora nodded. "She does. Every morning we have a little assembly line going at the kitchen table. Then she delivers them on Wednesdays."

"Gotta love the bonnet."

"She's seldom without one," Nora said. "Can I get you something to drink?"

"I'm fine, thanks. I just finished up a job down the road at the Dziuk's place. That last storm damaged a lot of windmills. I'm still trying to catch up."

"We have one that needs some attention, too," Nora said, relieved at the generic exchange of chitchat. If was helping to relax her. "My cousin Jack wants to check it out first, though. He keeps promising to get around to it."

"Let me know if I can help."

That's exactly what this is, Nora thought. *Safe, idle chit chat.*

They sat there for a moment, neither of them saying anything. Finally, Darcy said, "I was glad you called this morning. I thought maybe I would hear from you last night after the game."

"We had some people over last night."

Another awkward silence followed before Darcy said, "Are you sure you never got married?"

Nora shook her head. "I'm sure. I would've remembered something like that."

"My mother told me you did. After they sent me away, she wrote and told me you'd gotten married."

Nora didn't know how a mistake like that could have happened. Darcy was the only person she had been involved with until her second year in college. And even then she hadn't dated any guys.

With a shrug Nora said, "I had several cousins who got married right out of high school, so maybe she had me confused with one of them."

Darcy shook her head. "I don't think so."

Nora looked over at her and tried to get an idea from Darcy's expression what exactly she meant by that, but Darcy seemed genuinely perplexed by the conversation.

"Do you think I'm lying to you?" Nora asked.

Darcy sighed. "No. Not at all. I'm just having a problem dealing with the fact that my mother lied to me."

"Why would she do that?"

"To make sure I never came back to find you."

Nora felt a ripple of energy course through her body as all the old fear and speculation about what had happened that night in October returned to her. Darcy had just disappeared. No phone call saying good-bye and no letter or card indicating that she was alive and well somewhere. Nothing.

"I never knew what they did to you," Nora said in a low, quiet voice. "Your father dragged you out of that office like you were a rag doll and I didn't hear from you again."

"What happened to you after I left that night?" Darcy asked.

"I couldn't stop screaming at your father for hitting you," Nora said. "Mr. Szalwinski had to practically tackle me to keep me there in his office after your parents took you out of there. I begged him to help you, but he wouldn't do anything. I think both of us were in shock about what had happened."

"Did he tell your parents about finding us?" Darcy asked.

"After the way your father acted? I remember asking Mr. Szalwinski if he wanted the same thing to happen to me. I can honestly say he was pretty shook up. He knew he had made a mistake. There were better ways to handle that kind of situation than outing a kid to her parents."

"I remember being worried about you," Darcy said.

"You were worried about *me*? Why me? You were the one getting the stuffing slapped out of you!"

"I'd never seen my father get that angry before. He had hit me and my mother in the past, but never like that. I knew things would be bad, but not that bad. I didn't want the same thing happening to you. That was killing me inside."

"Well, nothing happened to me that night. At least nothing physical. So . . . uh . . . how bad did it get?" Nora asked. In a way she wanted to know everything about what had happened, and in another way she hoped to never have to hear all the details.

"I had a fat bruised lip and a bloody nose," Darcy said without emotion. "By the time I got to Denton, I had two black eyes, one of which was nearly swollen shut."

Nora was getting angry all over again. *A wheelchair is too good for that bastard now.*

"I look back on that night sometimes and I wonder why I didn't run away," Darcy said. "That's why there's so many gay kids out on the streets. They can't go home again. I wasn't welcomed back until my mom passed away several years ago. My father contacted the Red Cross so they could tell me. He said I could come home for the funeral."

"I'm sorry all of that happened to you," Nora said. "I remember being so worried. The next day after he beat you I called your house and each time I asked for you, your mother would hang up on me. I finally told my brother what happened and he went over to your house with me to see you, but your mother said you weren't there and told us to never come back. Then on Monday morning when you weren't in school, I had a terrible feeling . . . like maybe your father had killed you and thrown you in the river or something."

Darcy chuckled. "At the time I probably would have preferred that."

"Mr. Szalwinski really did feel bad about what happened," Nora said. "I was in his office Monday morning practically hysterical. I had waited all weekend to hear how you were. It was the longest two days of my life. I prayed that you were safe and well enough to come back to school. There were so many things I wanted to tell you. Mr. Szalwinski didn't know what to do with me that day. Then he found out that your mother had been to the office earlier and withdrew you from school." Nora could feel all those old, terrifying feelings of hurt, guilt, and devastation begin to seep back into her head. "It didn't seem possible to me that day that I would never see you again. But as time went by and there was no word from you, I didn't know what to do with myself."

Darcy pushed her cap back on her head. "Now let me get this straight. Mr. Szalwinski didn't tell your parents what he found us doing?"

"After the way your father exploded?" Nora said. "I practically dared him to, but he had seen enough. I'm sure he never made that mistake again with a student."

"He just let you go that night?"

"I stayed in his office and made him call your house to make sure you were okay, but no one answered the phone. Then a few minutes before the football game was over, he walked with me back to the stadium and bleachers where my parents were sitting. I made him promise that he would keep trying to check on you that night. Did he?"

"I don't know if he did or not," Darcy said. "I was on a bus to Denton bright and early the next morning." She shook her head. "It's so weird to hear your side of what happened. My mother led me to believe the whole town knew about what happened. She said I'd disgraced the family. I felt terrible for me and you and our parents. The shame of that night stayed with me for a very long time."

"No one knew about what happened other than your parents and Mr. Szalwinski," Nora said. "I'm not even sure he told anyone else about it." She sighed. "I had to tell my brother because I needed his help to see how you were." Smiling at the memory, Nora said, "He was such a cool, brave guy that day we went over to your house to see how you were. I'd forgotten all about that until just now." After a moment she added, "That experience sure taught me a lot."

"Yeah, me too."

"I never made out in a car again after that."

For Nora it was a relief to hear Darcy laugh. She remembered Darcy as always being so serious about everything. She thought it would be nice to get to know her as an adult.

"So you're *sure* you never got married?" Darcy asked again with a smile.

"Oh, I'm sure."

"Are you with anyone now?"

"There was someone in Dallas I was seeing for a while, but it wasn't working out. She agreed that we needed to see other people."

"Whew," Darcy said, pretending to wipe sweat from her brow. "You said *she*."

"Oh, yes. Always a she. How about you? Anyone in your life?"

"Nothing but broken windmills. That's all I've had time for since I came back here."

"What about before that?"

"I had a few women in my life, too, but the Army didn't make that very easy either."

"Maybe you should try and make time for other things besides windmills."

"Maybe I should."

Are we flirting? Nora wondered. *If so, I always thought I was better at it than this.*

"Would you like to have dinner sometime?" Darcy asked.

Nora was relieved that she didn't have to ask first. "Sure," she said. "We could go to the Dairy Queen or Sonic. All the local eateries close at two in the afternoon."

"I noticed that. Then perhaps lunch would be a better idea," Darcy suggested.

"Or you could come over here for supper sometime. My mom's a great cook."

"I'd like that." Darcy looked at her watch. "Unfortunately, I have another windmill waiting for me." She stood up and adjusted her cap. "Let me know about dinner. I'll have to make some arrangements for my father while I'm out."

"How about tomorrow?" Nora asked. She didn't want to take a chance and lose the momentum.

"I'll see what I can arrange. I'll call you later. Would that be okay?"

"Sure. I'll talk to you later then."

Chapter Sixteen

After Darcy left, Opal came out on the porch with two tall glasses of iced tea. She handed one to Nora and sat down beside her in the swing.

"It's a little frightening to hear about some of the things you kids got mixed up with when you were younger."

"You heard all of that?"

"I'm sorry. My snooping didn't start out to be intentional, but once I got a snippet, I couldn't stop myself."

"Then that'll save me from having to tell you about it now." Nora took a sip of tea. "I was crazy about her, Mom. So crazy that I was willing to be careless to be with her. We ended up paying the price for it, only Darcy paid a bigger price than I ever did."

"So I heard," Opal said.

"I think a part of me has been wondering all this time if she blames me for what happened. For years I only blamed Mr. Szalwinski for catching us and then calling Darcy's parents, but as

I got older I knew most of the responsibility had to land on me. Sneaking off somewhere to make out was always my idea." With a slight groan, Nora ran her fingers through her hair. "It was only a matter of time before we got caught."

"She didn't seem to be interested in pinning blame on anyone."

"Maybe we didn't have time to get into that yet."

"How do you feel about her now?"

Nora shrugged. "That's hard to say. I find her interesting and attractive, but those are such superficial things. I don't know her anymore. She's not the shy pool goddess I remember, but I've outgrown that type anyway."

They laughed together for a moment.

"Oh, and I invited her over for supper tomorrow night."

"I heard that, too."

"Do you think it would be rude to have some other people over then, too?" Nora asked. "Maybe that would make it seem less like a date or something."

"Depends on who you invite, I imagine. Probably wouldn't be wise to invite the Szalwinski's over."

"Holy crap!" Nora blurted out. "What a disaster that would be. I gave that man 'the look' every time we made eye contact after that night. I'm sure he was glad to see me graduate."

"So what's wrong with just having her over for supper by herself?"

"I don't know," Nora said with a shrug. "I guess I'm a little nervous about it. She knows you'll be here, so it's not really like a date. It'll just be a meal."

"Is that what you think she had in mind? Eating with you and your mother?"

"I don't know."

"Well, I don't think so," Opal said. "It sounded to me like she asked you out for a date."

"Really?"

"We can invite Jack over too if you like," Opal suggested. "I'll explain the situation to him. If nothing else, he'll be able to talk about windmills with her or something."

114

Nora made sure the house looked extra nice. She dusted all the chicken trinkets in the living room and cleaned the bathroom. When Darcy called the evening before to say she had found someone to stay with her father for a few hours, Nora thought she sounded excited about the invitation.

She's probably been stuck at home with the old man ever since she came back to town, Nora thought. *Anything would sound exciting.*

"I've got a pound cake baking for dessert this evening," Opal said when Nora went into the kitchen.

"Why don't you rest while I take care of things in here?" Nora said.

"I just might do that. I'm still feeling tired."

When her mother gave in so easily to Nora's nap suggestions without any type of fuss, it was easy to see that she wasn't feeling well. Looking around the kitchen at the pile of tomatoes and cucumbers on the counter that needed to be tended to along with a sink full of breakfast dishes, Nora got right on it. Staying busy would hopefully keep her from thinking too much.

Once she settled down at the kitchen table to snap some green beans, her cell phone rang.

"Hello."

"Where are you?"

Nora mentally thumped herself for not checking the caller's phone number before answering. She had avoided no less than eight calls from Dr. Sally Ortega already since the move, so it was just a matter of time before they caught up with each other again this way.

"Sally. How are you?"

"I can't believe you moved and didn't tell me!" Sally said. "How could you do such a thing? Then I tried to find you at work and they told me you quit your job! What's going on?"

"Calm down, will you?"

"Don't talk to me that way! I'm furious!"

"I can hear that," Nora said. "Look, we agreed to start seeing other people and—"

"That was your idea."

"You said it was a good idea at the time, remember?"

"I can't believe you moved and didn't tell me! Even if we're not lovers on a regular basis anymore, don't I deserve to know where you live? Where you work? How you're doing?"

Nora let those questions hang in the air between them for a few awkward moments. Her not answering them should have been all the answer either of them needed.

"Did you get the messages I left on your cell phone?" Sally asked.

"I did."

"But you chose not to call me back."

"I've been busy with the move."

"Is there someone else? Is that it?"

"No. Of course not."

"Then why won't you tell me where you are?"

Nora knew this woman better than anyone. Sally wasn't about to let any of this drop. She would keep calling her until she got the answers she wanted. Finally, Nora broke down and told her where she was and why she was there.

"Now was that so hard?" Sally asked in a sweet and smug tone.

"I really don't have time for this."

"Where does your mother live again? Some tiny town outside of San Antonio, right?"

Nora didn't answer, but instead asked, "How's that little nurse from pediatrics doing? Weren't you seeing her for a while?"

"Who told you that?"

Nora laughed. Her main reason for suggesting that they see other people was so Sally would find someone else to help occupy her time. Sally was a wonderful person and a good doctor. Her unselfish work with the homeless was unprecedented in the medical community. But she was too intense for Nora. Most emergency medicine physicians were cool and calm during a crisis. The potluck characteristics of emergency medicine with its innumerable types of patients and problems required a versatility that

116

worked its way into a physician's approach to patient care. But Dr. Sally Ortega always seemed to be charged up and running on adrenaline when she was working. She took the rush and excitement of trauma along with the variety of skills and knowledge needed to work in such a setting to another level, causing all of that to spill over into her personal life as well. At times she could also have a flair for the dramatic which added another unusual dynamic to any relationship. Sally had worked her way through medical school by doing commercials and modeling. She was a beautiful, talented woman and Nora was always mentally exhausted after spending any time with her. She found herself encouraging younger nurses to ask Sally out, thinking they would have more energy for her. Helping to keep Sally busy with new friends seemed to work for both of them for a while, too. Nora had been living with her mother for two weeks already and Sally had just recently noticed that she was gone.

"Will you be coming back to Dallas at all?" Sally asked.

"Probably not."

"What about seeing your niece and brother again?"

"They'll come here instead."

"How convenient for you. So invite me down for a weekend."

Nora shook her head. *This woman has no shame*, she thought.

"You would hate it here."

"How do you know that?"

"Because I know you."

"Nora, Nora, Nora. You're not getting rid of me that easily."

"I'm not trying to get rid of you at all," she said.

"Then answer my calls in the future."

"I will."

"I mean it!"

"I will!"

"I have to go. There's a trauma coming in. Call me sometime."

"I will," Nora said again. She closed her phone and felt relieved to have that over with. As she went back to snapping beans, she wondered about the trauma that had been on the way to the hospital. It was the first time Nora had missed being at work since quitting her job and moving back home.

Retirement had only been one option for Nora when she came back to Prescott. She would still be able to help her mother out and work part time if she wanted to. She wasn't sure how long farm life would keep her occupied before she needed to find something else to fill some of her time. Nora had invested her money wisely over the years, so working wasn't a financial necessity, but she happened to like her work and imagined she would actually like it more if she could set her own hours. *Maybe I'll check into that,* she thought. *A part time job would still keep my skills up and allow me time to help Mom when she needed me.*

Nora finished putting the vegetables away, and before starting on the dishes and getting the kitchen floor swept and mopped, she called her brother.

"Have you found Mom a truck yet?" she asked once she got Greg on the phone.

"One of my clients owns a dealership," Greg said. "He's getting me a good deal on a new Ford pickup, a small one. I'll get a few bells and whistles added to it so she can get in and out of it easily. Anything bigger than what she has now would take all of her hard earned egg money to fill up with gas."

"I didn't think about that."

"So Holly and I will drive it down the first chance I get once I sign the papers on it."

"Excellent. I bet Mom will only be mad at us for a little while once she drives it," Nora said. "We should've insisted on doing this years ago. So how are the negotiations going for science camp?"

"Got her registered already. I had to put my foot down to make it happen, but it was worth it. She gave me the silent treatment for a while, but she's just starting to lighten up on that a little."

"Okay. Well, I've got stuff to do around here. Talk to you later." Nora closed her phone and looked down at the worn tile on the kitchen floor. It had been years since there had been a shine on it. All the wax in the world never helped either. *And there certainly won't be any shine on there today,* she thought with a smile. *Sweep and mop. That's it!*

Jack arrived first and parked his truck next to Opal's old pickup in the front yard. Nora could hear a Johnny Cash song playing so loudly when he pulled in that it got the chickens all stirred up.

"Am I too early?" Jack called from the porch steps.

"Never," Opal said. "Get in here."

"How are you feeling today, Aunt Opal?" Jack gave her a hug. He wore his usual starched jeans with creases so sharp they looked dangerous, tan boots that had a fresh coat of polish on them, a crisp white shirt, and a new Fleming Feed and Seed cap. His lean, tanned face was strikingly handsome. Nora still couldn't imagine him staying single for very long.

"We need rain," he said.

"Spoken like a true farmer," Nora replied.

"Maybe so," Jack said, "but we do."

Nora heard another truck coming down the driveway. *She's here and on time,* she thought. It was a relief to have her mother and Jack there with her. Nora felt less inclined to be nervous knowing she wouldn't be alone with Darcy right then.

Darcy parked her pickup next to Jack's as the three of them stood there on the porch waiting for her to emerge. There was a nice breeze blowing and Nora felt eager to have this first official meeting behind them.

"We look like three linebackers protecting the house," Opal noted. She went to sit on the swing, leaving the other two there to greet the guest.

Darcy got out of the truck. She wore tan slacks, a pale yellow shirt, and brown loafers. Carrying a box with a turtle cheesecake in it, her engaging smile made Nora glad she had extended the invitation.

Out of the side of his mouth Jack whispered, "Are you sure she's here to see you?"

"I'm sure," Nora whispered.

"If you change your mind, let me know," he whispered back.

Nora chuckled. "You wouldn't have a chance in hell, kiddo."

Chapter Seventeen

If Darcy was surprised to see Jack there, she never let on. His presence struck a nice balance for the evening as the topic of discussion changed frequently, giving them no time for awkward silences. The laughter came easily, and by the time supper was ready, Jack's curiosity and questions about windmills left them all knowing more about the subject than Nora ever imagined or even cared about. Darcy's declaration that windmills settled the Southwest sparked another interesting conversation as they passed a heaping platter of chicken fried steak and bowls of mashed potatoes, gravy, and honey-glazed baby carrots around the table.

"You really think so?" Jack asked.

"Without the ability to get water to places that don't have it readily accessible," Darcy went on to explain, "the Southwest would look totally different today and wouldn't have been settled as quickly. Not only that, but the state's economy would have an entirely different structure to it."

"You're probably right," Jack said with a shrug.

"Along the coastal bend, the fresh water table is right on top of the ground in a lot of places," Darcy said. "We're not that lucky here. Sometimes people think there's something wrong with their windmill when in fact there's just nothing there to pump up anymore. The water table drops too low during a drought. In parts of this state the ability to pump water means more than the ability to pump oil."

She has so much confidence now, Nora thought as she listened to the conversation. Nora managed to keep from staring at her, but she felt drawn to this new Darcy she was seeing and listening to. *Whatever it is she used to have that pushed all the right buttons for me,* Nora admitted, *she's still got it. The years have been good to her.*

"I understand that you spent some time in Iraq," Opal said.

"I did. I was there for almost a year."

"Do they hate us over there as much as we've heard and read about?" Opal asked.

"The Iraqi people appreciate us and the children adore us. We're doing so many good things that never get reported on by the American press. I can say this without question, though. Living in a tent for a year can certainly make you appreciate the comforts of home and our way of life here. Going to Iraq made me a better soldier and a much better American, but I can't say I was sorry to leave."

"Did you ever get used to being there?" Opal asked.

"The heat was draining, but I learned to make the best of things just like everyone else did." Darcy ate slowly and didn't seem to mind the attention. "I remember my first few days there. It was a lot like where am I going and why am I in this hand basket? The military does its best to prepare you for it, but they certainly can't prepare you for everything."

"I think going to another country that's being ravaged by war would have to be one of the most frightening things in the world," Opal said. "I just can't imagine."

"You can't really think about that too much," Darcy said.

"You'd never get anything done. We have a job to do there. Time goes by faster if you think of it that way and just do what's expected of you."

Nora passed the bowl of mashed potatoes to Jack and followed that with the gravy bowl.

"I'm usually not a fan of cooked carrots," Darcy said, "but these are delicious, Mrs. Fleming."

"Aunt Opal is an excellent cook," Jack said as he scooped another pile of mashed potatoes on his plate.

"My cooking talents begin with whatever canned goods I find in the pantry," Darcy confessed. "When I lived alone and didn't want to go out for a meal, I had soup for dinner and supper and Spam and eggs for breakfast."

"Spam?" the other three said in mock horror.

"That canned stuff with the icky jelly on it?" Jack asked.

"What food group does Spam fall into anyway?" Opal asked.

"Probably has its own food group," Nora said. "I bet it also has its own shelf in the grocery store because the other canned goods don't even want to stand next to it."

"I heard that the word Spam stands for something," Opal said over the chuckles going around the table.

"It stands for something posing as meat, Mom," Nora said.

The fun and silliness reminded Nora of having her brother there for a visit. They always laughed a lot whenever Greg was around.

"Spam and eggs are good," Darcy said, obviously seeing the need to defend her occasional choice for breakfast. "But I've had to refine some of my culinary skills since I've been home. My father doesn't much care for soup twice a day."

"I'll be taking biscuit-making lessons from Mom soon," Nora said. "I've watched her make them for breakfast all my life and never really paid that much attention to what all went into it, so I guess it's about time I learned."

Darcy cut her chicken fried steak and said, "Pancakes were the staple at our house for breakfast when I was a kid."

"Ours, too," Jack said. "It was because of a pancake that I had to go to the hospital once." He smiled and set the gravy bowl down after smothering his mashed potatoes in a brown pool. "Here's a story I never told anyone else."

"Oh, I just love true confessions!" Nora said.

Jack smiled. "I was in the fourth grade and I had a spelling test at school that day. I hadn't studied for it like I was supposed to, of course. So I'm sitting at the kitchen table before school complaining about not feeling well. A headache was usually easier to fake than a stomach ache, so I was torn between which one I should be pretending to have. My mom stuck a thermometer in my mouth and when she wasn't looking I poked it under my pancakes to get the temperature up there where I thought it needed to be, but I must've left it in there too long. When my mom finally got around to checking my temperature she looked at the thermometer, showed it to my dad, and without saying a word, my dad yanked me up, put me in the truck, and rushed me to the doctor. The next thing I knew I was having my tonsils out." Jack looked up with a sheepish grin. "There. That's my pancake story."

"Oh, lordy!" Opal said.

"I remember when you had your tonsils out," Nora said. "So it was the pancake's fault, eh?"

"Got me out of a spelling test," he said proudly.

Nora was happy to let her mother and Jack continue to carry on the conversation with Darcy even as they moved out on the front porch after supper where it was cooler. Nora and her mother sat in the swing while Jack and Darcy pulled up wooden rockers so they could sit closer to them.

"If we were at my father's place right now," Darcy said, "we'd all be listening to the police scanner."

Nora's involuntary snort made them all laugh.

"That's what I listen to in the evenings," Jack admitted. "I like knowing what's going on."

"Me too," Opal said.

"Hey, then how about we turn the scanner on so everyone feels right at home then?" Nora suggested. A part of her had only been kidding, but she smiled and shook her head when Jack opened the screen door and reached in to switch the scanner on.

"Did your father enjoy the basketball game the other night?" Opal asked Darcy.

"Oh, yes. That's all he would talk about for weeks before it got here. Finally, a customer gave me some tickets, so that worked out well."

"How many business cards did you pass out that night?" Nora asked. Darcy's eyes met hers and they both held the look a little longer than necessary. Nora felt a vaguely familiar rush of emotion sweep through her, snapping the very core of her body to attention.

Finally, Darcy said, "Several."

Crickets chirping in the yard and the occasional creaking of a rocker on the porch were sounds that Nora associated with home and her childhood. She felt safe and loved there, and at that particular moment she couldn't imagine being anywhere else.

"I was just wondering," Jack said quietly, interrupting Nora's thoughts.

"What were you wondering, young man?" Opal asked.

"I was just wondering how long we have to wait before we can have dessert?"

Nora volunteered to bring out the dessert and was pleased when Darcy offered to help her.

"What does everyone want?" Nora asked. "We've got cheese-cake and pound cake."

"Yes," Jack said, which made his Aunt Opal chuckle. "I'll have some of both, please," he clarified.

"Me too," Opal said. "Small slices for me."

"Big ones for me," Jack said.

"Fresh drinks for everyone?" Nora asked. "It's kind of late for coffee, but there's some tea left."

They got everyone's order and Darcy followed her to the kitchen. Nora got plates out of the cupboard while Darcy sliced the pound cake.

"This has been a wonderful evening," Darcy said. "Thanks for inviting me."

"It's been fun. I'm glad you could make it." Nora took the cheesecake out of the refrigerator and set it on the table. "Who did you get to take care of your father?"

"The local VFW," Darcy said. "He's playing bingo there tonight. I have to pick him up at ten."

Nora glanced at the rooster clock on the kitchen wall by the stove and was relieved to see that it was just a little after eight. They still had time.

"Your cousin Jack is quite a character."

"He has his moments," Nora said. "He's really close to my mom. She thinks of him as one of her own."

"Where does your brother live now?"

"In Dallas with his teenage daughter."

"What does he do?"

"Greg is a CPA with an accounting firm," Nora said. "He's a tax-loophole genius. I can't even begin to count the amount of money he's saved me over the years. Finally he's good for something."

"I might be in the market for some tax advice. Which one of these do you want?" Darcy asked, pointing to the two desserts with a serving knife.

"A small piece of both," Nora said. "I've had too many desserts lately. That along with my mother's cooking will have me out shopping for bigger clothes if I don't do something about it soon."

"You look fine to me," Darcy said.

The comment hung in the air between them for a moment. Nora felt a huge sense of relief hearing the remark—not so much for its implication that she didn't look overweight, but for the fact that Darcy had noticed her at all.

"I was wondering," Darcy said as she carefully placed a slice of cheesecake on one of the dessert plates. "Would you be free for lunch tomorrow?"

"Tomorrow?" Nora repeated. Trying to recall what plans she already had, Nora quickly remembered what the next day would consist of. "Oh. Tomorrow's not good. I'll be helping Mom deliver eggs most of the day."

"Ahh."

Nora put some ice in a small pitcher and filled it with tea from the refrigerator. She waited for Darcy to suggest another day for lunch, but instead Nora noticed that she was busy cutting the pound cake. Nora jumped in. "How about lunch the day after tomorrow? Would that be possible?"

"I'm sure it'll be fine," Darcy said. "What time?"

"Noon-ish?"

"Sure."

Nora reached for a tray on top of the refrigerator and set the pitcher and four glasses on it. Darcy set two of the dessert plates on the tray also.

"Where's a good place for lunch around here?" Nora asked.

"It's either fast food or nothing," Darcy said. "At noon we might get a table at the Dairy Queen. Most of their business is for to-go orders."

"Then Dairy Queen it is."

As they carried the desserts and drinks out to the porch, Nora was happy knowing she would be seeing Darcy again. *We have a lunch date*, she thought. *There's no mistaking it or jumping to conclusions this time. She definitely asked me out.*

Chapter Eighteen

Early Thursday morning Jack dropped off the extra fresh vegetables he had picked from his garden and helped Nora load up the tables they'd be using. On Thursday, Friday and Saturday was open market time for vendors at the Prescott town square. In the late spring Opal and Jack pooled their extra fresh vegetables so that Opal could sell them. She and Jack split the profits and Opal got to see old friends and relatives she hadn't seen in a while.

Nora followed her mother to town in her car and helped her set up. She was once again impressed with her mother's people skills. Opal didn't go to all this trouble just for the extra money. Nora knew this was a social event for her.

"Let me get this straight," Nora said as she pulled one end of the sheet of plywood out of the bed of the pickup and struggled to set it on the two saw horses she had already placed on the grass. "You spend a good forty-five minutes loading up this stuff then setting it all up once you get here, then you sit behind a table for five hours and Jack gets half of what you make. Is that the way it goes?"

"That's correct," Opal said as she tossed one end of a white table cloth in the air and let it float down perfectly on top of the plywood table. "That's the way we do it. I'm gonna be here anyway. Might as well sell his stuff, too."

"Okay. Just checking."

Nora tried not to get too hot and sweaty setting up this adventure. She would be leaving the vending area close to noon for her lunch date with Darcy and wanted to look and smell as good as possible.

"What else do you need for me to do?" Nora asked as she glanced around their immediate area.

"Get the veggies in the baskets and try to look friendly."

"I *am* friendly!"

"The closer it gets to noon," Opal said, "the grumpier you'll be. We don't need grumpy at the table. We need our friendly these-are-the-best-veggies-in-town faces on."

With a furrowed brow, Nora said, "I'm not sure I have that face."

"You do. In fact, I bet you'll have that face on after your date's over."

Vegetable sales were swift and steady. Once again Nora was delighted to see her mother in action with old friends, neighbors and a string of relatives that Nora had forgotten even existed. Off and on during the course of the morning, Nora had to keep going back to the truck to get more tomatoes and okra. She had learned earlier that her mother and Jack grew different things in their gardens so they would have a bigger variety of things to sell.

"Do you ever run out of this stuff?" Nora asked. She had no idea that the six boxes in the back of the pickup were filled with cucumbers and tomatoes until her mother sent her after more vegetables to fill the empty baskets.

"We'll probably run out by Saturday afternoon," Opal said, "but then we've also got tomatoes getting ripe on the vine right now, so there's still plenty to do and enough to go around for a while."

There was another rush at Opal's table as cars continued to pull up or slowly drive by to check out what was available. While Opal talked to the customers and took their money, Nora bagged up their purchases.

"Why aren't these people at work?" Nora asked when a cluster of customers left their table to shop with the other vendors at the town square.

"Most of them work downtown, but some are just old like me," Opal said. "Only they can't do their own gardening anymore."

"Speaking of diets," Nora said, "I need to go on one. I've gained seven pounds since I've been here."

"Stop worrying. It looks good on you."

"Hey, I know me. The next thing I know, it'll be ten pounds and then fifteen and before long it'll be all out of control and I'll have nothing to wear."

Opal rearranged the vegetable baskets on the table and then sat back down in her lawn chair. Holding up her arm and pointing to the saggy flesh that hung there, she asked, "What can I do about this?" She moved her arm a little as they both watched the swaying flesh. "It's like my skin doesn't fit me anymore."

Nora chuckled. "I'm sorry, Mom. There's nothing short of plastic surgery that'll help it. After a while it all starts to hang."

"Most of that hanging stuff I can cover up," Opal said, "but not always the arms. It gets too hot for sleeves in the summer."

They had another steady flow of customers and before she knew it, Nora had ten minutes to meet Darcy. She scurried around and got the vegetable baskets full again, and then remembered to get her mother's lunch order.

"Call me if you need anything," Nora said as she pulled her keys out of her pocket. "I shouldn't be very long."

"Call you with what?" Opal asked. "I can't leave here to find a phone. Besides, I can't imagine me needing anything. Just go and have fun. I'll be fine. I've done this hundreds of times without you, dear."

She doesn't have a cell phone, Nora realized. *How do people function without a cell phone these days?*

"Here," Nora said. "Take my phone."

"What for? Just go to lunch with your friend. I don't need a phone."

"I insist."

"What? Are you kidding me?"

"I'll feel better if you have it," Nora said. "I can't believe you've been out delivering eggs all this time without any way of calling for help if you needed it. Greg and I need our butts kicked for not getting you a cell phone."

"I've delivered eggs for thirty years without a cell phone," Opal reminded her. "Besides, if I did have trouble, how many people in this town do you think would stop to help me?"

"How many? All of them."

"That's right. All of them. So I don't need a cell phone."

"Oh, just take it, please. It'll make *me* feel better. Okay?"

A new truck and a cell phone, Nora thought. *We'll get her all fixed up soon. She'll be the envy of all her friends.*

Nora pulled into the Dairy Queen parking lot and almost couldn't find a place to park. She looked around, but didn't see Darcy's truck anywhere. *Mom was right,* Nora thought with a chuckle. *Darcy can't call to tell me she'll be late because I gave my cell phone away!*

A few minutes later Nora smiled when she saw Darcy's truck pull in. She parked along the highway and got out with her sunglasses on. Nora met her at the door and tried to catch her own reflection in the glass. Giving her hair a little toss with her fingers, Nora said, "I've been schlepping tomatoes and cucumbers all morning."

"I know," Darcy said as she opened the door for them. "I had a nice chat with your mom when I called your cell phone to let you know I'd be a little late."

"Good for her!" Nora said delightedly. "We had a dry-run on how to answer it and place a call before I left her downtown. She kept holding it like the thing would bite her or something."

"Oh, grab that table over there," Darcy said. "Those four kids are leaving. I'll get our orders. What do you want?"

Nora scanned the menu hanging up over the counter and made a quick decision on what she wanted to eat. *So much for starting a diet anytime soon*, she thought.

By the time Nora got the table and seats cleaned off to her satisfaction with a pile of paper napkins, Darcy had placed their orders and was already carrying their drinks to the table. The line at the counter was three-people deep now and the drive-thru line outside was almost hanging out onto the highway. They both slid into the hard plastic booth on opposite sides of the table and looked at each other for the first time that day. Darcy's blue eyes set off her dark, salt-and-pepper hair. She was no longer the shy, awkward teenager Nora had been crazy about so many years ago.

"You look great, by the way," Darcy said. "Schlepping tomatoes must agree with you."

Nora fiddled with the back of her hair again, feeling certain that she was blushing. "Thank you," she said quietly.

"What does your mom have for sale today?"

Nora rattled off the list of vegetables they had brought with them.

"I think the farmer's market in the town square is a great idea," Darcy said. "Not everyone has time for a garden."

"Business there is good. That's for sure. What have you been doing today?" Nora asked.

"I got a windmill fixed on the Baumann Ranch. The part I needed came in yesterday. I have two more to look at for estimates this afternoon."

"You're probably working more now that you're retired than you did before."

Darcy's smile showed off her perfect teeth. Nora liked the way Darcy's hair covered her ears and fell across her forehead in thick layers of black and gray. She had always tanned easily and Nora could see herself getting caught up in her attraction to this woman all over again.

"I like having a full schedule," Darcy said. "My father and I get along a lot better when we're not around each other for too long."

Nora nodded. "It's just the opposite with my mother and me. The more time I spend with her, the closer we seem to get. I'm really enjoying our time together."

Darcy sat back and rested an arm along the top of the booth. "Got any plans down the road?"

"What kind of plans do you mean?"

"You're officially retired then?"

"Oh, that," Nora said. "I'm thinking of getting a part time nursing job. Maybe at the new county hospital. Just a few hours a week to keep my skills up. What about you? What's your mission? Keeping all the windmills in South Texas going no matter what?"

"I need to get my father's business straightened out. He knows all there is to know about windmills, but next to nothing about running a business."

"How hard has all of this been on you?" Nora asked.

"What's that saying—when the winds of change blow, you need to adjust your sails." Darcy looked down at the small ticket they had given her at the counter. "That's what I find myself doing every day now. Adjusting my sails."

"You're not happy here?"

"I'm not sure I've ever been happy." Darcy folded the small ticket and let it fall on the table. "Well, that's not entirely true," she admitted. "I remember being happy that summer with you."

There it is, Nora thought. *The first real mention of that summer.* "That was a lifetime ago," Nora said.

"I remember how brave you were. I'll never forget that."

"Brave?" Nora repeated. She took her straw out of its wrapper and poked it through the lid on her drink. "When was I ever brave?"

"That's just one of the things that always stood out in my mind whenever I would think of you. How you talked to Mr. Szalwinski that night in his office. I was petrified, but not you. There you were, all up in his face."

133

"Sometimes we show our strongest side at our weakest moments," Nora said. "Believe me. I was plenty scared that night. Scared and furious."

"Have you had any therapy because of all that stuff that happened?"

"Sure," Nora said. "I think we could all use some therapy no matter what happens to us. Just being human should be the only prerequisite needed for a good dose of therapy."

"Yeah, I guess you're right. I know therapy helped me forgive my parents. I was able to go on and lead a relatively normal life after that."

"What's the longest relationship you've been in?" Nora asked.

"Two years."

Lowering her voice, Nora asked, "What's that in lesbian years?"

Their laughter was genuine and easy. Nora felt good being with her.

"I'm good for about three months at a time," Nora admitted, "then I tend to get bored. At least that's been the pattern for me so far."

"I found myself settling for things just to keep from being alone so much," Darcy said. "Therapy helped me with that too. Growing up emotionally was a lot harder than it probably should have been. I spent a lot of money getting to know myself."

"Money well spent, I'm sure. What did you learn?"

"I found out that I'd rather want something I didn't have than have something I didn't want."

"Wow," Nora said. "Now that's profound. You got that out of therapy?"

"I sure did."

"You certainly got your money's worth then."

"I should have. It cost me a fortune."

The time passed quickly and the hour was up long before Nora was ready for it to be. She couldn't quite get a handle on the mood that was in the air, though. She found it frustrating to try and define exactly who Darcy was and where she had previously fit into her life. *Who are we now?* Nora wondered. *Old friends? Old lovers? High school acquaintances? We aren't exactly old lovers,* she thought. *We never actually slept together. And as far as being friends, I kissed her long before I got to know her very well. There's also the possibility that our old relationship has been overly romanticized because of the way Darcy was shipped off to relatives. It's like she and I have some unfinished business,* Nora mused. *Whatever it was that we could have had together—it got interrupted.*

Darcy neatly folded her burger wrapper and napkins and placed them in the red plastic basket with the reminder of her French fries.

"I don't suppose you'll be available for lunch again tomorrow," Darcy said.

"I'll be schlepping more tomatoes and cucumbers tomorrow."

"Is that a yes or a no?"

"Let me see how my mom did today while I was gone. Can I get back to you on that?"

"Sure," Darcy said.

Someone behind the counter called the number for Nora's to-go order for her mom. Nora held up the small rectangle-shaped ticket. "That's me. I guess I should get going."

"Yeah, me too."

Nora took her time getting her things together.

"I don't know what it is," Darcy said, "but I hate leaving you. There's something inside of me that's so worried that I'll never see you again."

Nora felt a fluttering in her stomach. It was like Darcy had taken Nora's unspoken words and feelings and made them her own.

"That's sort of freaking me out, too," Nora admitted.

"Ever since I saw you at the basketball game, I've been trying to unravel my feelings. Unfortunately, they seem to be a lot more complicated than they should be."

"Complicated how?"

Darcy looked at her as if she were trying to memorize her face. "We're not kids anymore."

"I know."

"The way I felt about you that summer," Darcy said, "was so new and exciting. No one else has ever made me feel that way. And now here we are almost twenty-five years later and all of those emotions are bubbling up inside of me again. It's very unsettling."

Nora closed her eyes and sighed. "You're not alone, Darcy. I'm feeling some incredible things, too."

"I keep telling myself to take it slow . . . that eventually you'll do something that'll wake me up so I can shake off this fog I'm in."

"Something like what?"

"Oh, I don't know," Darcy said. "Like maybe if I found out you're a Republican or something. Or that you're no longer a feminist. Something that goes against everything I believe in. Then maybe I could get past this infatuation I have with you."

"Infatuation?" Nora said.

"That's just the word I'm calling all of this," Darcy said with a wave of her hand.

Nora didn't know what to say. She remembered how deep and intense her feelings for Darcy had been that summer they were together, but somehow the word "infatuation" didn't seem quite appropriate. *All I know,* Nora thought, *is I want to spend more time with her. There are a few things inside of me that have been dormant for a very long time and they've suddenly been nudged awake again.*

"I don't expect you to feel the same way," Darcy said. "All I'm asking for is a chance for us to get to know each other again."

Nora picked up her cup and the ticket for her to-go order. "I probably want that more than you do."

Darcy's smile tugged at Nora's heart. It was a relief to know that they were both interested in the same thing even if neither of them could find a good word to describe what it was.

Chapter Nineteen

It was Thursday evening and Nora and her mother sat in the swing on the porch. The rude static interruptions from the police scanner didn't make her jump as much anymore, but Nora still found it incredibly annoying.

"Sold completely out of yellow squash today," Opal said. "Jack might have picked more this evening."

"I don't know how you've done all this stuff by yourself all these years," Nora said. "I'm exhausted."

"Even after that nap you took when we got home?"

"Too much relaxation wears me out, I guess. Along with all that smiling I had to do for your customers today."

"Smiling," Opal said with a grunt. "Big chore that is. You didn't say too much about your lunch with Darcy today. How'd that go?"

Nora shrugged. "I think we're both toying with the idea of trying to pick up where we left off years ago, but it's a scary thing, Mom. Except for the night we got caught, all of my memories of that time are good. I'm not so sure it's wise to fool with that. Some things are better left alone, you know?"

"Maybe. Then again you might be missing the chance to make better memories in the long run."

"I probably didn't need to hear that."

"You need to do what's right for you," Opal said. "That bad experience you two had together no doubt made you both stronger people in many ways. You also might discover that you make better friends than anything else. I know I like her. She has a good heart and she wants to do the right thing on many levels. Not only that, but she's taking care of someone who hasn't always treated her well. That says a lot about the kind of person she is."

"I have no doubt that she's a good person," Nora agreed. "She was a great person as a kid, too. Always quiet, polite and smart. I'm sure I was a bad influence on her," she added.

"You were never quiet, but you were always polite and smart," Opal said. "You have to stop feeling guilty about what happened with her. She was just as responsible for getting caught as you were. You didn't drag her to the car that night. Sounds like she was a willing participant. You both need to share the blame for it."

The dispatcher's voice crackled over the police scanner, giving Nora a start. They both listened to the report about pigs in the road on one of the highways south of town.

"The Ferguson pigs are out again," Opal said. "They'll be rootin' in the neighbor's garden by morning if someone doesn't round 'em up tonight."

"Might be good for our farmer's market business tomorrow," Nora said. "Someone else's misfortune could be putting money in your pocket."

"Don't be thinking of it that way!" Opal said with a chuckle. "Shame on you."

After a moment they settled back down again. Nora felt restless and uncertain about what to do as far as Darcy was concerned. The attraction between them was obviously mutual. Even after all these years there was still something in the air for them—something left unresolved, and in Nora's mind, the circumstances that had brought them together again were more than a coincidence. She was convinced that fate was leading them in this direction, but Nora wasn't sure she was ready to just jump back into things so quickly. *In a way,* she thought, *not a lot has changed for either of us. We're both still living with our parents, for crissakes!*

"What are you thinking about all serious-like over there?" Opal asked.

"Pigs in the garden."

Opal laughed.

"What should I do, Mom?" Nora asked suddenly. "I'm drawn to her, but I don't know if it's the right thing for either of us. The thought of her getting hurt again really worries me. I can't let that happen. She's been through so much because of me already."

"It's unlikely that her father will be slapping her around now."

"True, but it's not the physical pain I'm thinking about."

"I know, dear, but she looks like she can take care of herself. Besides, there's a reason you're both here now. Don't rush into anything. Just see how it all plays itself out. Once you get to know her better, you might notice some qualities in her that you don't like. She could be one of those nose-pickers at a stop light or something. That would sure make me have second thoughts. You're both different people now, but you won't know anything unless you give it a try."

Nose-picking at a stop light? Nora thought with a little cringe.

"Roger that," the dispatcher blurted out into the cool, quiet night. "It's the Ferguson pigs again."

Startled by the verbal intrusion, Nora acknowledged her mother's snicker with a groan.

"See?" Opal said. "I told you. The Ferguson pigs are out. They're bustin' loose all the time."

Opal went to bed, but Nora's racing mind kept her awake. She replayed lunch with Darcy and how they both had been tip-toeing around the fact that they were interested in pursuing a relationship. *We're gun-shy*, Nora thought, *and with good reason. The first time for us was so painful I hope to never experience anything like it again.*

The police scanner crackled an update on the Ferguson pigs. Nora got up to switch it off just as her cell phone rang. It was Darcy.

"I hope it's not too late to call," Darcy said.

"Not at all. I'm still up."

"My father's settled in for the evening. This is about the time of night I finally get to relax."

"Did you finish your estimates today?"

"I did," Darcy said. "One of the reasons I wanted to call was to let you know I have to go out of town tomorrow. There's no way I can meet you for lunch."

"I see," Nora said, feeling a twinge of disappointment. "Well, maybe another time."

"I was hoping you would say that. Other than lunch tomorrow, what would be a good time for you?"

"You're the one that's busy. You tell me. I'm retired, remember?"

"Hmm," Darcy said. "I'm sensing some attitude here. Is this a bad time to call?"

Nora took a deep breath and sat down in the swing again. She realized that she felt more than disappointed that Darcy cancelled their lunch date. All those "should we or shouldn't we" thoughts and discussions she had been having with her mother weighed on her. Nora didn't do well with uncertainty in her life. She liked knowing the answers to her questions.

"Hello? Are you still there?" Darcy asked.

"Look," Nora said, immediately hearing the irritation in her voice. She took another deep breath to calm herself down a little. "Look," she said again, only more quietly this time. "If I can't see you for lunch tomorrow, then is there a way I can see you tomorrow night? Or even now? Is that possible? Can you come over here this evening? I think we need to talk."

There was a moment of silence before Darcy said, "I don't like leaving my father alone at night once he's in bed. If he needs something, I have to be here."

"Of course. I'm sorry. I forgot about your father."

"But maybe you could come over here for a while," Darcy suggested. "I'd really like to see you and I agree that we need to talk."

"I can be there in fifteen minutes," Nora said, relieved at the invitation. Suddenly, the thought of seeing her again was more important than anything else.

"That's great. You know where I live, right?"

"By the river. Yes, I know."

"Be careful on your way over," Darcy said. "I hear the Ferguson pigs are out."

Nora's mind was racing as she drove to the Tate house. She knew where Darcy lived just like she knew where most long-time Prescott residents resided. Giving directions to someone in the country usually consisted of remembering old businesses that no longer existed, but that everyone still knew about or other old landmarks that only a native from the area would know. Directions usually went something like "take the first road after Junior's Ice House (even though Junior no longer owned it and the ice house already had another name) then take the third gravel road after you pass old man Carpenter's hay barn." It also didn't matter that old man Carpenter had been dead for fifteen years and someone else now owned the barn. It would always be known as old man Carpenter's hay barn.

This was just one of the things Nora loved about living in the country again. Regular words meant different things there too, like "dinner" and "supper." No one but a stranger in town would have lunch at lunchtime. In the country they had dinner at lunchtime. It was a more simple way of life, which was something Nora had missed more than she thought possible. She had adjusted well to being home again.

While driving down the highway, Nora saw red lights flashing up ahead. *They must've found the Ferguson pigs*, she thought as she took another route to Darcy's house. It was good to see Darcy waiting for her on the front porch when she finally arrived.

"No trouble finding me?" Darcy asked.

"Not at all. I know where the Ferguson pigs ended up, though."

"They don't get that far down here when they get out," Darcy said as she held the screen door open. "They figured out we don't have a garden."

The living room was big and had two recliners, a loveseat and a matching sofa all facing a large flat screen television. There was a desk in the far corner of the room with a computer on it and built-in bookcases covering one entire wall. Nora noticed a fireplace on another wall with a nice mantel where pictures of Darcy at various ages were lined up like a chronological story of her growth and accomplishments. The room was tidy and welcoming. Nora immediately felt comfortable there.

"What a nice home you have," Nora said.

"Thanks. Can I get you anything?"

"No, I'm fine."

"Have a seat. I'm glad you could come over."

Nora sat down on the loveseat while Darcy sat in a recliner.

"How's your father?"

"He's doing well. He doesn't necessarily like physical therapy, but he'll be the first to admit that he's doing much better because of it."

"Does he know how lucky he is to have you?"

Darcy smiled shyly. "We're both lucky. I couldn't stay in the Army forever and it was nice to know I still had a home to come back to."

"You're a wonderful person and a good daughter. Don't forget that."

Darcy looked at her with a flicker of surprise in her expression. "Where did that come from?"

Nora shook her head and shrugged. "Forgive me for not being a fan of your father's. The most vivid memory I have of him—" She stopped and decided not to get into any of that.

"It's okay," Darcy said. "There are times I'm not that crazy about him either. I love him, but I don't necessarily like him some of the time. He's always been a grumpy old man. Even when he was younger. You know how some people just aren't happy unless they're bitching about something? Well, that's him. Bitching is like a hobby."

Nora smiled. "How did you grow up to be so normal?"

"Normal? I'm a lesbian. What's normal about that?"

"You're a well-balanced, normal lesbian," Nora said. "At least that's what I see. Unless you got kinky since I knew you back then."

"Kinky?" Darcy repeated. "No. Nothing kinky about me. That's hard to pull off in the Army. I'm about as vanilla as they get."

Nora realized she was flirting as she leaned her head back against the loveseat. She wanted to go forward with this. No more treading water to see how deep it was. Plunging in head first was beginning to make more sense. "Vanilla happens to be my favorite flavor," Nora said. Their eyes met and every time that happened lately, Nora's heart turned over. "I see what a truly remarkable woman you've become," she added. "I feel lucky to have had you in my life."

"It almost sounds like you're saying good-bye."

"We both went through a lot, Darcy. Some people don't recover from things like that." Nora sighed. "I can't stand the thought of hurting you again . . . or me being hurt either for that matter. It took me a long time to get over what happened. In some ways I've never gotten over it."

"Neither have I." Darcy sat up straighter in the chair. "Let me ask you something. We're all grown up now and we're not kids anymore. Between the two of us, I'm sure we have a lot more life experiences than most people our age. Are you at all curious about what things could be like with us now?"

"Curious?" Nora said. "Oh, I'm curious about a lot of things."

"Like what?"

Nora shrugged, feeling shy all of a sudden.

"Tell me something you're curious about."

Forcing herself not to think too much before speaking, Nora decided to dive in. "For one thing," she said, "I'd like to know if kissing you can still make me feel like swooning."

"Swooning?" Darcy said. They both laughed. After a moment, Darcy got up from the recliner and went to sit next to her on the loveseat. "You never told me anything about swooning."

"Maybe swooning isn't the right word," Nora said, embarrassed. She felt silly having confessed such a thing. "Besides, it's not really something I would've talked about back then anyway." She was thrilled at being so close to Darcy again. It was something that felt new and exciting to her. When they were younger, Nora had always been the aggressor, the one to mention parking or sneaking up to the balcony in the theater so they could make out. Nora had always felt desperate to be with her, as if something deep inside had been directing her actions. Now to have Darcy sitting beside her, lightly touching her hair was suddenly like wading through a dream. Her limbs felt heavy, but at the same time the rest of her body was light enough to almost float across the room. *Ohmigod*, Nora thought. *She hasn't even kissed me yet and I'm already swooning.*

"Tell me something else you're curious about," Darcy whispered.

Nora closed her eyes and tilted her head ever so slightly as the back of Darcy's hand caressed her cheek. Nora caught the faint scent of a pleasing perfume, but couldn't identify it. She was glad to know it was a fragrance unfamiliar to her. Nora wanted to always remember it as Darcy's.

"Tell me," Darcy whispered again, but Nora didn't want to talk anymore. She opened her eyes long enough to find Darcy's lips and leaned forward to kiss her.

What started out as a surprisingly gentle kiss, making Nora quiver at its sweet tenderness, slowly became a merging of such delicious passion that it sent shock waves through Nora's entire body. Her calm was shattered with the hunger of Darcy's lips and she savored every moment of it. In the deep, dark recesses of her swirling mind Nora remembered feeling this way before.

Darcy seemed to also give herself freely to the passion of the kiss. Just the hint of Darcy's tongue sent shivers of desire racing through Nora's body. As Darcy's kisses moved to the pulsing hollow at the base of Nora's throat, Nora felt carried away by her own response. The prolonged anticipation of finally being able to make love with her was almost unbearable. A sense of urgency drove her to reach for the buttons on Darcy's shirt. Nora wanted to feel this woman's body against her. They had waited a lifetime for this moment.

"Follow me," Darcy said in a low, husky voice. "We're doing this the right way."

She took Nora by the hand and led her down a dark hallway and into a bedroom. Switching on a lamp on the nightstand revealed a huge four-poster king-size bed. Darcy closed the door and turned to look at her. Nora's whole being was filled with want and desire as she saw the heart-rending tenderness in Darcy's gaze.

"It feels like I've waited forever for this," Darcy said.

Nora felt a brief shiver ripple through her body as she met Darcy halfway. *Finally*, she thought. *Sometimes dreams really do come true.*

Chapter Twenty

Darcy's demanding lips found Nora's then moved to nibble at her earlobe before returning to kiss her again. Darcy's mouth sent new spirals of ecstasy through Nora's body to the point that she wouldn't be able to stand up very much longer. In between hot, smoldering kisses there were hands fumbling with buttons and zippers along with the tugging and flinging of various articles of clothing. Nora had a burning desire and an aching need to feel Darcy's warm skin against hers. *We've never had that before*, she thought as she slipped her panties off and pulled Darcy toward her. *We never really got a chance to make love when we were younger.*

Darcy eased her down onto the bed and for the first time their bodies touched the way they were meant to. Nora reached up to caress Darcy's face and searched her eyes looking for the searing desire she knew would be there. Finding it made her heart skip a beat as they both took a moment to gaze and bask in the reality of what was about to happen. Nora rose up and rolled her over, then kissed Darcy with such passion that she thought for sure her heart would explode. Nora had never wanted anything as badly as she wanted this.

Darcy's finely toned body was soft where it needed to be. Nora's lips found one of Darcy's nipples with tantalizing possessiveness and she enjoyed hearing the low moan that came from deep in Darcy's throat.

"Oh, God you feel good," Darcy whispered. She wrapped her long legs around Nora, pulling her closer. With a steady rocking motion they settled into a rhythm that had them both wild with sensation in no time. Darcy pushed up against her while Nora's hand seared a path down her abdomen like a heat-seeking missile. She opened herself, letting her fingers enjoy the wetness she found there. The less than gentle massage sent currents of desire rushing through her before she touched Darcy in the same way, slowly slipping her fingers inside. They came together quickly with a release that left them both breathless.

Nora laid her head on Darcy's chest and listened to her racing heart. Darcy tightened her arms around her as a single warm tear scampered down Nora's cheek.

"That was worth waiting for," Darcy said a few minutes later. Nora rolled off of her and they crawled under the covers. "At least it was for me," Darcy said.

Nora turned on her side and propped her head up, gazing lovingly down at this incredible woman. With an index finger she gently touched the end of Darcy's nose.

"I'm speechless," Nora whispered, her voice full of emotion. "There's a part of me that can't believe I'm actually here with you. Does that make sense?"

"It makes perfect sense," Darcy said. She reached over and gently outlined the circle of Nora's breast. She paused to kiss her and with an unspoken need, Darcy eased Nora on her back. Her hands lightly traced a path over her skin and explored the soft lines of her waist and hips.

The way Darcy was looking at her made Nora feel cherished

and adored. *Yes*, she thought as Darcy's lips stopped just long enough to tease her navel with the tip of her nose, *I'm still crazy about her. Crazy, crazy, crazy.*

Nora pressed her head back against the pillow and reached down to find Darcy's hair with one hand, running her fingers through its silky softness and then gripping it as Darcy slowly moved down her body. With her other hand Nora squeezed her own marble-hard nipples, sending jolts of pleasure shooting through her body. Darcy matched her urgency with nips and nudges along the way to where they both wanted her to be. Nora opened her legs even more in an unspoken invitation that Darcy gladly accepted.

For Nora this was no longer the teenage sweetheart who had so abruptly been taken away from her. The woman who was gathering her close and moving down her body searching for and finding those tantalizing pleasure points was a master at this. Nora felt as though she had known Darcy before in another lifetime and she would keep finding her over and over again though the ages. They were two beings who had been separated for reasons unknown to either of them, but they were together now and that was all that mattered. Nora intended to make the most of it, and she was determined to let Darcy know how much she meant to her. But for the time being, all Nora could think about was how Darcy's tongue was teasing and playing her . . . playing her like a finely-tuned instrument ready to break out into its very own symphony. Nora squeezed her nipples again and let go of Darcy's hair so she could use both hands on her breasts.

"Ohmigod," Nora heard herself say. "That feels wonderful. Right there. Right there. Ohmigod!"

Nora rode the building crescendo of pleasure and writhed around on the bed as Darcy probed, licked and sucked her way to an explosive orgasm. Nora's body shook with blinding sensation and kept soaring higher until it shattered into thousands of glowing stars. The world seemed to spin and careen on its axis as she arched up against her. Nora let go of her rock-hard nipples and filled her hands with Darcy's hair before grinding herself into her as she cried out her pleasure. She gasped as waves of explosive passion electrified her very core. Involuntary tremors shook Nora's body as Darcy kissed her swollen clit and slowly circled it with her tongue.

As Nora tried to get control of her breathing, she was filled with an amazing sense of joy and completeness. She savored that contentment while Darcy gently kissed her way back up Nora's body. Nora took her in her arms and held Darcy close. The warmth of her soft skin was intoxicating.

"Just give me a minute," Nora whispered shakily as she kissed Darcy's cheek and smoothed her hair away from her brow.

"Hold me," Darcy said. "I've thought about this moment for a very long time. I need to feel your arms around me."

Nora held her and liked the way their bodies fit together. Her hands moved gently down the length of Darcy's back and it didn't take her long to convince Darcy that it was her turn to be explored and ravished. Nora wanted to show her how she felt. Before the night was over, Darcy Tate would know what it was like to be taken over the edge.

Nora woke up in Darcy's arms with no sense of time or place.

"Hi," Darcy said sleepily.

"Hi," Nora answered. She couldn't stop smiling as she stretched and propped her head up with her tingling hand.

"I wonder what time it is?" Darcy said then turned to look at the clock on the nightstand. "Oh, my. It's two already."

"Really?" Nora said, shocked. They had been asleep a lot longer than she thought. She had to be up early to help her mother load more vegetables on the truck in the morning. "I hate to break this party up, but I need to get home."

Darcy pulled her into her arms for a warm hug. "I know. I have to get up early and drive to Pearsall to see about a few windmills."

They started kissing again and before long Nora was on top of

Darcy caressing her swollen nipples with the tip of her tongue. Together they found the tempo that bound their bodies and Nora felt Darcy's raw need and emotion consume them both. A golden wave of passion and desire flowed between them as they rocked and rubbed against each other. Exploding in a downpour of fiery sensations, Nora grabbed Darcy and kissed her in a thrilling release of pleasure. Shivers of delight followed as the heat spread to her heart. Nora buried her face into the soft hollow of Darcy's neck and kissed her there until she was too exhausted to move any longer.

Darcy held her and kissed the side of Nora's face. "We're much better at this now than we would've been then."

Nora smiled. "Oh, you don't know that for sure." She rolled over and lay beside her again.

"Well, one of us was greener than goose shit back then."

"I guess it's safe to say we both were," Nora admitted. "I really need to get going and you need some sleep if you're driving in the morning."

Nora forced herself to get out of bed and gather up the clothes that she had thrown about the room. Darcy got up and put on a robe. She watched Nora get dressed and sat back down on the bed.

"If I were a smoker, I'd need a cigarette right about now," Darcy said.

"Me too."

Nora finished getting dressed and came over to kiss her again. "I hate leaving you." She slipped her hands inside the robe and cupped Darcy's breasts.

"If you keep that up I'm not letting you go anywhere."

"Can I see you when you get back into town later?" Nora asked just before taking a sweet, hard nipple into her mouth. She sucked gently on the other one as well before giving Darcy another kiss.

"Come over after my father goes to bed," Darcy whispered. She stood up, letting her robe fall open. Nora wasn't about to let an opportunity like that go unnoticed. She stepped into her arms again and then let her hands move down Darcy's warm, soft skin. Nora put her hand between Darcy's legs and was rewarded with a delicious intake of breath from her. Darcy lay back on the bed as Nora knelt down between her legs. As if a choreographer had whispered directions to each of them, Darcy draped her legs over Nora's shoulders. Nora was delighted to find her lover wet with arousal and excitement. She feasted on her as if she were a starving beggar at a banquet. Darcy arched up to meet her thrusting tongue while Nora craved the taste of her sweetness. When Darcy finally came with a thrashing wild display of urgency and need, Nora was ecstatic to have gotten her that far again. They had so many things to learn about each other and Nora was definitely looking forward to it. Time was on their side now.

At dawn, back in her own bed, Nora got up once she determined the young rooster wasn't going to let her get another ten minutes of sleep. She took a shower and loved the way the warm water felt against her breasts. Memories of her night with Darcy kept her in the shower a lot longer than usual, but she couldn't stay in there all morning. She eventually got out and pampered herself with baby powder. Nora then blow dried her hair before making an appearance in the kitchen.

"Good morning," she said to her mother. "Did I wake you up last night?"

"Me? No. Why? What did you do?"

Nora smiled and shook her head. "I didn't *do* anything. I went over to see Darcy after you went to bed. I didn't get back until about two thirty."

"In the *morning?*"

"Yes, in the morning. I turned off my headlights when I got close to the house so I wouldn't set off the rooster."

"Well, I didn't hear a thing."

Nora poured herself a cup of coffee and sat down at the kitchen table.

"What were you doing there until two in the morning?" Opal asked.

"Uh . . ." Nora was certain her cheeks were glowing.

151

"Uh-oh," Opal said. "You two were . . . uh . . ." As her mother searched for the word she wanted, Nora continued to turn red. Finally, Opal said, "In his house? You two were . . . uh . . . in his house?"

"Yeah, in his house," Nora admitted sheepishly. That particular fact hadn't occurred to her until her mother mentioned it. They had made love in the windmill man's house!

"Well, under the circumstance, I guess he deserved it."

"He was asleep the whole time."

"I'm sure he was."

"I didn't go over there with that intention in mind," Nora said. "Things just sort of—"

"I know. Your hormones have been in overdrive since you saw her at that basketball game."

"Oh, they have not!" Nora said indignantly. They were both laughing now.

"If it had been anyone else but that ornery windmill man, I would be wagging a finger at you," Opal said, "but he's a whole different story. I think you've both gotten a little revenge in on him now. Just be careful. He's not a nice man."

"I know. I know." *Jesus*, Nora thought. *Me and my big mouth.*

Nora heard a truck pull up outside. They both went out on the porch to see who it was. Jack got out wearing his usual starched jeans, denim shirt and white straw hat.

"I've got more yellow squash and green beans," he said. "I'll be back this afternoon to help you unload the tables."

"Can you stay for breakfast?" Opal asked.

"Already had breakfast. Thanks."

He put three boxes in the back of Opal's truck and tipped his hat to them. They went back inside the house as he drove away.

"What we don't sell today," Opal said, "I'll have to can this afternoon and tomorrow. We'll have more fresh stuff by Thursday anyway."

Once they were back in the kitchen, Opal took the biscuits out of the oven. "Let's eat and get on downtown. I don't want anyone getting my spot."

Vegetable sales were swift and steady. There were still customers mingling about as vendors kept stalling to pack things up, hoping to make another sale. Nora and Opal sold out of yellow squash and okra again.

"I think I'll make a batch of fourteen-day pickles," Opal said once they started to break down their vending area.

"What about all these tomatoes that are left?" Nora asked.

"The ones that won't keep until next Thursday I'll have to do something with," Opal said. "I could stew them then put 'em in the freezer for spaghetti sauce, but eating tomatoes that way makes me gassy."

Nora folded up a card table and had to lean against another one as a fit of laughter overwhelmed her. A sudden memory-flash of a spaghetti discussion when she was in middle school made her nearly double over in hysterics. For years, Thursday nights at the Fleming house was saved for a big spaghetti supper with Opal's homemade meat sauce. Nora and Greg always ended up going to school the next day with the most awful gas. Once they were old enough to figure out that it was the fresh tomatoes in the spaghetti sauce causing the problem, spaghetti night had to be moved to Fridays.

"I know what you're thinking about," Opal said as she folded up the white tablecloth. "You kids getting on the school bus every Friday morning with gas attacks."

"Greg and I could sure make that big old school bus seem mighty small!"

"Maybe I'll use these tomatoes for something else."

Nora rolled the window up in her mother's truck to keep out the road dust. Someone ahead of them kicked it up in huge clouds, so Opal slowed down to avoid being engulfed in grit.

"We need rain," Nora said.

"Spoken like a true farmer's daughter," Opal said as she rolled up her own window to keep from choking on dirt.

Nora coughed. "How much did you and Jack make this week?"

"We get to split five hundred and thirty dollars."

"Wow." Nora knew they had been busy the last four days but not *that* busy. "Wow," she said again. "That's a lot of veggies."

"Word gets out this time of year. City people will drive a long way for garden-fresh stuff." Opal slowed down to turn into the driveway. She stopped the truck so Nora could get out to check the mail.

"Water and electric bill," Nora said as she smacked the dusty mail against her thigh and got back in the truck.

Opal drove over the cattle guard and as they got closer to the house, Nora saw the white truck parked next to her car.

"Wonder who that is?" Opal said.

Nora broke out into a smile when she saw her brother and niece sitting on the front porch.

"Will you look at that?" Opal said. "Did you know he was coming today?"

"Not exactly."

Opal parked her pickup and got out to give her granddaughter Holly a hug.

"How long have you been waiting here?" Nora asked them.

"About sixty seconds," Greg said.

"That was you throwing all the dust on us?" Opal said.

"I'm sure it was," Nora said. "You know how he drives."

"Can I give them to her, Dad?" Holly asked excitedly.

"Sure you can," Greg said and gave his daughter the keys.

"Grammie!" Holly said. She took Opal by the hand and led her to the new white truck. "This is for you."

"What's for me?"

Holly gave the keys to her grandmother. "We bought you a new truck."

"I didn't know you could drive."

"I can't drive yet, Grammie. This is your truck. Not my truck."

"What?"

Greg took his mother's hand and closed it with the truck key in her palm. "Nora, Holly and I bought you this truck, Mom. It's yours."

"Mine?"

"Yes. Yours."

"What have you kids gone and done now?!"

Chapter Twenty-one

As Darcy drove down the highway on a service call, she didn't like the feelings of frustration that piled up as the days and weeks passed. She wanted to spend as much time as possible with Nora, but that wasn't as easy to do now that Nora had taken a part time job at the new county hospital in Fairfax. Nora worked only a few days a week but it was still time that they couldn't spend together. Darcy also learned that Nora's niece would be there for most of the summer, which would make it even harder for them to find time to be together. The arrangement they had now—a few hours snatched here and there together—just wasn't working out. Darcy wanted more but she wasn't sure how to get it.

For Darcy, being involved with someone she couldn't see whenever she wanted to leveled off into a series of eye-opening realizations as time went on. She felt too old to still be dating. She was ready to settle down and get on with her personal life. How was it possible for someone in their mid-forties to still be having so many adolescent complications to deal with? Neither one of them truly felt as though they had their own space anywhere. They lived with a parent in a house that had been paid for several years ago. And both she and Nora had personal items and furniture in storage with nowhere to really call their own.

There was also a certain amount of sneaking around going on for both of them that reminded Darcy too much of the relationship they'd had as teenagers. There wasn't the same amount of secrecy involved since Nora's mother knew what Nora was doing but there was no way Darcy could let her father find out. She felt the need to keep her private life to herself for a lot of reasons, especially since she had a business that served the local farming and ranching communities. Darcy had been in the closet her entire life, so staying there was easy for her. But Nora was out to her family, which was a surprisingly huge portion of the Prescott population once the number of cousins, aunts and uncles were factored in. Darcy imagined it wouldn't be long before the rumors about their relationship leaked out. She would deal with that when it happened and hope for the best. Not only did she feel too old to still be dating, she felt too old to still be in the closet. She had to admit that she felt more comfortable there. She needed to sit down and figure out what she wanted out of all this.

Anxiety accompanied Nora's late evening visits to the Tate home. One night when Darcy was alone, she had a dream about her father coming into her room in his wheelchair with a rifle in his lap, ready to shoot them both as she and Nora lay sleeping in each other's arms. It was such a vivid dream that Darcy put a lock on her bedroom door the next day. It was the first time in years that she had been afraid of her father. He was a sound sleeper and she and Nora were always careful about making too much noise when they made love, but the dream still had Darcy on edge.

She didn't have any answers, only a lot of questions. She looked at her watch as she drove down the two-lane country road and imagined that Nora and her mother were out delivering eggs already. Darcy was on her way to a small town west of San Antonio where a five-hundred-acre ranch had three windmills that needed some work. She checked her cell phone for a signal there in the Hill Country and decided to give Nora a call.

"Hello," Nora said.

"Hi. It's me."

"Hey there. Where are you?"

"On my way to a ranch near Geronimo."

"My mom isn't feeling well today," Nora said. "I'm doing her egg run by myself."

"How did you convince her to let you do that?"

"She couldn't get out of bed this morning, so she didn't have a choice."

"I'm sorry your mother's sick. Is it her lupus acting up?"

"Yes. I'm just glad I'm here to help her. She calls me every few minutes or so to make sure I'm at the right place at the right time. If I screw this up, she'll never let me do it alone again no matter how sick she is. The only good thing about all of this is she's learning to use the new cell phone I got for her."

"So tell me something," Darcy said. "Are you wearing a bonnet? Do you look like the Egg Lady?"

"No," Nora said. "Sorry. No bonnet. I don't look anything like the Egg Lady right now. I can tell you this much, though. My mother's customers absolutely adore her. I've got a stack of notes to give her and jars of jellies and jams, plates full of turnovers, a link of dried sausage, a set of chicken salt and pepper shakers and a yellow sign that says 'Chicks Live Here' on it. No telling what all I'd be dragging home if they had known she was sick. This is just her ordinary egg-delivery-day haul. I almost felt bad making them pay for the eggs."

Darcy had often wondered what it would be like to have such personable parents. Both of hers had been in their forties when Darcy was born. They were told early on that having children would be nearly impossible, so Darcy was a complete surprise to the Tates. When she was in the first grade and her mother would come to school for whatever reason, the other children thought she was Darcy's grandmother. Then there were the times when little Darcy and her mother would go shopping together. Darcy could remember women patting her on the head and then asking her mother how old her granddaughter was. Even though Darcy was young, she knew how uncomfortable these remarks were for her mother. If they were embarrassing for her as a kid, she could only imagine how awful it must've been for a parent. *It's no wonder they were both always so grumpy*, Darcy thought.

"Anyway," Nora said, "I'm on a mission. Wish me luck."

"Good luck then. I'll talk to you later."

In her pickup, Darcy followed the rancher down an overgrown road that had cows on both sides of it. To her it was more like a cow trail than a road, and it was mostly up hill, but it was getting them where they needed to go. Huge rolls of feed hay dotted the pastures every hundred yards or so. The property was dry and rocky, typical for the Texas Hill Country. No one had gotten the rain they had needed in the spring. Everyone all over South Texas had to feed their cattle and water their crops already.

She saw a clearing up ahead and then noticed the windmill. This was the first of the three the rancher wanted her to check out. Keeping windmills properly maintained was vital when wanting to get the most out of them. All windmill owners knew that, but fooling around with their upkeep was time-consuming and could even be dangerous. It was easier to call someone else and have them do it. That's how Darcy's father had made his living and why Darcy now had more money than she would ever need. It was also the reason she had no time to spend any of it either. Fixing and maintaining windmills was a lot of work.

"It's got a new squeak to it," the rancher said when he crawled out of his truck. "Lost a few blades, too. I saw some feathers around here. Thought maybe an owl might've flown into it or something."

Darcy had her binoculars handy to give the windmill a good

inspection from the ground. She wouldn't be climbing up there any sooner than she had to.

"You have hunters around here?" she asked.

"No. Shouldn't be any. The property's posted for no trespassing."

"You've got bullet holes in the tail vane and helmet. Have those always been there?"

"What?! Lemme see that."

He took the binoculars she handed to him and focused in where she told him to.

"Well, son of a—" He stopped and shook his head.

"Hunters love practicing on windmills," Darcy said.

"How much harm was done?" He gave the binoculars back to her.

"You'll need a new helmet," she said as she looked back through the binoculars again. "You've got oil leaking out, so that's not good. I'd recommend rebuilding it." She focused in on the wheel section of the windmill to see what was going on there. "When was the last time you were out here to see about it?"

"A week ago," the rancher said. "Your dad always said to check 'em at least once a week to make sure they were pumping water. Everything seemed fine and the tank was full. Then I brought the hay out a few days ago and I heard this one squeaking."

"Are the other windmills squeaking, too?" Darcy asked.

"No. It's just time for their yearly maintenance. There better *not* be any bullet holes in 'em!" He walked back to his pickup. "Let's go see how they're doing. I never thought about checking them with binoculars. I'll be sure to do that from now on."

She followed him in her truck along the cow trail to the other windmills on the ranch, but there was no evidence of vandalism on either of the other ones. Just the usual annual maintenance on those. Windmills were dependable and usually didn't need much attention. After the original expense of installing one, the operating costs were next to nothing. Some windmills had been pumping water for over forty years, so changing the oil once a year and

160

tightening all the bolts was about all the maintenance they needed as long as bad weather kept flying objects out of the way and hunters used something else for target practice. A properly maintained windmill would pay for itself quickly and was more reliable than an electric pump. They were cheaper to operate too.

Darcy started on the last one he showed her. The binoculars helped her locate a wasp nest nearly as big as a softball about halfway up. She kept a case of wasp spray in her truck just for such occasions. Insect stings were one of the biggest hazards of her job.

Darcy was already tired when she got in her truck to drive to the last windmill. She was glad she had finally gotten her legs in shape for climbing up and down and even staying on top of a windmill long enough to do what needed to be done to it. Those first few weeks on the job once she took over for her father had been miserable. The Army had kept her in good physical condition, but all the climbing she had to do on a daily basis was an entirely new experience for her body. She concentrated exercises on her calf and thigh muscles and bought good, sturdy work boots to help keep her feet from getting too tired on the rungs every day. She was in the best shape of her life and Darcy was finally comfortable with fixing windmills.

She had just come down from the second windmill when the rancher drove up to check on her. Driving another truck with bales of hay on it, he asked her how the other two windmills had looked.

"They'll be ready for a few new parts next time," she said, "but they're fine now. Just make sure they keep pumping water. That's the best way to tell if everything's working all right."

"How long will the other one be out of commission?" he asked. "Will I need to move my cows?"

Darcy rolled the window further down on her pickup. She wiped her greasy, oily hands on a rag and tossed it in the seat beside her. "A few hours. I should have all the parts I'll need with me if it's just the helmet that needs replacing. We probably caught the problem in time to keep from wearing out other parts. I won't really know until I break it down and see what damage the bullet did."

"You're like a windmill doctor," he said. "I'll be back to check on you in a while then. I've got some hay and salt blocks to deliver."

By the time Darcy had the last windmill repaired and put back together, she was tired and hungry. Not only that, but the hundred-mile drive back home was still in front of her.

Her father was unusually chatty when Darcy finally got home. She had to get cleaned up, make some supper for them, return whatever work-related calls she'd gotten during the day, do the week's bookkeeping on the computer and get the river depth readings for her father so he could report them to the National Weather Service. There hadn't been any rain in the area, so that was one less thing she had to worry about. Hopefully she would have time later to call Nora and ask if they could see each other after things settled down a little. Darcy wasn't sure she would be able to stay awake very long, but she needed to spend some time with her.

She took a ham out of the refrigerator and sliced off two nice ham steaks. Darcy decided to peel some potatoes and add a bit of onion to the skillet. Within minutes the kitchen smelled good enough to bring her father in searching for food.

"What did you have out there today?" he asked, rolling right up to the kitchen table in his wheelchair.

"Poachers taking pot shots at one of the windmills," she said. "Had to replace the helmet and plug a hole in the tail vain."

"You don't have to worry about the tail vain. Waste of time. It'll catch the wind just fine."

"I don't do it for the wind," Darcy said as she added black pepper to the potatoes and put a lid on the skillet. "I do it for the windmill. If I plug the hole, the hunter doesn't win."

162

"That's silly."

Darcy ignored him. If she was the one doing the repairs now, then she would do them her way.

"How was physical therapy today?" she asked him.

"Grueling."

"Did you watch any of the movies I rented for you?"

"One of the John Wayne's. Then I got sleepy."

"What did she make you for dinner?"

"Grilled cheese."

They talked about Darcy's day at the ranch. She told him step by step what she had done and how she did it. Darcy and her father had different ways of doing things, so most of their meals together consisted of him punctuating teaching points with his fork, while Darcy listened attentively, but would continue doing things the way that worked best for her. In Darcy's mind, keeping him a little agitated about her approach to fixing windmills was her way of making him want to get better. He longed for the day when his legs would work well enough again to where he could climb and fix things. Occasionally she would tell him something totally inappropriate for windmill repair just to get him riled up. He sounded more like his old grumpy self then, which made her think he really *was* getting better.

After supper she did the dishes and got him settled in with the John Wayne movie he didn't finish. Darcy drove down to the river near their property and took a reading. *No change*, she thought, and got back in her truck to go back home. Her cell phone rang as she started her pickup. It was Nora.

"How's your mom doing?" Darcy asked.

"I got her moving around after the egg run. Hopefully she'll be feeling better in a few days. Are you too tired for a visit later?"

Darcy smiled. "I'm not *that* tired."

"Then I'll give you a call when I get mom tucked in for the evening."

Chapter Twenty-two

Darcy woke her father up after she had finished the nightly bookkeeping on the computer. The John Wayne movie was still on so she turned off the DVD player and the television.

"There's something about that movie that puts me right to sleep," he said. "I'll try watching that one again tomorrow."

Darcy pushed his wheelchair down the hallway to the bathroom and waited outside the door until he called for her. She had a fresh pair of pajamas waiting for him and helped him get dressed for bed.

"Did you have any calls earlier?" he asked.

Darcy's eyes flew open as she remembered the call she had received from Nora. Then she realized that he was referring to business calls about windmills.

"I've got one left to see from yesterday and two more from today's calls," she said. "They're local, so I should have estimates on all of them by tomorrow afternoon."

She helped him into bed and covered him up. Darcy switched on the ceiling fan and turned out the light.

"Goodnight, Dad."

She heard him grunt in the darkness and imagined that he was already asleep before she even had the door closed.

After her dream about him coming into her room with a rifle, Darcy kept his two guns in her bedroom closet. The effect of the dream was fading—at least enough for her to feel better about having Nora stay over again. *Guilt has been messing with me,* she thought with a shake of her head. *But there's not a lot I can do about it. I won't stop seeing her and we still need a place to be together.*

She glanced at her watch and decided to work on the computer some more, adjusting the inventory while she waited for Nora to come over. They hadn't seen each other in a few days but they talked on the phone several times each day. Nora liked her job and her hours, but for Darcy it just seemed like they weren't able to spend much time together. *Not a lot I can do about that either,* she thought with a sigh. But she needed to discuss this with Nora and see how she felt about all of it. Maybe Nora was happy with the way things were going for them.

Darcy met her out on the front porch and took Nora in her arms for a slow, sweet kiss.

"I've missed you," Nora cooed in her ear.

"How's my junior Egg Lady?"

Joy bubbled in Nora's laugh as they went in the house holding hands.

"I'm kind of proud of myself actually," Nora said. "I gave out my mom's cell phone number to a few of her favorite customers who were really worried about her and she's been on the phone all day with them. She's even a little social butterfly when she's at home in bed. I told her to turn the phone off when she got sleepy so it wouldn't disturb her."

They stood in the middle of the living room still holding hands.

Darcy wasn't sure whether to have a seat so they could continue talking or lead the way to her room where they could make love.

"How long can you stay?" Darcy asked.

Nora leaned closer to kiss her. "A few hours," she said. Her tongue traced the soft fullness of Darcy's lips. "Let's go to your room. I promise to be quiet."

Darcy smiled and led the way. *To hell with guilt*, she thought. *I deserve to be happy.*

Once they were in her room, Darcy switched on the lamp by the bed and then locked the door. It was easy to forget about everything else when they were together. She longed for the day when they would be able to wake up in each other's arms in the morning.

Nora kissed her again and sent Darcy's stomach into a wild swirl of sensation. It always amazed her the way her body reacted to Nora. Even when they were teenagers Nora could make her feel desirable and happy with nothing more than a look or a smile.

"Did I mention that I've missed you?" Nora whispered while nibbling at Darcy's neck and throat.

"You did," Darcy managed to say. She unbuttoned her shirt and let it fall to the floor. Nora's hand went immediately to Darcy's breast, circling her nipple with her thumb.

"Sports bras," Nora said. "The next best thing to real skin."

Darcy pulled the sports bra over her head and a small moan escaped from her throat as Nora's warm, sweet mouth captured her nipple. It was hard to think about anything but getting Nora out of her clothes before it became too difficult to remain standing. She fumbled with the buttons on Nora's blouse and got that off, then went to work on Nora's bra.

"You don't need to wear so many clothes when you come to visit," Darcy said.

Nora took her mouth away from Darcy's breast and kissed her with such heat and passion that they would both need to be on the bed soon. Darcy maneuvered them in that direction and worked on getting Nora's shorts off. They finally got undressed and Darcy eased her back on the bed.

166

Lying side by side with hands and lips exploring each other, Nora whispered, "I should just show up here in my going-to-get-laid outfit? Sneakers, shorts and a T-shirt?"

"That outfit's already become a favorite of mine."

Nora brought her leg up so Darcy could touch her while they kissed. She was so wet and ready that Darcy felt another flutter in the pit of her stomach as she slowly found Nora's swollen clit. The moment Darcy touched her there Nora sucked Darcy's tongue into her mouth. With her free hand she reached between Darcy's legs and it was all Darcy could do to keep from coming right away. She wanted to prolong the stroking and the exquisite intimacy. She wanted to make this wild but delicate act of sharing last as long as possible, but a mutual sense of urgency made it harder than she thought. Darcy pulled her mouth away from Nora's when she started to come. She buried her face in the side of Nora's neck as hips and fingers flung them both into a vast sea of pleasure.

Darcy felt overwhelmed with emotion and throbbing euphoria as Nora kept her fingers deep inside of her. Nora's entire body trembled with the power and force of her own orgasm. They stayed that way for several minutes with nothing more than a thin layer of sweat separating their bodies.

"You have a way of zapping every ounce of energy out of my body," Nora whispered in a weak, sexy voice.

They both withdrew their fingers and settled easily into each other's arms. Darcy had no idea what time it was when she finally woke up again. She kissed Nora on the nose and rose up to look at the clock.

"What time is it?" Nora asked sleepily.

"Midnight."

"Oh, it's early then."

"How long can you stay?" Darcy asked. She moved a lock of blond hair away from Nora's droopy eyes.

"Actually, I probably should be getting home. I might be handling the farmer's market alone in the morning. My mom might not be feeling well enough to go with me."

Darcy was suddenly sorry she had looked at the clock at all. She didn't want Nora to go. Darcy propped her head up with her hand and asked, "Do you ever think about our situation? The sneaking in and out? Not being able to wake up with each other? Not being able to have a decent meal together that doesn't come in a plastic red basket? Or that doesn't happen unless it's bingo night at the VFW?"

Nora smiled and looked at her closely. "I've thought about it some, but I also know what is and isn't possible for us right now."

"Right now," Darcy repeated. She knew what that meant, but neither of them wanted to put it into words. As long as Darcy's father was alive, this was about as much as they could have together—a few hours stolen in the middle of the night. It felt more like an affair than a real relationship but she knew Nora was right. This was all that was possible right now and they'd have to deal with the complications.

"You're an incredible woman, Darcy Tate," Nora said with a quiet voice still laced with sleep. "I've known that since I was a six-teen-year-old pool bunny." She touched the side of Darcy's face with the back of her hand. "If this is what we have to do now to be together, then we'll be careful and keep it all quiet. Things will be different some day. It won't always be like this. I promise."

"It's just nice to know we both want the same thing," Darcy said.

"Of course we do." Nora kissed her to bring home her point. "We've waited too long to be together. We can wait as long as it takes."

Darcy felt a deep sense of relief as they settled in, snuggling and cuddling. By the time Nora had to leave, Darcy was ready for some much needed sleep.

Darcy was home earlier than usual the following evening. She had finished the three estimates and already had a list of other cus-tomers either wanting advice about their ailing windmills or need-ing an estimage. There were many times Darcy got calls from farmers or ranchers who wanted to save money by trying to make their own repairs. It was almost a sure thing that these people would eventually be calling her back. The more the average user knew about windmills, the better they tended to operate, but that didn't mean technical problems weren't to be taken seriously. It was too easy to let a simple thing go which could eventually have the potential to make the whole thing shut down production. So free advice usually meant that a service call was just being postponed for a little while.

"What did you do today?" her father asked. They were having an early supper of ham, eggs and toast.

"I'm just about caught up from the last storm," Darcy said. "It's been a few days since I've gotten any calls on that."

"Some of those fools probably don't even know their windmills are broken."

"Did you watch that movie today?" she asked, changing the subject. Darcy didn't like hearing him refer to their customers as fools. They were all hard working people who needed to cut expenses just like everyone else did.

"No. I've been saving it for later."

Darcy was glad to hear that. It would keep him occupied for a few hours while she spent some time out in the shop on one of her welding projects. There hadn't been much time for things she liked to do, so whenever she got the opportunity to tinker with one of her sculptures, Darcy took advantage of it.

After supper she got her father settled in front of the television and gave John Wayne another try. Once the movie was going Darcy went out the back door and into her workshop. Before she got the door unlocked, her cell phone rang.

"Hi, it's me," Nora said. "I can't come over tonight. We've got company."

Darcy could hear the disappointment in her voice. "Oh. I'm sorry to hear that. How's your mother feeling?"

"Better. She was up and out of bed most of the afternoon. Some of my cousins heard she was sick and came over with a boatload of food for us. I guess they think I'm totally inept in the kitchen. It's like we've both been here starving since my mother is too sick to cook."

"Did they bring anything good?" Darcy asked.

"Frozen casseroles to heat up later—chicken, sausage, brisket, you name it. My mom insisted they all stay for supper, so it'll be one of those Fleming family all-nighters. They have the family photo albums out now. I already know there won't be a chance for me to get away later. Someone will have to practically fall over in a pan-rattling snore before they'll get the message that it's time to leave."

"I understand."

"But I do have some good news for you, though," Nora said. "My mom wants you to look at that windmill we have out in a back pasture. The corn isn't doing well there, so she wants to turn the cows out in it a few weeks from now. She was feeling well enough to move them up from the creek earlier this afternoon and they'll be ready for moving again soon."

"I can probably look at it tomorrow. Will you be around to take me back there?"

"I will in the afternoon. Tomorrow's Saturday. I'll be schleppin' vegetables at the town square in the morning."

"Then I'll call you," Darcy said.

"And I'm sorry about tonight. This is a spontaneous bunch that likes to visit."

The next day, Darcy took care of business and finished two of the repairs just after noon. Summer was a lot closer than she liked to admit and the heat was already taking its toll on her. They needed rain, but other than a tropical storm eventually making its way into the Gulf, there didn't seem to be anything promising on the way. This time of year was relatively boring as far as her volunteer duties with the National Weather Service were concerned.

With her father finally well enough to make the calls and give the reports once Darcy collected the daily information for him, that was one less thing she had to do each afternoon. It was nice to see him taking an interest in things again. She wondered how long it would take him to suggest he ride with her when she made initial calls on windmill customers. In a way she was looking forward to that day since it would mean he was a lot better, and in another way she wasn't. Once her father was up and around again, he would be telling her how to do things and wanting to run the business his way. Darcy knew it was a no-win situation, but she would do what she thought was best for her, him and the business regardless of what her father wanted.

Darcy parked next to the new white pickup in front of Opal Fleming's house. She saw Nora and her mother sitting on the porch swing.

"Hi there," Nora said. "We've been waiting for you."

Darcy climbed the steps and was surprised when Nora came over and kissed her lightly on the lips. Darcy could feel the heat in her face and knew she was blushing. Never in her life had she ever been kissed that way in front of someone's mother!

"How were things at the town square this morning?" Darcy asked, hoping she sounded less flustered than she felt.

"Better than expected," Nora said. "We're still getting okra, tomatoes, and cucumbers off the garden every day, so that's keeping us in business."

"How are you feeling, Mrs. Fleming?" she asked. Nora held Darcy's hand, which also made Darcy feel uncomfortable. Such open displays of affection were foreign to her. The military was too firmly engrained in her heart and her head for her to enjoy it as much as she would have liked to.

"I'm feeling better," Opal said. "Thank you for asking. I'd like to take up my regular activities in a few days. My girls miss me."

"She means her chickens," Nora said. "You ready to see about our windmill?" Without waiting for an answer from Darcy, Nora asked her mother if she wanted to go with them.

"I'll just wait here," Opal said. "I don't feel like climbin' steps or gettin' in and out of a truck right now."

"We'll be back then," Nora said. "Can I get you anything before we go?"

"No. I'm fine. Take the old truck if you like," Opal said. "We've got some ugly ruts down there."

"Darcy's truck sits up high. We'll be okay."

Darcy was still a bit stunned by Nora's kiss and hand-holding. In many ways she was very old-fashioned. It just didn't seem right to be carrying on that way.

"You okay?" Nora asked.

"You kissed me in front of your mother."

"So?" Nora looked over at her and arched a brow. "What's the matter? I've always been affectionate with my girlfriends in front of my family."

"I can honestly say I've never experienced anything like that before."

"You look like you've just seen a ghost."

"I guess you surprised me."

"Well, get used to it, my dear."

Darcy took a deep breath. "Promise me one thing. Please promise me you won't ever do anything like that in front of my father."

Nora threw her head back and laughed. "Jeesuuus, Darcy! I might be out, darlin', but I'm not stupid."

Chapter Twenty-three

They were getting closer to the last gate leading to the back pasture on Opal Fleming's property. Darcy was impressed with the size of the Fleming spread as they drove around overgrown branches bordering the faded road. Nora told her stories about growing up on the farm and got Darcy so distracted that she missed a hole that sent them bouncing around in the cab of her truck.

"I remember one time Greg and I were down by the creek and I wanted to get some water to drink," Nora said. "I'm not sure I would drink it now, but we didn't think anything about it back then when we were kids. The creek's so clear you can see right to the bottom. Anyway, so I have my little bucket ready and each time I try and get some water, Greg would stick his toe in the creek."

"He was barefoot?"

"Yeah. We'd been fishing and swimming. We'd fish until we got too hot or bored, then we'd piddle in the water for a while and scare all the fish away. Neither one of us could sit still very long. So anyway, I'd dip my bucket in the creek and there his toe would be, so I had to wait a while for his toe-water to go on down stream." She waved her hand around pantomiming water flowing down a creek. Nora's laugh was delightful. Darcy could tell that her childhood memories still brought her much joy. "I wasn't about to drink any toe-water," Nora explained. "Each time I'd dunk my bucket in the creek, there Greg's toe would be. Boy, was he pissing me off, but yelling at him wasn't doing any good." Nora chuckled at the memory. "Then the next time I dunked my bucket I saw a crawdad reach up with its pinchers and grab him by the toe. Ohmigod! Greg let out a scream and started yelling that a snake had bit him. So off he went running up the hill. I was laughing so hard I couldn't holler loud enough to stop him. He sure could run a lot faster than me, too. By the time I got to the house to tell them it wasn't a snake my mom was putting on her going-to-town bonnet and was ready to take him to the hospital."

Nora's laughter made Darcy laugh too.

"And to this day my brother still isn't convinced that it wasn't a snake. He *hates* snakes. But I'll tell you one thing. He never stuck his toe in the water again when I wanted a drink."

"So that's what I missed by not having a brother."

"What? Never having to drink toe-water? At the time I would've given you my brother without even blinking an eye," Nora said, "but I kind of like him now so I'm glad I've kept him."

They reached the last gate and Nora got out of the truck to open it. Darcy drove through and waited for her. In front of them was a pasture of cornstalks in desperate need of rain. Off to the right Darcy saw an old Samson windmill standing at the edge of the cornfield. There weren't too many Samsons around Prescott anymore. Seeing it brought a smile to her face.

"How long has this windmill been here?"

Nora shrugged. "As long as I can remember. When we were kids we used to take pot shots at it with our BB guns."

Darcy lowered her binoculars and turned to look at her. "You had a BB gun?"

"Didn't everybody?"

Darcy raised the binoculars to get a good look at the windmill again. "I took you for the Barbie and Ken type."

"Oh, I had those, too, but BB guns were more fun than pretending my Ken doll was a really butch girl. Besides, I liked being outside a lot more. Sometimes we'd go hunting for lizards with our BB guns." Nora came over to stand next to her and looked at the windmill. "So what do you see up there?"

"I'm sure it needs at least a lube job and an oil change."

"How is it you can make that sound so sexy?" Nora whispered as she leaned closer to her.

Darcy lowered the binoculars and glanced down in time to see Nora's engaging smile.

"It might've been the word *lube* that got my attention," Nora said.

"I see. Uh . . . when was the last time anyone checked on this windmill?"

"I'm not sure. My mom would have left that up to my cousin Jack. He's been promising to fix it ever since that last bad storm. I can call and ask him."

While Nora got her cell phone out, Darcy walked over to the holding tank to see how much water was in it. Her visual inspection with the binoculars told her the windmill needed oil at the very least and every nut and bolt checked out for wear and effectiveness. She wouldn't be able to tell if there were other problems until she climbed up the tower for a closer look.

"Wow," Nora said. "Jack is really mad."

Darcy got her tool belt out of the truck and put it on. She attached a few other things she would need and pulled on her work gloves.

"Ohmigod," Nora said breathlessly. "You even have a tool belt. Be still my heart."

Darcy shook her head and chuckled. "What's Jack mad about?"

"He said he would fix it. We didn't need to call you." Nora looked up at the windmill again. "Maybe he's worried about the cost. He and my mom would have to split the bill." She slowly leaned over and kissed Darcy lightly on the lips. "Or perhaps my windmill-fixin' girlfriend will let me pay it off in another way."

"You've got a one track mind today."

Darcy reached for a can of wasp spray and stuck it inside her shirt. She made that mistake once and she wasn't taking any chances.

"I'll know more when I come back down," Darcy said.

As she climbed the windmill tower, Darcy looked down to see Nora watching her. Darcy could only imagine how clumsy and awkward she looked from the ground. Where as she had made great progress in getting her legs in shape for this job, her upper body strength wasn't where she wanted it to be. But by taking her time and changing positions often, Darcy was able to keep herself from getting too tired before finishing a job. That was one reason she liked doing estimates in between maintenance or repairs. It gave her body and muscles time to recover.

Once she reached the top, Darcy glanced down to see Nora walking into the cornfield. The rows were close and compact, with barely enough room to walk between them. *Too bad they'll lose the crop if we don't get rain soon*, she thought.

Darcy checked the helmet for damage. Taking off a glove and thumping it with her knuckle, she knew from the hollow sound it made that it needed oil. On closer inspection she noticed that new wheel arms were needed, too. She checked the hub next and decided to replace that as well. Luckily she had all the parts she would need with her in the truck.

Darcy held on to the tail vane and glanced down at the cornfield again and looked for Nora. Squinting to see better, she noticed that the cornfield wasn't but about fifteen yards deep on all four sides. In the middle was another crop, but from where she was perched on the windmill, Darcy couldn't tell what the other crop was. *Too tall for beans*, she thought, *and too short for okra, but it sure is green.*

176

Then she saw Nora's blond head at the edge of the corn as she walked out into the middle of the other crop with her hands on her hips. Darcy wished now she hadn't left the binoculars in the truck.

Turning her attention back to the windmill, she secured the tail vane and took the helmet apart. Before she got too far into it, Darcy heard a vehicle in the distance and then saw a pickup roar to a stop behind her truck. Jack got out and slammed the door just before she noticed Nora storming out of the corn. It was amazing to hear how well their voices carried in the wind.

"Damn, Nora! What are you doing out here?" Jack yelled.

Darcy looked down to see Nora in front of him with her hands on her hips again.

"I can't believe this!" Nora said. "How long have you been growing pot out here?"

Pot? Darcy thought. She peered over the top of the windmill to get a better look at the crop in the middle of the cornfield. *Well, well, well,* she thought. *Old Jack has a part-time job!*

"You shouldn't have come out here!"

"I want it gone, Jack. Get rid of it now."

"I can't. At least not yet. It's not ready."

"It's not ready for what?"

"To harvest."

"Harvest?" Nora yelled. "What the hell do you think you're doing? How *could* you?" She was about six inches shorter than Jack, but Nora was right there in his face. "You're growing pot on my mother's property! What could you *possibly* be thinking?!"

"I make sure she gets her share."

"Don't for one minute think that my mother would approve of this! She trusts you! How could you betray her this way?"

"We need the money!"

"She doesn't need drug money! What do you think this looks like from up there?" Nora yelled, pointing to the sky. "Whose door will the DEA be knocking on if they find it?"

Jack threw his hands up in the air. "Drug money! Stop thinking of it like that! There's no way I can scratch out a living for us by planting watermelons and corn. I can make more money off one marijuana patch than I can from five watermelon seasons."

"It's against the law, Jack," Nora said as if talking to an obtuse child. "It's against the fucking law. You could go to jail! My mother could go to jail! Get that stuff off of her property now!"

"I *told* you not to come out here. Why didn't you listen to me?"

"Get rid of it."

"I told you already. I can't. I've got bills to pay."

"You know, Jack, it's one thing if you want to do this sort of thing on your own and take the chance of getting caught, losing your land and house and everything your family's worked so hard for all these years. You can plant your marijuana and pretend it's all fine and dandy. Right now you can be as *big* a fool as you want to be, but the minute you involve my mother in your little scheme, I have to draw the line. It's no longer just you being a fool. Now it's you involving someone who loves you and trusts you to do the right thing." Nora leaned in closer to him and poked him in the chest with her finger. "*That's* what I'm pissed off about! Now either *you* get rid of it, or I'm driving that tractor down here myself and I'm plowing the whole thing up. Do you understand me?"

"Ah, Nora! You're *killin'* me here!"

"What do you think this would do to my mother if she knew what you were up to?"

"You can't tell her."

"You don't think she has a right to know what you're doing on her property? And just who are you selling that stuff to anyway? High school kids?"

"No! Of course not!"

"Then who?"

"I'm not discussing this with you." He turned around and stomped off to his truck, slamming the door again.

Darcy watched him drive away. If there had been pavement instead of grass and dirt, she imagined that Jack would have squealed his tires and left about an inch of smoking rubber behind.

178

She looked down at Nora on the ground with her arms folded across her chest.

Darcy took her time and lowered the helmet down with a rope. She would repair it on the tailgate of her truck so she could help Nora. *If people only knew how far their voices carried out here,* she thought. *My goodness. There aren't any secrets in the wind. That's for sure.*

Chapter Twenty-four

The rooster was relentless. Nora glanced at the clock and saw that it was already after seven. *He let me sleep longer than usual*, she thought. Stretching until she heard bones pop back into place, Nora got out of bed and shuffled to the bathroom. She and her mother had eggs to deliver today.

"Good morning," Opal said to her in the hallway.

Nora gave her mother a sleepy kiss on the cheek. "How are you feeling this morning?"

"Much better."

"Then let me get the truck loaded up before I take a quick shower. Can you throw us some breakfast together? I'm starving."

"What time did you get home last night?" Opal asked on her way down the hall toward the kitchen.

"Early. About one thirty. Darcy was tired."

"I imagine so," Opal said. "We'll just leave it at that."

Once she was out of the bathroom, Nora threw on yesterday's

clothes and carried the two huge ice chests out to her mother's new truck. She had worked an uneventful evening shift at the local hospital the night before and then stopped off to see Darcy on her way home afterward. They were getting to know each other better, which made for some wild, passionate lovemaking. Nora caught herself smiling off and on during the day whenever she recalled their evenings together.

It had been a long time since Nora had thought so much about sex. Memories of Darcy's hands and mouth sent shivers up Nora's spine and made her squirm in her seat wherever she was. She often wondered if there would come a time when they could be together without being so tired. It was always late and inconvenient to have to get up, get dressed and drive home again. Nora also wondered what it would be like to actually do normal things with Darcy— things like waking up on a Sunday morning and reading the paper in bed or falling asleep at night with the TV on. *Maybe someday we'll have that*, she thought.

After a quick breakfast of fried egg sandwiches and coffee, they were ready for their egg run. Opal wore her yellow bonnet and a matching yellow sun dress, while Nora wore denim shorts, a white T-shirt and white sneakers. Her hair was still a little damp from her shower, but it would dry soon with all of the getting in and out of the truck they would be doing.

Opal started up her truck and headed down the driveway. "First stop is Jack's place."

Nora let out a little groan and hoped to have a word with him about his extracurricular activities. She wasn't about to let any of that drop.

"We sure need some rain," Opal said, glancing in her rearview mirror. The pickup left a cloud of dust behind them.

Opal drove down Jack's limestone driveway and parked beside his truck. He came out on the porch in his starched jeans, a white shirt, tan boots and a straw hat.

"Mornin'," he said, tipping his hat to them.

"We need rain," Opal said. She got out of the truck so slowly that Nora wondered if her mother would be able to do the entire egg run today.

"We'll get it eventually," Jack said. He came down the steps and kissed his Aunt Opal on the cheek.

Nora walked around the back of the truck and handed him a carton of eggs out of the ice chest. "Did you take care of that problem we discussed?" she asked him quietly.

"Kind of," he said, matching her secretive tone of voice.

"What does that mean? Kind of? You either did or you didn't."

"It means kind of. Like I said."

"You coming over for supper this evening?" Opal asked him.

"Got plans already," Jack said. "But thanks anyway."

"All righty then. Maybe later in the week." Opal got back in the truck just as slowly as she had exited.

Nora stared him down on her way back around her side of the pickup. "We're not finished with this."

"Sure we are," he said and then gave her that Fleming smile that reminded Nora so much of her brother. At that particular moment it did nothing more than irritate her. She got in the truck and Opal waved to him then backed up and headed out for the rest of their egg run.

Nora was the first one to wake up from a nap, but her mother got up soon afterward. They had come home to a voice mail message telling them that Greg and Holly would be flying down for the weekend. After that Holly would be staying there with them until mid-July. Nora was certain everyone but Greg was looking forward to that. He missed having Holly at home with him in the summer.

"Let me fix supper," Nora said through a yawn.

"I might just let you do that," Opal said.

"What are we having, by the way?"

"The cook's asking me what we're having," Opal said with an amused laugh. "I thawed out some pork chops earlier. I'll leave you in charge of them. I'm off to spend time with my girls."

Before Nora got supper going, she made a decision to go down to the field in the back and see what Jack had done about his marijuana crop. Every time she thought about it, she got angry all over again. She took her mother's old truck and drove through the pastures over the worn road. When she finally got down to where the back pasture was, Nora understood immediately what Jack had meant when he said he had "kind of" taken care of the problem. On the last gate she found a huge padlock and a heavy chain securing it. Fuming and outraged, Nora climbed over the gate and landed with unusual grace on the other side. She could hear the windmill turning, which made her a bit less furious. Darcy's little tune-up had fixed it, which would make her mother happy.

Nudging her way through the corn stalks, Nora found the marijuana crop exactly as she had left it. She shook her head and decided to pay Jack a visit after supper. Apparently he wasn't taking her seriously.

Nora tried to get control of her anger as she turned the pork chops in the skillet. Jack's solution to the problem was so totally unacceptable to her that it wouldn't take much for Nora to lose her temper when she went to see him later. *And that won't get us anywhere*, she thought. *We also can't be snipping at each other in front of Mom either. She'll catch on to that pretty quick once she gets to feeling better.*

Her mother came in, moving slowly, with a basket full of eggs. "Sure smells good in here," she said, taking off her bonnet. "I'll have Holly help me clean out the hen house when she gets here this weekend. I know how much you hate that."

"How about you supervise while Holly and I do it?" Nora suggested.

"Okay."

Opal agreed so quickly that it made them both chuckle. She washed her hands and helped Nora set the table.

"Need to do some shopping tomorrow," Opal said. "Greg and Holly drink sodas and we don't really keep those here for us. There might be one or two in the fridge, but we need to stock up."

They sat down to eat and Nora tried to get her mind in a better place.

"Make a list and I'll get whatever we need," Nora said. She poked at her baked potato without any enthusiasm. Getting this situation with Jack cleared up was becoming more of a necessity than she first thought. Eventually her mother would hear the whispering and snarling going on between them.

"You had a long day," Nora said. "How are you feeling?"

"Tired."

"Maybe you should skip the farmer's market tomorrow. Or I could do it for you."

"Trying to take all my fun away?" Opal asked wearily. Nora noticed that she wasn't eating very much. "Besides," Opal said, "you'll chase all my customers away. I'd have to call you every thirty seconds or so to remind you to smile."

Nora was able to convince her mother that a smile would be a permanent fixture on her face at the vegetable and plant sale the next day if Opal didn't feel well enough to go. Even though Nora believed that smiling at potential customers wasn't the secret to her mother's success, she didn't offer her opinion. Nora figured out that first day she helped with the farmer's market that it was her mother's bonnet that drew customers in. The bonnet was like a customer magnet, instilling confidence in the product being offered. But Nora let her mother continue thinking it was a good old-fashioned smile that did the trick.

Opal went to bed right after supper and Nora made sure her mother knew she'd be gone for a while over to Jack's house. She hoped he was alone since he had hinted earlier in the day that he had plans. When Nora pulled up in front of his house, Jack came out on the porch to meet her.

"I guess I've been expecting you," he said. He held the screen door open for her.

"I found the lock on the gate," she said. "The only thing that really accomplished was pissing me off even more."

"I *know* you," he said. "You would've driven that tractor down there and did me in for sure." He motioned toward a wooden rocking chair in the living room. "Have a seat. Excuse me for a minute while I get out of this."

He walked over to the computer on the desk. With just a glance, Nora could see that he was in a chat room. She sat down and was surprised to hear how fast he could type. It wasn't long before he pulled the desk chair over to the other side of the living room close to where Nora was sitting.

"Can I get you something to drink?" he asked.

"No. I'm fine. Thanks."

"What did Aunt Opal have for supper?"

"We had pork chops and I cooked."

"Oh, good. Then I didn't miss much."

Nora didn't take any offense to the comment and they both laughed.

"I didn't accept her invitation earlier because I didn't want to see you," Jack admitted, "but now here you are."

"Jack, I—" Nora started.

He held up a hand and she stopped talking.

"Let me say something first," he said. "You have to know how much your mother means to me. I would never do anything to hurt her. You have to believe that."

"I do."

"This is how it is for me. I don't think of things in terms of hers and mine. I think of things—and I mean all the things we have on the farm—I think of them as ours. I plant melons here. I plant melons there. I plant corn here. I plant corn there. We buy cows. We buy chickens. We buy pigs. If the tractor breaks down, either I fix it or we pay to have it fixed. If we're ready to put a cow in the freezer, we both pay to have it processed. What's mine is hers and what's hers is mine. That's how it is and that's how it's always been ever since your dad died."

"So you're saying that's my *mother's* marijuana crop out there?"

"No!" Jack said. "That's not what I'm saying. She doesn't know anything about it. Are you kidding me?"

"I like my mom just fine as the egg lady. I couldn't handle her being the pot lady, too."

Once again they shared a laugh before turning serious again.

"Anyway, as I was saying," Jack continued, "you hammering me about planting marijuana in your mom's pasture hurt me to the core. I never thought of it that way before. It just seemed like the best spot to do it this time. I didn't think of it as her place."

"Wait, wait, wait a minute," Nora said. "Back it up there, kiddo. You said 'this time.' Does that mean there have been *other* times? *Other* crops?"

Jack leaned forward in his chair. She noticed for the first time that he had an invisible band around his head from wearing his hat all day.

"Didn't you hear anything I said to you yesterday?" he asked simply. "I have bills to pay. Seed bills, vet bills, truck payments, credit cards, crop insurance. The list goes on and on. I can't pay for this stuff on what we bring in from selling melons or corn. I need the money, and with one marijuana crop I can make some very *good* money. That little patch of pot allows me to do what I like to do. It lets me grow melons, hay, or whatever, and have a garden that can feed a family of ten the way I like to."

"Maybe it's time you did something else, Jack," Nora said, refusing to fall for his pity routine. "The Flemings have always been farmers," she said. "I was raised by a farmer. All of our grandparents were farmers. But there's a reason you're the only farmer left in the family, Jack. It didn't pay squat then and it's not paying you squat now unless you break the law."

"Nora, this is all I know," he said, leaning back in his chair. "It's like you said. Farmin's in my blood. I've been on a tractor my whole life. My daddy held me on his lap while he plowed the field when my mom had errands to run. I can't imagine doing anything else. I don't *want* to do anything else. Don't be mad at me for finding a crop that finally pays well."

Nora looked at him as he attempted to play on her sympathies, but he wasn't fooling anyone.

"What would your father say if he knew what you were doing?" Nora asked him. "What would *my* father say if he knew you'd planted marijuana in one of his fields?" She waited a moment for that to sink in a little. Jack would no longer look at her. "So this is the deal, Jack," she said. "Take the lock off the back pasture and get your crop out of there as soon as possible. If the cops find it before that, you have to own up to who it belongs to."

"Why would the cops find it?"

"Sometimes they just get lucky, and if they do, I can't let my mother get involved in it. So do whatever it is you have to do and then you need to promise me something."

He looked up at her then. Nora could see the guilt and sadness in his light blue eyes.

"Promise you what?"

"You have to promise me you'll never involve my mother in any of your drug schemes again. To include giving her any of your drug money. Split the melon money with her, but keep the drug money. I can't allow Prescott's egg lady to end up in jail because you prefer being a pot farmer."

"Nora, I—"

"That won't happen on my watch."

"I'm not a bad person."

"You have no idea what you're doing! I've seen what drugs do to people, Jack. I've seen babies born to crack mothers. I've seen teenagers die of heart attacks from a night of cocaine use. All those people don't start out on heroin or crack. They all started out smoking pot. So maybe you didn't *used* to be a bad person, but you're now the enemy in this boondoggle the government calls the

187

war on drugs. You're where it all starts. So you do whatever it is that you have to do, but I can tell you this with some absolute certainty. I'm disappointed in you and I'm ashamed of what you've become. And if my mother or either one of your parents, God rest their souls, knew what you were doing, they'd feel the same way."

They sat there in silence as her words bounced off the walls in Jack's living room. He put his hands over his face and took a deep breath.

"Let me ask you something," Nora said. "Is this why your wife left you?"

He rubbed his eyes and then slowly leaned back in his chair again. Jack sighed heavily and looked straight ahead. "She wanted nice things," he said in a voice laced with emotion. "Nicer things than I could afford growing melons."

"So you found a way to make more money?"

He nodded. "I made more money, bought her nice things and she left me anyway."

"I'm sorry, Jack."

"Yeah, me too." He cleared his throat and shook his head. "I've got several credit cards to pay off and some bills from jewelry stores. She liked having diamonds."

"A lot of women do," Nora said. "I don't suppose you got any of that back when she left?"

"She took it all with her." He ran his hand through his sandy-colored hair. "I need something to drink. Can I get you anything?"

Nora got up and followed him to the kitchen. It was always a nice feeling being in Jack's house. It was like her mother's house in so many ways that she never failed to feel comfortable there.

"No dishes in the sink?" Nora asked.

"They're out on the back porch in case Aunt Opal wanted to come in this morning." Jack opened the refrigerator and looked to see what was in there. "I've got sodas and beer."

"Anything diet?"

He handed her a can of Diet Pepsi and got a regular one for himself. They sat down across from each other at the kitchen table.

"I don't like you being disappointed in me, Nora, and hearing that you're ashamed of me is . . . is . . . well . . . I just can't have that. I don't know what to do."

"It's comforting to know you care about my opinion of you," Nora said.

"I guess I never realized how much I *did* care until you started yelling at me."

"When was I yelling?"

"In the field yesterday."

"Oh, then." Nora nodded. "Have you thought about getting the diamonds back from her?"

"Nah. They were a gift."

"She's with another guy and wearing diamonds you're still paying for," Nora reminded him. She could see the hurt in his eyes and instantly regretted mentioning it.

"People probably think he bought 'em for her," Jack said.

"Probably."

"How could I get them back?"

Nora shrugged and sipped her Diet Pepsi. "If she wants a divorce bad enough, trade a signature on the divorce papers for the diamonds. Then sell them and get your money back."

"Nah," he said. "She'd never go for it."

"You won't know until you try."

He held his Pepsi can up in a little toast. "I'll think about it." Jack took a sip and then set his drink down on the kitchen table. "This is what I'll do, Nora. Let me get rid of this marijuana crop and then I'll be out of the pot business. I'll just have to learn to live within my means. Our fathers did it and raised a family scratching out a living on melons and corn. I can do it, too. Even though I've been at this for a while, it's always made me nervous."

Nora let out a sigh of relief. She didn't like being angry at him and it was good to know he wasn't happy with their situation either.

The telephone on the kitchen wall rang. Jack looked at his watch before answering it.

"Aunt Opal!" he said. "Are you okay?" He glanced over at Nora. "Yeah. She's here. Just a minute."

He handed the phone to Nora.

"Hi, Mom. You okay?"

"I'm fine, dear. You have a visitor."

"I do? What's Darcy doing there? I was going over to her house as soon as I left here."

"It's not Darcy," Opal said quietly. "It's Dr. Ortega from Dallas."

"Sally!?" Nora said, her voice sounding more like a squeak. "Holy crap! How did she find me?!"

Chapter Twenty-five

On the drive back to her mother's house, Nora couldn't stop wondering how Sally had been able to find out where she lived since rural route addresses weren't very specific. In her mother's area, addresses were listed as a county road number that was usually only shown on one small sign off the closest major highway. A post office box number on the mail box off the county road where a person lived was the only other thing to identify where a house might be. There was seldom a name on the box and even someone familiar with the area could spend a lot of time searching for the right house. Nora was impressed with Sally's resourcefulness in tracking her down.

And what is she doing here anyway? Nora wondered. She called Darcy's cell phone to cancel their plans to get together later, citing the arrival of more unexpected company. Sally Ortega was the *last* person Nora wanted to see right then.

"It's probably just as well you don't come over," Darcy said.

"I'm bone tired tonight. I wouldn't be good for much more than cuddling anyway."

"Hey, I love to cuddle," Nora said, struggling to contain her mounting irritation with Sally. "Get some rest, okay? I'll talk to you tomorrow."

Disappointed at not being able to see her later, Nora closed her phone and shook her head. "Sally, Sally, Sally," she mumbled into the darkness. "What the hell are you doing here?"

Nora parked next to a Volvo that seemed totally out of place beside her mother's old pickup. The living room light was on and she could hear voices coming from the house as she stepped up on the porch. Her mother opened the screen door for her.

"There you are," Opal said. "I told Dr. Ortega you were just next door."

"Surprise," Sally said. She got up from the sofa and came over to where Nora was standing and kissed her on the cheek. Sally was an attractive woman, about ten years younger than Nora with long black hair that was up off her neck in a loose bun. She was dressed casually in tan shorts, a matching crew neck blouse and tan sandals. "You aren't happy to see me," Sally said with a pout. Within seconds the pout turned into an amused smile that made it obvious to Nora how much she was enjoying this.

"I'm . . . I'm . . . I'm speechless, I guess," Nora stammered. *What am I supposed to do now?* she wondered. *Is this just a little drive-by on her way somewhere else? A spur of the moment visit? Is she staying here tonight? What the hell is going on?*

"Well," Opal said. "I'm going to bed. I'm sure you two have a lot to talk about. Nice meeting you finally, Dr. Ortega. I've heard so much about you."

"I'm not sure *that's* good," Sally said with a smile. "Please call me Sally and it was very nice meeting you as well."

Nora attempted to give her mother that don't-leave-me-alone-with-her look, but Opal must have seen it coming and shuffled on down the hallway to her room before any eye contact could be made.

"I must say, this is indeed a surprise," Nora offered. "How did you find me out here?"

"I knew your mother's name and there has to be at least thirty Flemings in the Prescott phone book. The second person I called gave me excellent directions once I realized where the third dirt road after the tractor shop was. Your neighbors were then nice enough to give me further directions."

Oh, great, Nora thought. *Hilda will be over here grilling Mom about this the first time she catches her here alone.*

"Have a seat," Nora said. "How long can you stay?"

She really wanted to ask how *long* she was staying, but thought better of it. Nora also imagined that a certain amount of bluntness might eventually be needed if it became necessary to get a specific point across to her. Sally was known for going after whatever she wanted and Nora wasn't convinced yet that this was merely a social call.

Sally sat down on the sofa and crossed her shapely legs. "That depends on you. I have a few days off and an interview tomorrow."

"An interview?" Nora asked. "Where? What are you interviewing for?"

"Where? That new county hospital you're working at. I thought it would be fun to do some moonlighting here a few days a month."

Nora sat down with a little thud in the recliner. "How did you know I was working at the new county hospital?"

With a sweet smile Sally said, "I have my sources."

"Aren't they giving you enough hours at Parkland?"

"You know I set my own schedule there. I get as many hours as I want."

Nora shook her head and didn't like where this was leading. There were so many things she wanted to ask and say, but Nora didn't want to give Sally the impression that she was interested in much of what she did or where she did it. To inquire about her future plans might send the wrong message and that was never a good idea. Sally Ortega usually got her way when she set her mind to something, and Nora wanted there to be no misunderstandings about anything that involved the two of them.

"You could make better money moonlighting in Dallas," Nora reminded her.

"This isn't about money."

"It isn't? Since when? It's always about money with you."

Sally laughed. "You're right. It usually is about money, but not this time."

"What's different about this time?"

Sally smiled again and made Nora a bit uncomfortable with a lingering look. "You've been avoiding me," Sally said. "You've tried setting me up with all sorts of women. I'm on to you. It might have been a flash of brilliance on your part, but shame on you for assuming I could be so easily distracted."

Nora rolled her eyes in response, thinking that distracting her had worked for three months already so that "flash of brilliance" had apparently come in handy and done the trick for a while there.

"I have to admit, though" Sally continued, "the drug rep from Merck was very interesting. And don't even *try* pretending you didn't have anything to do with that."

Nora smiled. "Now you're getting a big head. That one would suck-up to anyone if there was even a remote chance they would use her products."

"She had some very nice . . . products."

After a moment they both chuckled.

"The pharmacist on three seemed genuinely interested, too, by the way," Nora reminded her.

Sally nodded. "The pharmacist on three and the radiology resident were both interested, but none of them are you," she said in a simple, even tone. "The more women I went out with, the more I wanted to be with you. That's just one of the things I've learned over the past few weeks." She opened her right hand to casually inspect her nails. "You'll never know how much it hurt me when you quit your job without telling me. That was bad enough. But then when I realized you had moved away without telling me . . . well . . . that was another story all together. You and I are not finished yet. You know that, right?"

Finished? Nora thought. *What does that mean? She can't be saying what I think she's saying. We dated! It was never serious!*

"Why are you really here?" Sally asked. "I've met your mother. She's in fine spirits and remarkable shape for someone her age. Not to mention someone also having to deal with lupus."

"I won't have her forever," Nora said. Just saying the words made her heart feel heavy. "Besides, you saw her on a good day. Earlier this week she couldn't even get out of bed. She has bad days and I plan to make things as easy for her as possible. That's why I'm here."

Nora pursed her lips, amazed at Sally's ability to turn everything around and make all of this about her now—as if Nora's leaving Dallas had been some desperate way for her to be rid of Sally. *When in fact that was only a very small reason for leaving,* she thought. Nora decided to try another approach.

"When was I supposed to discuss any of my personal plans with you?" Nora asked her. "In between your dates with the pharmacist on three, the nurse from pediatrics, or the radiology resident?"

Sally gave her a look of amused surprise. "You and I were lovers, Nora. We had something good. I don't deserve to be treated this way. You can't just shut me out of your life like this. I care about you and I wouldn't have *been* with those other women if you hadn't made yourself so unavailable."

"Seeing other people was a mutual decision."

"Is it really mutual when one party insists on something the other party doesn't want to do?"

"That's not the way it happened. On the other hand, which one of us went on to actually see other people?" Nora took a deep breath and couldn't believe she was getting all agitated over this. *Let her think she's right,* Nora mused. *It'll be easier that way.*

"There's something I need to ask you," Sally said. "Is there someone else? Is that why you left the way you did?"

"There wasn't initially," Nora said. "Look. I'm sorry I didn't tell you I was leaving. I already apologized for that the last time you called."

"Initially," Sally said. "You didn't slip that word past me. What does *initially* mean in this context?"

"It means I found my first lover again after I moved here. We've been spending time together."

Sally slowly inspected the perfect nails on her left hand. "Tell me more."

"Are you sure you want to know more?"

"Are you in love with her?"

Nora met Sally's steady gaze. "I've been in love with her since I was sixteen."

"Ouch," Sally said with a grimace. "But you say she's not the reason you moved here."

"I moved home to be with my mother. Meeting Darcy again was an accident."

Sally folded her hands in her lap. "Then I'm happy for you. I see something different in your eyes. At first I was hoping that seeing me again had put it there."

"I am glad to see you," Nora said, surprised at how much she suddenly meant it. In her mind Nora had always thought Sally would make a better friend than a lover. Sally was too high maintenance for her. The sex had been good and they shared a common interest in medicine and health care, but all that had never been enough for Nora. Sally needed someone who could make her their entire focus, which wasn't something that had ever interested Nora. She and Sally didn't have the same goals where a personal relationship was concerned.

"Let me ask you another question," Sally said. "I'd like an honest answer."

"Of course."

"If you were ever in Dallas again, would you look me up? Or give me a call?"

"I can't imagine why I would be going back there."

"You have a brother and a niece who live there."

196

"Oh." Nora had forgotten Sally knew so much about her. "That's true."

"I suppose that answers my question then." Sally crossed her tan, shapely legs the other way and looked at her with a serious, pensive expression. "I'm not ready to give you up yet. I would like to see us working together again, and that can happen here if it's the only way I can see you."

Nora shifted in the recliner. She was suddenly uncomfortable again with the conversation and knew it would have eventually gotten to this point. The time for bluntness had arrived.

"You know there can never be anything intimate between us again, right?"

Sally smiled. "Never say never."

Nora looked at her to try and gauge the degree of seriousness in her body language, but Sally wasn't that easy to read. *Well, crap,* Nora thought. *This can't be good!*

"When I'm moonlighting down here," Sally continued, "I'd like for us to work together. I'll make sure we have the same shifts."

"A few runny noses and some crying babies? It's usually dead at this hospital," Nora said, hoping that the lack of patients in the emergency department would discourage her. She knew how much Sally liked the excitement of a busy shift. "No real traumas are routed through us. We would med-evac them out to University Hospital in San Antonio if anything too serious came along."

"Then it'll be easy money and there should be more time for us to catch up on things."

Nora took a slow, deep breath. "All of that sounds fine as long as you understand there can't be anything else. We would be friends with a professional relationship. That's it. Nothing more."

"I hear what you're saying. Can we talk about something else now? You haven't asked about any of the old gang at Parkland. Some of them were even more upset than I was when they heard you had left without telling anyone."

Nora didn't know what to say and she didn't like being put on the spot. They got up and went into the kitchen in search of drinks and snacks. Sitting down at the kitchen table, they shared a bag of pretzels and each had a Diet Pepsi while Sally talked about people they knew. Nora inspected the eggs her mother had gathered that day and asked a few questions about old coworkers. After a while Nora embarrassed herself with a huge yawn, which made them both laugh.

"I'm sorry," Nora said. "My nap this afternoon must've worn off already." She stretched and then put the eggs away. "Let me show you where you'll be sleeping. My brother's old room has a really comfortable bed."

"Your brother's old room," Sally said with a shake of her head.

Nora looked at her and nodded. "Yes. My brother's old room. Oh, and you can't turn the bathroom light on after it gets dark outside or none of us will get any sleep."

Sally arched an eyebrow.

"It's a rooster thing. We've got one that even crows at a full moon."

Nora had slept well and wanted more than anything to just turn over and catch another ten minute nap, but she needed to see how her mother was feeling. If Opal was having another bad day, then Nora would be setting up the tables at the town square by herself for the farmer's market.

She tossed the covers off and slipped on her house shoes. Smelling coffee, Nora went to the bathroom and then followed that fresh coffee aroma all the way to the kitchen.

"Good morning," Opal said. "I told Sally you'd be up soon. That rooster won't be quiet until you're out of bed every morning."

Nora asked how everyone had slept and then gave her mother a good-morning hug. "How are you feeling today?"

"I'm fine. Want to try your hand at biscuits again?"

Nora smiled. "With a guest here?" She reached into the cupboard and got the biscuit-making bowl down. Over her shoulder she said to Sally, "She wants you to experience my biscuits first so you'll really appreciate hers the next time."

Sally's playful expression as she held her coffee cup caught Nora's attention.

"Next time," Sally said. "I like the sound of that."

"Oh, your biscuits are coming along nicely," Opal said to her daughter.

After taking a sip of coffee, Sally set her cup down on the table. "I'm actually looking forward to your biscuits." Her smile had a teasing, flirtatious hint to it. Nora rolled her eyes and got the flour out of the cupboard.

Breakfast consisted of good food and "chicken chat" as Nora liked to call it. There was always a never ending flow of chicken stories—some that Nora had even forgotten about.

"We had a rooster once that loved to chase Nora," Opal said. "If anyone else was with her, she was fine, but if that old rooster caught her out by herself it wouldn't be long before we'd hear her yelling out in the yard somewhere."

Opal and Sally laughed.

"We found her in the old hackberry tree one day screaming so loud it brought her daddy in from the field. He heard her yelling over the roar of a tractor." Opal was trying to keep her enthusiasm for telling the story in check. "That rooster just flew right up there after her and peck, peck, peck, then yell, yell, yell."

"Let's just say I wasn't sorry to see him go," Nora acknowledged with a shake of her head.

"Hey," Opal said as she snatched her napkin off her lap. "I need to get going. Would you load the tables up for me?"

"What time is your interview today?" Nora asked Sally as she and her mother got up from the table.

"At two."

"Good. Would you like to go to town and help us sell some

vegetables? We'll be back here around twelve thirty. Plenty of time for you to get ready for your interview."

Sally's helpfulness surprised Nora. She pitched right in to set up the tables and kept the display baskets full of fresh vegetables. Sally's fluency in Spanish was an added bonus—with Sally's ability to bring in the Mexican shoppers along with Opal's bonnet appealing to the more traditional fresh vegetable seekers, there was never a lull. At about ten o'clock Nora went back to her mother's truck for more tomatoes when she saw Darcy crossing the street.

"Hi there," Nora said. "How's it going?"

"I tried to call you this morning, but all I got was voice mail."

Nora retrieved her cell phone from her pocket and checked it. "Hmm. I never heard it ring, but it says I have a message."

"Who's that at the table with your mom?"

"An old friend from Dallas," Nora said. "She's interviewing for a job this afternoon. Follow me back over there and I'll introduce you."

Nora carried a bag of tomatoes to the table and immediately started filling display baskets.

"Hello, Darcy," Opal said. "Good to see you. How's your father doing?"

"He's fine. Thanks for asking. Looks like you're feeling better, too."

"I am."

Another customer wandered over and Opal turned on the charm right away.

"Sally," Nora said. "This is Darcy Tate. The woman I was telling you about."

Sally smiled and nodded. "Nice to meet you."

"Good luck with your interview today," Darcy said. Turning back to Nora, she said, "I just stopped by to say good morning. I had to pick up a part at the shop. I'm working at a ranch close to Graytown."

200

Nora filled the last basket and went with Darcy back to her truck. The town square was the usual buzz of activity for a Friday morning.

"I'm not sure I can get away tonight either," Nora said as she fell in step beside her. "I don't know when Sally's leaving and Greg and Holly are flying in this evening for the weekend."

"Is she just a friend or was she a lover?" Darcy asked.

"What?"

They had crossed the street and were standing beside Darcy's truck. Nora's thoughts were racing all over the place. Suddenly her life had more people traipsing through it than she could ever recall and all she wanted to do was find a way to spend more time with Darcy.

"It's an easy question," Darcy snapped. "Is this Sally person someone you've slept with in the past?"

"In the past, yes, but we're friends now."

"She doesn't look at you the way friends look at each other."

"I can't help the way she looks at me."

Darcy opened the door to her truck. "How long ago were you and Sally lovers?"

"What does that have to do with anything?" She could tell that Darcy was upset, but Nora was annoyed by her interrogation.

"Call when you have time for me," Darcy said. She got in her truck and drove away.

Chapter Twenty-six

On her way back to the table Nora wondered what had just happened. She had never seen this side of Darcy before. Things had been going so well between them but this little display of jealousy caught her off guard. She didn't know who to be more irritated with at the moment—Darcy for being jealous or Sally for just being Sally.

"We need more okra," Opal said when Nora got back to the table.

"I've got some right here," she said, but okra was the furthest thing from her mind.

She filled more display baskets and noticed Sally talking to an older Hispanic couple who had just purchased some fresh tomatoes while Opal took money from a man with a bag full of pickling cucumbers. When she finished filling baskets, Nora walked far enough from the table to call Darcy in private.

"Hello," Darcy said.

"I don't understand why you're so upset." Nora could tell from the background noise that Darcy was in her truck. "Hello?" Nora said. "Can you hear me? Are you there?"

"I'm here."

"What was that all about? Sally is just a friend."

"A very attractive friend."

"I have some unattractive friends, too. Should I just hang out with them?"

"Funny, Nora. Real funny. I've gotta go. I'll call you later."

Suddenly Nora found herself standing there holding her phone with no signal. *What the hell? What's going on here? She hung up on me!*

Nora selected an old copy of *Family Circle* from the stack of magazines and thumbed through it while sitting in the waiting area of the Connally Memorial Medical Center. She had volunteered to drive Sally to her interview knowing it would be easier to take her there than try and give directions to the next town.

The idea of working with Sally again wasn't as unappealing as Nora had initially thought it would be. Her professional relationship with her had always been a highlight in their dealings with each other. In a way, Nora missed the busy shifts and the thrill of a true medical emergency. Nora found herself less reluctant to admit any of that and was, deep down, glad to have Sally there.

She looked around the atrium and noted how strange it felt being at the hospital and not going to work. She was at odds over the idea of working with Sally again a few days a month. Nora didn't doubt for a minute that it would be fun and help maintain her skills. Not only was Sally an excellent doctor, but she was also a good teacher. Working with her again might just be that extra something Nora had been looking for.

Nora set the magazine down when she saw Sally and the hospital administrator walking toward the waiting area.

"Nora," Gabe Moreno said. "I understand you and Dr. Ortega will be working together."

Nora stood up and smiled. "That's what I've heard."

Gabe had also been a part of the interview process when Nora had applied for a position there. She liked him as far as hospital administrators went. His main focus was keeping a bare-bones staff on hand and saving the hospital money. He did it by hiring part-time physicians and nurses instead of staffing the emergency department with full time employees.

"I wanted to show Dr. Ortega our emergency department," he said as he led the way down the hall, "and give her a brief orientation. She tells me you two have worked together before."

As Gabe gave the guided tour, Sally and Nora followed along behind him.

"Looks like it went well," Nora whispered.

"Mr. Moreno was very accommodating," Sally said. "We're working every third Saturday of the month," Sally said, "and the last Friday of the month. We're set for the evening shifts, so mark your calendar."

"Your confidence and manipulative ways never cease to amaze me," Nora said dryly while shaking her head.

"You can pretend all you want that this is cramping your new style, but you'll see I'm right."

"What are you right about now?" Nora asked.

"You'll be glad to see me each time I come back. We both know you will."

Nora was amused by how predictable they each thought the other one was.

After Gabe showed them around the emergency room, Nora and Sally thanked him and walked out to their cars together.

"You're more than welcome to stay with us when you're in town," Nora said to Sally. "My mother and I would love having you."

"That's a very nice offer," Sally said. "I see southern hospitality is alive and well."

And my girlfriend will just have to get used to having you around, I guess, Nora thought. *How do I get myself into these situations anyway?*

❧

Traffic wasn't too bad as Nora and her mother followed Sally to the airport in the new pickup. After dropping off her rental car, they drove Sally to the main terminal and found a good parking place. As it turned out, they would be meeting Greg and Holly's flight not long after Sally's plane departed, so spending more time with Sally this way seemed like another fine example of Southern hospitality—on the surface. Nora had her mother settled in one of the only comfortable waiting areas near the passenger screening section at the airport. With Opal occupied, Nora stood in line with Sally as they inched closer to where eventually only ticketed passengers were allowed to be.

"Remember what I said, Nora. We aren't finished yet."

"We agreed to see other people," Nora reminded her. "That's the part *you* should be remembering."

"I know." Sally looked at her nails again. "I can't believe how you tricked me into doing that."

"Tricked you?" Nora repeated with amusement. "I'm sure you tricked yourself all over that nurse from pediatrics."

"Forget about the nurse from pediatrics. You have to stop doing that. Those other women meant nothing to me."

"Sally, I'm still not even sure why you're here. This moonlighting job will bore you silly. You don't need the money and it's a lot of traveling for very little benefit."

Sally switched her carry-on roller bag to her other hand. "You're not a dense woman, Nora, so why are you pretending to be one now? I told you before, darling. You and I are not finished yet. If I get my way, I intend to see to it that we're just beginning."

With a furrowed brow Nora asked, "Beginning what? You aren't making any sense. We're not beginning anything."

"Not true. We're beginning . . . at . . . the beginning." Sally's delightful laugh just confused Nora even more. "You'll see soon enough."

"We're beginning at the beginning," Nora repeated. "Oh, that clears up a *lot* of things!"

As they moved closer to the ticket inspectors, Nora stepped out of the line and gave Sally a final wave.

"I've been a fool lately," Sally admitted. "That won't happen again." She leaned closer and kissed Nora on the cheek. "I'll talk to you soon."

She handed her ticket and driver's license to the inspector and then put her bag in the little tunnel to be x-rayed. Sally walked through the metal detector and then waved one last time before she left to find her gate.

Less than an hour later they spotted Greg and Holly in a group of passengers coming out of the gate. Nearly everyone rounded the corner with a cell phone up to an ear. Nora and Opal went to the baggage claim area with them. After that ordeal was over, the four of them fit nicely in Opal's new truck.

"How often do you drive that old clunker now?" Greg asked his mother as he heaved several suitcases into the back of the pickup.

"My old clunker is a real farm truck now," Opal said. "I drive it down to the creek and back every now and then. Or move the cows to another pasture with it. That's about as far as it goes these days. Still plenty of things to use it for."

"She wouldn't *dream* of taking the new truck down to the creek," Nora said. "A cow might accidentally rub up against it or something." She tousled her niece's blond hair and gave her a hug. "How was the last day of school?"

"I'm free!" Holly sang.

"She must've packed those suitcases thirty times this week," Greg said over his shoulder. He was driving and adjusted the rearview mirror as they pulled out of the airport parking lot.

"If you're anything like me," Opal said, "then your pills need their own luggage."

"There's more to packing than throwing a few pairs of clean jockies in a gym bag, Dad," Holly noted. "There's an art to packing properly."

"An art, huh?" Greg mumbled under his breath.

"That's all you brought?" Opal asked her son. "Clean jockies?"

"With all the luggage your granddaughter had, I'm lucky they let me take those!"

They had supper at a popular Mexican restaurant where strolling mariachis were a staple. Even though Nora had spent several hours staying busy with friends and family, she still missed being with Darcy. Before their food arrived, she excused herself from the table and went outside to call her. Darcy answered on the second ring.

"Are you still mad at me for having attractive friends?" Nora asked in a light attempt to smooth things over from their last verbal encounter.

"Why is my discomfort and pain so amusing to you?"

Uh-oh, Nora thought. *Big mistake trying to "make nice" with a little joke. She's still upset about this.*

"I'm sorry," Nora said. "I don't want to argue. Tell me about your day."

"Is she still there?"

"Who? Sally? She flew back this afternoon."

"I see."

Come on, Nora thought. *Lighten up a little here.*

"We're having supper with my brother and niece now," Nora said. "I miss you. It seems like forever since we were together."

There was silence for a moment then Darcy said, "I miss you, too."

"It's silly for you to be jealous of anyone. Don't you know that by now?"

There was more silence. Finally, Darcy asked, "When can I see you again?"

"Well, not tonight, unfortunately. I need to spend time with my brother. Tomorrow's Saturday, though. Can you get away for lunch or something? I'll be at the town square with my mom again at the farmer's market in the morning."

"I'll let you know."

Nora could hear the resignation in Darcy's voice. "I'll call you later if it's not too late when we get home," Nora said.

"Yeah, sure. I'll talk to you later then."

Nora closed her phone and went back inside the restaurant. She had very little patience for moody people. She also didn't care for Darcy's streak of jealousy. *We can work through it*, she thought. *All things are possible when you care about someone.*

They arrived at Opal's house a little after eight. Nora helped her brother carry in Holly's luggage while Opal and Holly changed the linens on the beds.

"Seen any snakes around here?" Greg asked no one in particular as he set one of the suitcases on the ground.

"Not lately," Opal and Nora said at the same time.

"Lord, help me."

There were three huge suitcases that barely fit through the front door, along with two carry-ons that Holly took care of. Nora struggled with one of the bigger luggage pieces, but eventually got it rolling down the hallway toward Holly's room.

"Tell her she can't buy anything else while she's here," Greg said behind her.

They left Holly and Opal in charge of unpacking while Nora and Greg went to the kitchen for dessert. Unpacking for the summer was a little ritual that Opal and her granddaughter looked forward to each year, so Greg and Nora left them alone.

Once they were in the kitchen, Greg asked, "How's she doing?" referring to their mother. He kept his voice low so there wasn't a chance of the other two hearing him.

"Some days she hurts too much to even get out of bed," Nora said.

He sat down at the kitchen table and pulled the sugar bowl close to him. "No piss ants. That's a relief."

Nora came back to the table with a huge piece of chocolate cake for him. She was still too full from supper to eat anything else.

"That bug incident was a fluke," Nora said. "We had the place sprayed and we haven't had any other problems."

"So do you think your moving here was premature?" Greg asked. "Things don't seem as bad as I thought they were. Maybe I spazzed-out over nothing."

"Mom's not as bad off as we first suspected," Nora admitted, careful to add the word "we" instead of "you." She sat down at the table across from him. "Moving here when I did was best for me. The time was right."

"Then this arrangement is working out for the two of you?"

Nora smiled. "I think so. I'm getting settled in and we have a routine established already. Mom's a lot more fun than I remember."

"I've opened up a checking account for the two of you," Greg said. "I have a friend who'll be at the bank tomorrow so we can go by and sign some papers." He took a bite of cake. "I'll put five thousand dollars in the account in case either of you needs anything in a hurry. Sometimes it's not easy to reach me."

"You don't have to do that! We're fine. I have money and mom has money."

Greg smiled. He had a chocolate frosting smudge on his nose which made him look younger, but Nora didn't bother telling him it was there.

"I'm not really doing it for you or mom as much as I'm doing it for me," he said. "I'll feel better knowing you have it. Does that make sense?"

"Yeah, it does, but stop worrying so much. We'll be fine."

"I can't even begin to tell you how relieved I am to have you here with her. I'm sleeping better at night and I don't dread a ringing phone." He took another bite of cake and shrugged. "But then with a fifteen-year-old girl in the house, the phone seldom rings for me anyway, but you know what I mean."

"Yeah, I know what you mean. Stop worrying, okay? We're fine."

Chapter Twenty-seven

The rooster got them all up early and Opal seemed more like her old self as she made breakfast for her family. Nora imagined that for her mother, some of the best medicine in the world involved having Greg and Holly there with them.

"You want to learn how to make biscuits this summer?" Nora asked Holly. "Your Grammie's still teaching me, but you'll probably be a better student than I am."

"Dad would like that."

"I'm real proud of you, son," Opal said to Greg. He was sitting at the kitchen table drinking coffee with his hair still wet from a quick shower. "You remembered not to turn the bathroom light on last night and get that rooster going again."

"That could be because Nora put duct tape over the light switch," Greg replied.

Opal and Holly snickered while Nora looked at him with an amused expression. "You know, that very well could be the reason we all slept so good with you in the house, big brother."

Having Holly there always reminded Nora of growing up and spending so many fun times at the kitchen table. That was where they entertained company when it was too cool to sit on the front porch and where they did their homework at night after supper. When their friends or cousins came over, the kids never went to their rooms for privacy or had to stay out of the way when grown-ups were around. They hung out at their own end of the kitchen table snacking on pie or cookies, sometimes playing cards or board games. The more time Nora spent at home, the the more she felt it was a good thing to do .

It wasn't long before they finished breakfast through a constant string of chatter and left early enough to stop by the bank to sign the papers Greg had mentioned. Nora didn't know why, but it always surprised her to learn how many old high school friends her brother still had there. They were mostly football teammates that he kept in touch with, but all of them still got together a few times a year to talk about the good old days. It was almost like the wrong sibling had moved back home since Greg was the one with all the local connections outside of the family.

After taking care of business at the bank, which had been opened up especially for them as a special favor to Greg, they got back into the truck for the short drive downtown to set up their spot at the farmer's market. Once they arrived, they found Jack waiting for them with more tomatoes, green beans and squash.

"I missed you this morning," Jack said as he set some crates full of vegetables in the bed of Opal's truck. "You left early. Good to see you again, Greg." He tipped his hat to Holly. "You out of school already, young lady?"

"I'm free!" Holly sang.

"Come over for supper tonight," Opal said. "We're having pot roast. One of your favorites."

"Then you know I'll be there," Jack said with a wide smile.

Nora briefly explained to her brother and niece what needed to be done before they helped her set things up the way Opal liked it.

They were ready for customers within five minutes. It didn't take long for Greg to see someone else he knew while Holly, as usual, happily greeted customers and helped her grandmother fill their bags. With everyone else busy, Nora was able to slip away and give Darcy a quick call.

"Are we still on for lunch?" Nora asked.

"That's the plan," Darcy said. "I'll come by and pick you up."

After the call, Nora calculated that the soonest she would be able to spend some quality time with Darcy again would be Sunday evening after Greg left. Getting away sooner than that just didn't seem possible. With Holly at the house with her grandmother in the evenings, Nora toyed with the idea of spending a few nights with Darcy. They had earned that and Nora was looking forward to it.

They stayed busy most of the morning and even ran into some cousins who bought a few things. Kit Fleming and her teenage son Wyatt picked out a wide assortment of vegetables while they stood there talking. It was nice to see how close Kit had stayed to the family after losing her husband Christian in the first Gulf War. Flemings tended to rally around each other during a crisis, so Nora was happy to see things hadn't changed.

She noticed right away how well Holly and Wyatt got along. She remembered hearing about them keeping in touch by e-mail throughout the year. Whenever Holly was there for the summer, she usually spent some time with Kit and her son riding horses on their ranch outside of town.

"If it isn't the queen of donkey basketball," Nora said to Kit. "How are you?"

Wyatt looked over at his mother and smiled while Kit gave Nora a hug.

"School is out for the summer," Kit said, "so we're doing fine."

"I'm free!" Holly sang again.

"How much for all these goodies?" Kit asked holding up the bag of vegetables.

"For you?" Opal said. "Nothing. It's on the house."

"Oh, I don't think so!" Kit said.

"I'll charge the next group of relatives double," Opal said. "How's that?"

Everyone at the table had a good laugh. "Why don't you and Wyatt come over for supper tonight?" Opal said. "We're having pot roast. It'll be fun."

Kit nodded. "That sounds great!" She pointed to the bag and said, "I'm paying for these, by the way, so how much do I owe you?"

After they left, Nora leaned closer to her mother and whispered, "Just how big is this pot roast you're cooking? That's three extra people you've invited over so far. You know how much Jack and Greg can eat."

"I've got it covered, so—"

Before her mother could finish her answer, Nora saw that Darcy was there to pick her up for lunch. With promises of returning with food for her hard working family, Nora was ready to go, but as luck would have it, Darcy became one more person Greg had known from high school. They had a short, friendly conversation before Nora could drag her away for their lunch date.

Once they were in Darcy's truck they had to decide where to go. "Dairy Queen, Sonic, or barbeque," Darcy said. "Those are our best choices."

"Sonic," Nora said. "We can stay in the truck that way."

Darcy drove the short distance to Sonic and parked toward the back. She placed their orders and kept the truck running so they could stay cool.

"What did you and Sally do together while she was here?" Darcy asked.

We're starting off with Sally already? Nora thought. *What's up with that?*

"She went for an interview and then we took her to the airport," Nora said.

"We?"

"My mother and me."

"Oh. Did she get the job?"

"Yes." Nora didn't want to talk about this. She could hear something in Darcy's voice that she didn't like.

"What does she do?" Darcy asked.

"She's a doctor. We used to work together."

"A doctor. I see." An uncomfortable silence followed. Darcy scanned the colorful drive-thru menu beside the truck. "Will she be moving here?"

"No. It's a part time position. She'll commute from Dallas a few days a month. Why are you—"

"I've been thinking, Nora," Darcy said, interrupting her. "Maybe this relationship isn't working out."

"What?" Nora was sure she must've misunderstood her. There was no way Darcy had said what Nora thought she had heard.

"I'm not happy with the way things are going with us," Darcy continued.

"Since when? You seemed happy enough the other night when—"

"This isn't about sex, Nora. That's not a problem for us."

"Okay, then tell me what this *is* about." She felt tears on the way and the shock of Darcy's declaration had zapped away whatever appetite she had. "How much of this has to do with Sally showing up here?"

"It has nothing to do with your old girlfriends."

Just the way Darcy uttered that statement told Nora differently.

"I don't understand what's going on here," Nora said. "You're breaking up with me? This is it?" she asked, hating the fact that her voice cracked and the emotion she felt could be heard so easily. "It's over? Boom! Just like that?"

Darcy didn't say anything, which made Nora furious.

"Tell me what happened between Tuesday night when we were

together and now," Nora said. "Things were fine the last time I saw you at your place. You can't tell me otherwise, so what the hell happened?"

"Watermelon royalty," Darcy said with a shake of her head.

"What? Watermelon what?"

"All I know is," Darcy said slowly, "I can't do this right now. It's high school all over again. We're sneaking around, snatching an hour here and an hour there. In one way it's too much and in another way it's not enough. I want to see you, but then I spend all my time worrying about whether or not my father will find out or an old customer will see us out somewhere and mention something to him about it. I can't let that happen right now. I have to think about him."

"Is this about that dream?" Nora asked with disbelief.

"I've had other dreams since then," Darcy admitted. "Look, I thought I could do it, but I can't. I'm sorry. It's not working for me."

"So we won't be seeing each other again? Just like that?"

"It's not working," Darcy snapped. "When are we supposed to see each other? Before we go to work each morning? After work in the evenings? Quickies at lunch? Like I said before. This isn't about sex, Nora. This is about my unwillingness to hurt my father. He's all I have left. Who knows how much time he's got and all this sneaking around and deception isn't where I want to be or what I want to do right now."

"Well, that's just great," Nora shot back. She took a labored, deep breath and attempted to control the feeling of devastation that rushed through her. *You've lost her twice because of that old fart,* she thought. *Twice!*

"I can't explain any of this to him," Darcy said in a less intense tone of voice, "and I certainly can't expect him to understand it. Right now I don't have time for anything outside of work and helping care for my father. I don't expect you to agree with any of this or know where I'm coming from. All I know right now is this isn't working for me."

"So once again your father wins," Nora said in a low husky voice, finally attempting to vocalize what she was feeling. "Once again he takes you away from me."

"Stop thinking of it that way. It's also about struggling with a lifestyle choice I thought I could handle. You're lucky enough to have a family who embraces you no matter who you are or what you do. Some of us can never have that. I've spent my whole life envying people like you."

"Sounds like you've given up on us before we even had a chance to—"

"It's better this way," Darcy interrupted. "Better for me at least. Please try and find a way to respect my wishes."

Nora didn't know what else to say. She felt betrayed and angry. "If that's the way you want it, then there's not much I can do about it."

Opening up the door to the truck, Nora got out and started walking the eight blocks back to the town square. She felt both relieved and disappointed when Darcy didn't try and stop her but the walk did her good and gave Nora a chance to get her emotions under control.

When she reached the vending area, a crowd of people nearly hid their table from sight, but the rush of customers didn't stop Greg from asking where his food was.

"I'll take everyone to lunch once we're finished here," Nora said.

"Oh," Greg said. "That'll be soon, right?"

"Let's hope so."

Staying busy occupied her mind, but Nora felt emotionally drained by the time they were ready to call it another successful day at the farmer's market.

"How often do you do this?" Greg asked his mother as he closed the tailgate on the truck.

"Four days a week when we have the extra vegetables," Opal said. She was moving slowly and had to be helped up into the front seat of the truck.

As Nora and Holly settled comfortably in the backseat, Nora was nearly overcome by a mixture of anger and sadness. *Ohmigod!* she thought. *Don't let me start crying now! How could I not even have a clue about how she was feeling? How did that happen? When did it happen? Maybe Darcy's a lot more upset about how things turned out that night in Mr. Szalwinski's office than she led me to believe. Her whole life was turned upside down, while all I had to deal with was missing her and worrying about whether her father had thrown her in the river or not. This sucks,* she thought with a sniff. *Oh, great. I'm crying now. Fucking fabulous.*

"Barbeque, right?" Greg said. He looked in the rearview mirror for confirmation that he was driving to the correct place for lunch.

"If that's what everyone wants," Nora said in as normal a voice as she could muster.

"Sounds good to me," Holly said.

Pull yourself together, Nora thought. *It's not the end of the world. Maybe Darcy's just going through a rough spell here. Give her some time to think about what this means and what she's doing. Maybe time will make a difference.*

A house full of company was the distraction Nora needed to get past all the doom and gloom that consumed her. Holly and Wyatt talked about horses and made plans to ride together on Monday. Jack was a bit more subdued than usual until it was time to eat. Making a fuss over his Aunt Opal's pot roast made him the favorite again. After dinner several tattered boxes of old family pictures were brought out and Wyatt got to see photos of his father as a little boy.

"Your dad and I used to go fishing in the creek out back," Greg said. He pulled out a picture of him and a young Christian

Fleming, both smiling into the sun, holding their homemade fishing poles. Wyatt held the black and white photo and looked at it for a long time.

"Would you like to have that picture?" Opal asked him.

Wyatt nodded.

"Then it's yours," she said. "We've got more of him in there somewhere."

Greg reached for another picture in the box. "I remember one time your dad and I went down to the creek to fetch Grandpa for supper. It was Christian's idea to sneak around to the other side of the creek and rustle the bushes to see if we could scare him."

"Now why would you boys wanna scare an old man?" Opal asked innocently.

"*Why?*" Greg, Jack and Nora all replied at the same time.

Grandpa's practical jokes were legends in the Fleming family. If a youngster could scare Grandpa even once, then they would've had bragging rights for a lifetime.

"So anyway," Greg continued as he handed Wyatt another picture, "Christian and I are on the other side of the creek making some noises that we hoped sounded like wild hogs or even a bear or something. The sun's going down—"

"A bear?" Nora repeated. "You were out there pretending to be a bear?"

"The closest bears to us are probably in Wyoming," Jack said dryly.

Over the chuckling going around the table, Greg said, "Let me finish this story, please. So anyway. Christian and I are shaking tree limbs and bushes trying to scare him when we hear Grandpa say, 'I sure hope that's not any of my grandkids over there, because I saw a giant rat snake crawl that way earlier.'"

Greg selected another picture from the pile and handed it to Wyatt.

"Well, you know me and snakes," Greg said. "I shot out of there like I had rockets tied to my feet. I wasn't sure if he had said rat or rattler, but either way I wasn't staying there. Christian was mad at me for messing up our chance to get Grandpa back."

"A bear," Nora mumbled as she shook her head. "You never were the sharpest tool in the shed. There's never ever *ever* been bears around here."

"Hey," Greg said. "Then a bear would've really scared him, I bet."

The chatter and laughter continued on through dessert and more boxes of pictures until finally Opal yawned.

"Don't mind me," she said as she got up from the table. "Keep at it as long as you want. Just don't turn on the bathroom light." She gave them all hugs and went to bed.

"It's a rooster thing," Nora explained to a confused looking Kim and Wyatt as she cut another piece of cake for Jack.

Chapter Twenty-eight

Darcy tried not to think about Nora and how much she had hurt her. A certain amount of guilt went along with her decision to break it off, but in her heart Darcy knew she had done the right thing for herself. There was no question that as long as her father was alive, there wasn't much chance for her to have a normal relationship with anyone. It also wasn't realistic for her to expect Nora to wait around until circumstances changed or the time was right, if such an opportunity were to ever present itself at some point in the future. Women demanded a lot of attention and Darcy wasn't at a place in her life where she could offer much in the way of time. She was running on emotional fumes and she had nothing extra to give right now.

Meeting one of Nora's old lovers hadn't helped the situation either. It had forced Darcy to admit that things just weren't working out. Her life felt too complicated and the concept of having any real free time to spend with anyone else besides her father had become foreign to her. Finding the time to be with Nora had evolved into sacrificing much-needed sleep or evenings where Darcy should have been trying to eliminate the mounting stack of paperwork for the business. There weren't enough hours in a day and there just wasn't enough of Darcy Tate to go around. It also hadn't helped matters any that such a profound jolt of jealousy had taken over every waking moment once she knew that Nora was still in contact with one of her exes. It was just one more thing that Darcy didn't want to deal with. She was overwhelmed physically, mentally and emotionally and she could feel herself teetering on the edge every day.

As a result of Nora no longer being a factor in her life, the fear of getting caught in a compromising position had disappeared, and Darcy was finally able to sleep better at night and concentrate more on her work. The dreams stopped too, so there were times when she was able to take things in stride without feeling so much pressure. When it came to personal matters, Darcy didn't multi-task well either. The less emotional baggage she had to deal with, the better she could function.

In reality, her relationship with Nora had forced Darcy to confront her own homophobia. Breaking up with her was no different than how Darcy had handled all of her relationships throughout her life. She felt safer with women who preferred remaining in the closet and there was no way to keep that kind of lifestyle a secret with someone like Nora. Darcy envied Nora's ability and desire to be exactly who she was no matter what the consequences were. Nora had admitted to her once that being in the nursing profession was a true blessing for her with its virtually unconditional tolerance of gays and lesbians. However, in Darcy's way of thinking, her own past and the beating she had received as a teenager were rooted too deeply in her psyche to be dealt with now. Besides, when would she have time for therapy anyway? Coming out would never be an option for her. Even the government and organized religions were against gays and lesbians, so staying in the closet was her way of survival and without a doubt the best place to be as far as she was concerned. If nothing else, it was the safest place to be. In her mind and heart, Darcy knew that breaking up with Nora had been the best thing for both of them in the long run. Nora would have eventually done something to bring their relationship out in the open or at the very least she would have resented Darcy's desire to keep it secret. *She kissed me in front of her mother, for crissakes,* Darcy thought with a cringe. *How could she have done such a thing and made it seem so normal? Not only that, but how can I ever look Opal Fleming in the eye again?*

On her way home from the last call of the day Darcy picked up fried chicken for supper. She was tired and looking forward to a hot shower and a relaxing evening, but as soon as she walked in the house, she was greeted by her father's list of things to do. She imagined he spent a good part of his day dreaming up chores for her when she finally got home each evening.

"The guineas are gone again," he said as he followed her into the kitchen in his wheelchair. "Look for 'em by the river when you go down there for the reading."

"I will," she said with a tired sigh.

"Those movies you picked out can go back tomorrow," her father said. "I watched them all today."

"I guess you need new ones." Going back into town to get more movies wasn't something she felt like doing either. *A hot shower and a relaxing evening,* she thought. *That's all I want.*

"The next time you're in town will be fine," he said. "I can just watch regular TV tomorrow."

Darcy decided to wait until after supper to check the messages on the office phone in the shop out back. That way her father couldn't quiz her about the jobs that were coming up. At least she could plead ignorance about them while they ate, but that didn't stop him from grilling her about what she had done that day.

"Bingo's tomorrow, right?" she asked. Getting him off the subject of windmills was always a main goal of hers in the evenings. Occasionally she was successful.

"They call the numbers too fast for me. I usually just go to see old friends. Not sure I'll be up to it tomorrow, though." He dug around in the chicken box looking for a leg. "Did you ever get in touch with that Opal Fleming about my mineral rights like I asked you to?"

"I told you before, Dad. No one gives up mineral rights."

"I'm willing to pay for them so it shouldn't even be an issue."

"Why do you want them anyway? They haven't pumped oil around here in years."

"That's not the point," he said, emphasizing each word with a chicken leg. "When a person owns property, they should own all of it. *All* of it! Including the minerals that are on it whether it's oil, gold, copper or whatever. I own the land. I wanna own my minerals, too!"

"Does anyone really own their property?" Darcy took a philosophical approach. "Stop paying taxes on it and see who really owns it. If you think about it, you're really just renting your own property back from the government. They can take it away from you if you don't pay that annual rent they call taxes. That's where you should put all this energy you have. Start a tax revolt instead of badgering Opal Fleming."

"I don't care about that tax stuff," he grumbled. "All I care about right now is getting my mineral rights. You said you would call her for me. She's not taking my calls anymore. See what she wants for them. Everything has a price."

"Calling her won't do any good," Darcy said, attempting one last time to talk some sense into him. Besides, there was no way she was going to call Opal—especially after just dumping her daughter. Absolutely no way!

"Just do it," he said. "I want my mineral rights even if I have to sue to get them."

Darcy shook her head and chewed her food without really tasting any of it. Maybe a good night's sleep would make her feel better.

❦

223

Darcy found the guineas down by the river in their usual spot when they weren't in the yard. After getting the reading on the river, she left a seed trail on her way back to the house to lure the guineas home. Darcy gave her father the information he needed to relay the report to the National Weather Service. While he was busy with that, she checked the messages on the phone in the shop. There were three of them, one of which was an inquiry about parts she might have in stock and another message was a report on a job she had done a few weeks ago where the rancher thanked her for taking care of a problem he couldn't resolve on his own. The third call was from a woman named Kit Fleming.

"I got your name from a family member who has spoken highly of you," the woman said in the message. "We have a windmill that isn't pumping any water. Our stock tanks are drying up and I really need this windmill working for my horses. My son did some tinkering with it, but that didn't help much. I'd appreciate a call back to see what can be done." The woman gave her number and her name again and Darcy wrote everything down.

"More watermelon royalty," she mumbled while dialing the number. *Kit Fleming,* she thought. *Has to be a cousin of Nora's. We went to school with a Kit Mason. I wonder if it's the same person? That's not a common first name around here.*

The woman answered the phone on the second ring.

"This is Darcy Tate returning your call about a windmill."

"Yes. Thanks for calling back so quickly."

Darcy asked a few questions and usually from the answers it was easy to troubleshoot a windmill problem over the phone.

"My son is more fluent in speaking windmill than I am," Kit said good-naturedly. "Do you mind talking with him?"

"Not at all. It might save us both some time."

Once she got Wyatt on the phone, Darcy was impressed with his knowledge of windmills. He had isolated the problem and already knew what parts were needed. Darcy got directions to the ranch from him and promised to be there the next morning.

∽

"Donkey basketball," Darcy said as soon as she got out of the truck. She would know Kit Fleming anywhere. Darcy, along with everyone else at the gym that night, couldn't keep her eyes off her during the entire donkey basketball game.

Kit was Darcy's height and dressed in loose-fitting stone-washed jeans. Her brown boots looked comfortably worn and her tan T-shirt was at least two sizes too big for her. Even though she might have been dressed for ranch work, there was no way to deny Kit's femininity. Her light brown hair was a bit scrambled from the wind, but Darcy found her to be a very attractive woman with a nice, friendly smile.

Kit admitted that donkey basketball was her one and only claim to fame. "Every year they need a female faculty member who can stay on a donkey and shoot hoops, so I'm what they end up with each time. None of the other women I work with want to do it."

"You were good at both, as I remember," Darcy said with a smile.

"This is my son, Wyatt," Kit said. "You spoke with him on the phone yesterday."

Darcy shook his hand and was surprised at how young he was. He couldn't be more than fifteen or sixteen at the most—Darcy had expected him to be older. As she looked at him Darcy was immediately reminded of some of the other Fleming boys she had known growing up. Wyatt looked a lot like Greg or Jack had at that age, with blond hair and classically handsome facial features. He was a good looking kid and very polite.

"Thanks to your help," Darcy told him, "I think I have all the parts with me that I'll need to fix it."

"We'll show you where it is," Kit said. "You can follow us out there."

Darcy was again surprised as Wyatt got behind the wheel of their truck while Kit rode along. Kit was the person Darcy remembered from school. She had been about three grades behind her and Nora, and if Darcy's memory served her well, Kit Mason had been dating Christian Fleming in those days. Darcy also remembered getting a letter from her mother while being stationed in Kuwait during the first Gulf War. Her mother said that a local Army reservist named Christian Fleming had been killed in Kuwait while riding in a jeep. His death had affected her mother in a profound way and it had also given Darcy even more reason to be careful during her tour of duty. Things hit too close to home in so many indirect ways. Darcy decided right then as she followed the pickup over a dusty road that she wouldn't charge Kit Fleming for anything. It wasn't often that Darcy could help someone who had been so tragically affected by the last few wars. Darcy thought of it as a privilege to have such an opportunity.

As she followed the truck over a cattle guard out behind the house, Darcy saw three pregnant mares standing by a nearly dry stock pond. Several cows in an adjoining pasture didn't look up from their grazing. The trucks came upon another cattle guard, drove through some brush and then reached a clearing. Off to the right Darcy finally noticed the windmill. She got out of her truck with her binoculars in hand.

"I'm thinking about putting in another windmill up front near that stock pond," Kit said. "Any idea how much that would cost me?"

"Depends on how far down they have to drill to reach water there," Darcy said. "You could probably get one up and running for about five thousand dollars. A little less if you could find a used windmill somewhere."

She focused in with the binoculars in search of wasp or hornet's nests. Walking over toward the holding tank, Darcy looked inside to see how much water was there.

"When was the last time you saw it working properly?" Darcy asked.

Kit and Wyatt looked at each other. Wyatt shrugged and said, "Probably before that last big storm we had."

"A lot of wind and lightning," Kit said, "but not enough rain to do us much good."

"That wasn't normal wind, Mom," Wyatt said. "Normal wind wouldn't pick up a burn barrel and move it someplace else."

"Several windmills were damaged in that storm," Darcy said. "Not from the high winds, but more from being hit by flying debris." She smiled at Wyatt. "I agree with you. That wasn't normal wind." She got her tool belt out of the truck, put some rope on her shoulder, tucked a can of wasp spray inside her shirt and walked over to the windmill.

Darcy was getting used to having people watch her work. She always wished windmill owners would just show her where the windmill was and leave her alone to fix it. Not being a graceful climber, she could only imagine how clumsy and bumbling she looked while up there, but she got the job done—despite her self-consciousness. As long as the end result was satisfactory, how she accomplished it shouldn't matter.

Up Darcy went, one rung at a time. She glanced down for a moment and saw both of them watching her. *Just get up there and take care of business*, she thought. *So what if you climb like a girl?*

Darcy had windmill parts all over the bed of her pickup and tailgate and found herself explaining to Wyatt the intricate details of how they all worked. His offer to help had been sincere, so she let him do a few simple things.

"I went on the Internet and found a diagram of how to put one of these together," he said. "It's really cool how they work."

"They're a lot more complicated than they look," Darcy commented.

"That's why we had to call you," Wyatt said. That made his mother laugh.

"I need to check on the other horses in the back pasture," Kit said. "You coming with me?" she asked her son.

"I'll stay here and help with the windmill," he said.

Wyatt went back to work on the helmet while Darcy couldn't

stop herself from watching Kit walk to her truck and get in. She continued looking as Kit drove away toward a wooded area and then disappeared through the trees. By the time Darcy turned her attention back to the windmill parts strewn about the tailgate, Wyatt had made good progress.

"Thanks for letting me help," he said. "This is a lot of fun."

"You like windmills?" she asked. Darcy picked up the pitmen arm and checked it for wear.

"I never really paid too much attention to them until this one stopped working," he said. "I thought I'd be able to fix it and then we'd be back in the water business, but that sure wasn't the case."

"I like to soak all these parts in oil while I'm checking them out," she said. Darcy poured some fresh oil in a pan and dropped nuts, bolts, gears and a variety of other parts in there while Wyatt put a few things in to soak as well. "What in particular got you stumped while you were tinkering with it?" she asked him.

As Wyatt explained the research he had done and how long he had spent trying to determine the problem, Darcy knew right away she liked him. He was smart, curious and had a genuine interest in the mechanics of windmills. By the time he got around to telling her how he had diagnosed the problem, Darcy had already hatched a plan.

"I don't suppose you'd be interested in a part-time job for the summer, would you?" she asked.

His blue eyes popped open almost as quickly as his smile appeared. "For real? I could help you fix windmills?"

"Could be some early hours," she said. "I'd pick you up in the morning and then sometimes we wouldn't get finished for the day until late." Even as the words were coming out of her mouth, Darcy was thinking, *If I had a helper, the days might not have to be so long!*

"I'd like that a lot," he said. "I need to check with my mom, though. Sometimes she needs me around here."

"I'm sure we can work something out."

Chapter Twenty-nine

Because of her stint in the Army as a non-commissioned officer, Darcy was used to supervising young people. In general she had thought the new generation of soldiers was a very "me" oriented group with an overall lackadaisical work ethic, but Wyatt Fleming was different. Darcy attributed that to his mother's influence and the possibility that he was actually doing something he enjoyed.

The first morning she picked him up for work, Wyatt and Kit were waiting for her on the front porch of their home. It was warm already and promised to be a hot day.

"I'm making him leave his cell phone behind," Kit said. "He has friends who do nothing but call each other all day long."

Wyatt turned a light shade of pink under their scrutiny as he set a small backpack in the bed of Darcy's truck.

"We'll see how you do today," Kit said to him.

Darcy reached in her shirt pocket and pulled out a business card. "My cell number's on there if you need to reach either of us for anything." She liked the idea of Kit having other ways of getting in touch with her. She had been in town over three months now and hadn't made many friends yet. Hopefully, that was about to change.

The first day went so well for Darcy and Wyatt that she wondered why she hadn't thought of hiring someone when she took over the business. Wyatt freed her up to concentrate on the more complicated, intricate aspects of windmill repair. Darcy had an average of three service calls a day and usually ran about a day behind in taking care of customers. With Wyatt's help she found herself staying on schedule and losing some of the stress over falling behind.

Conversation—that was the other thing she liked about having Wyatt along. He asked a lot of questions about windmills and she never had to explain anything to him more than once. He learned quickly and never complained. He was always ready when she picked him up and didn't mind working late or being her gofer.

Darcy's favorite part of the day was driving to the Fleming ranch to pick Wyatt up each morning. She got to see Kit that way and when she arrived there, she tried to think of something new to say to her each time, but her conversations were mostly with Wyatt.

Darcy made another dramatic change in her life. She hired a live-in housekeeper to help care for her father—someone to cook, clean and take him wherever he wanted to go. She ran an ad in the local paper and carved out time to do the interviews. Darcy interviewed only three people before she found Bonita Esparza. Bonita had been living with her son and his family, caring for her twin grandsons. The boys were starting school in September and Darcy had sensed Bonita's near desperation for the job. In a way, Darcy harbored her own desperation about finding someone her father would like. It quickly became an arrangement that worked out for everyone.

"He's a grouchy old man," Darcy remembered telling her during the interview.

"Then he probably just needs some attention," Bonita replied.

As it turned out, Bonita moved in with an impressive collection of old movies. She loved bingo, was an excellent cook, immaculate housekeeper and had the ability to let anything a grumbling Skip Tate did or said just roll right off. So with the addition of two new people on the payroll, Darcy was finally able to catch up with the bookkeeping as well as spend a little time with her iron sculptures in the evenings. She also took half a day off on Saturday and all day on Sunday. Things were beginning to come together.

Darcy had a standing rule when she and Wyatt worked together—Darcy was the only one who did any climbing. She didn't want to take the chance of having Wyatt fall off a windmill and get hurt. As long as he stayed on the ground soaking old parts in oil and helping put everything back together again, he was just as valuable to her.

One afternoon in late June as she showed him how to plug a bullet hole in a tail vane, she asked him if his mother had given any more thought to putting in another windmill.

"We're looking into selling some horses to pay for it," he said. "Once that happens then we'll be ready. She has an estimate on the drilling and we'll be running an ad for an old windmill soon."

"I might have one we can put together," Darcy said. "I've got a barn full of windmill parts at my place and all sorts of things out back. When we're finished with this we'll go check it out."

Darcy often wondered what Kit did all day when she was home alone. Almost every day when Darcy brought Wyatt home in the evenings, Kit thanked her. Darcy wasn't sure if her gratitude was for giving him a job to keep him busy during the summer or for bringing him back safely each time.

She and Wyatt finished their job and headed out to Darcy's

place. As soon as she parked at the side of the house, Bonita was at the back door looking for her.

"Your father wants to see you," Bonita said. She was a short, plump woman with shoulder-length black hair. She wore a white scarf around her head and had a feather duster in her hand.

"I'll be right back," Darcy said to Wyatt.

She went into the house and found her father in the living room watching The Weather Channel on TV.

"They're getting a lot of rain north of us," he said. "You need to be checkin' the river reading at least once every few hours or so."

"How much rain are they getting?"

"So far, eight inches in the Hill Country."

"Any of it coming this way?"

"We're under a severe weather watch," he said. His eyes were fixed on the TV screen. "Drive down there and get a reading now. It'll be a long night even if we don't get a drop."

It'll be a lot longer for me, she thought. *I'll be the one driving down to the river all night long!*

Darcy went back outside. "Let's go," she said to Wyatt. They got in her truck again. "There's something else I have to do first." She drove down to the river and checked the readings on the gauges. Wyatt got out of the truck with her.

"What's all this stuff?" he asked.

"Official weather watcher equipment," Darcy said. "My father reports things to the National Weather Service for this area."

"For real?"

Darcy smiled. "Yeah, for real. Apparently they're having some heavy rain up north of us. It can eventually affect the river here, so someone has to keep an eye on it."

Wyatt looked up at the clear blue sky overhead and then looked down at the slow-moving San Antonio River again.

"That's just too cool," he said.

Darcy wrote down the reading and they got back in the truck again. She returned to the house and took the information in for her father.

"He's been glued to that TV all morning," Bonita said.

"And he'll stay there until the storms are gone," Darcy said. "I'll be out back for a while."

Darcy and Wyatt spent about an hour in what Darcy liked to call the bone yard. It was a huge barn open on two sides where the tractor was kept along with enough old windmill parts to start an all together different kind of business. Behind the barn about a dozen or so windmill towers lay tangled up in grass and weeds.

"What's that?" Wyatt asked pointing at the metal sculpture Darcy had been working on over the past several months. "Did you do that?"

"Yeah. That's what I do in my spare time." Darcy had to smile at using the term "spare time." She couldn't remember having much of that until recently. She stopped to look at the sculpture with him. It was about eight feet tall and she had it set on a flatbed trailer to work on. The three wild horses with flaring nostrils and a cloud of dust behind them looked different to her in the daylight. Sometimes she worked on it when she couldn't sleep. A spider had taken up residence on top of one of the horse's manes. Darcy had a lot more to do on it yet, but it was the one project that was nearly finished.

"Who are you making it for?"

Darcy shrugged. "I don't know. Me, I guess. I haven't thought that far ahead yet." She turned around and glanced at all the windmill parts in the barn that were lined up on shelves, along the walls, and covering the floor. It didn't take too long to find everything they needed.

"You can let your mom know that we've got her a windmill once she gets the drilling taken care of. We can get it over to your place a piece at a time until that happens." Darcy pulled her gloves off and tucked them into her waistband. "Then I can show you how to install one and get it all set up from scratch. I haven't done too many of those in a while, but it'll be an interesting experience."

233

They walked back toward the house and Darcy's office. She checked the phone messages and decided to go on one more call for an estimate before taking Wyatt home for the day. She had the luxury of taking care of calls the same day now. The more she got done today, the less she would have to do tomorrow.

Kit came out on the front porch to meet them when Darcy pulled up to the house.

"We found a windmill for you!" Wyatt said as soon as he got out of the truck. "Darcy's got all kinds of stuff at her place."

"Oh, really?" Kit said.

As Darcy opened the door to her truck, she wished she had taken the opportunity to wash up a little and comb her hair. *Great,* she thought. *I look like I've been working on windmills all day.*

"We're having spaghetti," Kit said. "Can you stay for supper?"

"Hey, that's my favorite!" Wyatt said. "Can you stay, Darcy? Mom makes great spaghetti."

"I'd like that," Darcy said. "I need to make a phone call first, though."

She couldn't stop smiling inside and at that particular moment, she was so grateful that she hired Bonita. Darcy could actually be spontaneous without having to rearrange her whole life for a few hours. When she called her father, Darcy had to promise not to be gone very long and to remember to get another reading on the river when she got home. Those were small requests that she could live with. Spending some personal time with Kit and Wyatt was exactly what she needed for a change.

Over a heaping mound of pasta and tall, frosted glasses of iced tea, Kit asked them about their day. "Oh, by the way," Kit said as she scooped two meatballs out of the bowl before passing it to Wyatt, "how much is this windmill going to cost me?"

"It's like a Frankenstein windmill," Wyatt said. He and Darcy laughed.

"A what?" Kit asked, looking at both of them.

"We're putting it together from spare parts," Wyatt said. "You know. Like Frankenstein."

"Oh, I see," Kit said. "So we're getting a Franken-mill. Got it." All three of them laughed.

"How much is this Franken-mill going to cost me?" Kit asked.

Wyatt and Kit both looked at Darcy and waited for an answer.

"Cost?" Darcy said. "It won't cost you anything. I've got enough Franken-parts around my place to make ten or more windmills."

"I'd have to pay you something," Kit said.

"Why? It's an old used windmill lying around my barn. You'd almost be doing me a favor by helping me clean the place up."

Kit looked at her and then at Wyatt.

"If you insist on payment," Darcy said, "then I'll take a few more meals like this. You're an excellent cook."

"There you go, Mom. We'll trade spaghetti for a Franken-mill."

Kit smiled. "Now that I can do."

Darcy stayed until she heard the rumbling of thunder off in the distance, but even then she was reluctant to leave. She and Kit were out on the front porch with Kit sitting in a wooden rocker while Darcy sat on the banister.

"Maybe we'll get some rain after all," Kit said. "Sometimes I don't think those weathermen know what the heck they're talking about."

"We could sure use it," Darcy said. "I've been all over this part of the state and everywhere I go I see brown crops and dried-up creek beds."

"We've got one stock pond that still has a little water," Kit said.

"We'll have to move the cows back there if we don't get a good rain soon."

"Let me know if you need help doing anything like that," Darcy said. "Now that I have Wyatt helping me, I have more free time. I really appreciate you letting him work with me. He's smart and good with his hands."

"I should be the one thanking you," Kit said. "He usually gets so bored in the summer. Now with him occupied, I can do some tutoring and a few things around here that he wouldn't want any part of."

"Things like what?"

"Oh, like putting new tile down in the kitchen and wallpapering the back room," Kit said. "He likes being outside. All these inside projects I start in the summer give him claustrophobia, I think. So your job offer has been a blessing for both of us. I don't have to see him moping around and he gets to stay busy outdoors."

Another low rumble of thunder told Darcy again that it was time to go even though she didn't want to. *I could stay here all night talking to this woman*, she thought. Forcing herself up from the banister, Darcy got her keys out of her pocket.

"I should get going," she said. "Thanks for dinner. Your son's right. You make great spaghetti."

"It's even better the next day," Kit said. "There's plenty left over if you're interested in having it again tomorrow."

Darcy felt the gloom of having to leave suddenly brighten and blossom into another opportunity to spend time with the two of them. Darcy knew she was smiling like a fool, but she didn't care. She was making new friends and seeing things a lot differently now that she had more freedom. The feeling of being trapped in her father's vision of what her life should be was beginning to melt away. Darcy had a vision of her own to embrace now—and having that made all the difference in the world.

Chapter Thirty

Happy and whistling with each swish of the windshield wipers, Darcy drove home in a near blinding rain. Finding ways to spend more time with Kit was becoming her next serious focus and favorite pastime. Not only did she need more friends to take the edge off the loneliness, but Darcy enjoyed being with women who weren't ordinarily available to her or women who didn't even realize they were available. She felt a sense of calm surrounding her as she thought about the possibilities ahead.

Darcy had dated a teacher several years ago and enjoyed her intelligence and commitment to a job she loved. Darcy had also liked the fact that teachers usually preferred keeping their personal lives private. Thinking back on her own life as a careless teenager, it was a miracle she and Nora hadn't been caught earlier during their relationship. That one event involving Mr. Szalwinski had taught her so many things, mostly the value of staying in the closet and the importance of protecting her privacy. She couldn't have had either of those things if she had stayed with Nora.

Turning on to the main highway, she could see the red flashing lights up ahead. Darcy slowed down with the rest of the sparse traffic and sat there watching grown men chase the Ferguson pigs across the road in the rain. Before she could inch along any further, her cell phone rang. It was Bonita.

"Where are you?"

"Not far from home," Darcy said. "Why? What's wrong?"

"Your father's all antsy about the storm. He wants you to check the river on your way to the house."

"I will," Darcy said with a sigh. Not only did she have weather bureau chores left to do, but now she would have to get wet doing them. "I'll be home soon."

She closed her phone and slipped it into her shirt pocket just as it rang again. Darcy was past the loose pig area and picked up speed again. When she answered the phone this time it was Kit. Just hearing her voice lifted Darcy's spirits.

"Wyatt and I were worried about you getting home safely," Kit said. "It's really raining hard here."

"I'm almost home. It's raining hard here, too." Just the thought of someone other than family being concerned about her made Darcy feel better.

"Well, call us when you get there safely although it's probably not smart for us to be on the phone during a storm like this."

"I'll let you know. Thanks."

Darcy closed her phone, slipped it back into her pocket and started whistling again as she continued on down the road. Her life was less complicated now. She could finally see things coming together in a way that she could handle. *Yes indeed*, she thought. *Life is good.*

She drove out to the barn behind the house and slipped on a poncho in an attempt to keep dry when she went back down to the river. After leaving the barn, Darcy parked her truck close enough to the depth gauges by the river to shine her headlights on them.

She found a flashlight in the floorboard of the pickup to help her see the numbers better when she got closer, but the rain was coming down too hard to see much of anything.

She opened the door and could immediately hear the difference in the river. It was moving faster and the wind was blowing the rain so hard that it stung her hands and face. As she attempted to shield her eyes from the cold, pelting rain, Darcy lost her footing and fell into a puddle of ooze. It happened so quickly she was stunned for a moment. Each time she tried to get up, her boots went out from under her and down she went again.

Okay, okay, okay, she thought. *I'm way too close to the river to be flopping around in mud like this. Stop moving so much and get your butt back up to the truck.*

She took her time and used the clumps of grass in the immediate area to pull herself toward the pickup. She was caked in mud as she scooted and slid her way up the slight incline. After several minutes of heaving and tugging, she was able to stand up again. *This is not my idea of fun,* she thought as she carefully walked to the truck. *All this stupid poncho did was keep mud off my butt for about three seconds!*

Knowing she couldn't go back to the house without a reading on the river, Darcy got a rope out of the pickup and tied one end to the front bumper and the other end around her waist. By now the only good thing about the stinging rain was that it would wash off some of the mud that covered her.

She slowly made her way toward the gauges again and had no idea where her flashlight had ended up. Darcy could feel her feet beginning to slip out from under her once more only seconds before she landed on the muddy river bank again. She slid down the incline on her butt, holding onto the rope along the way with the poncho bunched up around her. Luckily she found her flashlight and used it to read the gauges. The river was up a foot already since the reading she took earlier in the day. The runoff from the rains in the north was finally beginning to catch up with them.

Darcy stuck the flashlight under her arm and pulled herself

back up the incline with the rope. She could hear her cell phone ringing in her pocket, but couldn't take the time to answer it. Once she was close to her truck again, she had to decide whether or not to get the cab all muddy. She could walk back to the house, but neither option appealed to her. She took off the poncho and threw it in the back of the truck. There was no way the rain would get her clean again and she was tired of being out in bad weather. She got into the pickup and drove to the house—mud and all. *Yeah, right,* she thought. *Life is good.*

"What happened to you?" Bonita asked when Darcy finally came into the kitchen through the back door.

"Don't ask."

Under normal circumstances, hearing her father's laughter would have made Darcy happy, but this time she wasn't in the mood for it. At the moment they had totally opposite ideas about what was and wasn't humorous.

"I need something to change into," she said, but Bonita and her father were laughing too loudly to hear her. She snatched up a dish towel and wiped her face off and attempted to dry her hands, but there was too much mud everywhere. *Great,* she thought. *These two are no help.*

She pulled her muddy boots off and discovered the only thing dry on her were her socks. *He's going to want you to go out there every two hours or so to get more readings,* she thought with a new sense of dread.

"You would be laughing too if you could see yourself," her father said. "What's the reading?"

Darcy told him and tossed the muddy dish towel in the sink. Skip scribbled down the numbers she gave him then said, "We'll need another reading in a few hours."

Darcy hated the idea of having to go back out again, but resigned herself to the fact that she had no choice. "Yeah, I know," she said and walked across the kitchen floor dripping muddy water with each step.

"Hey!" Bonita yelled. "Look at the mess you're making! Stand still. Let me get you something."

Skip took a sip of coffee and looked at his daughter. "When did you lose your sense of humor?"

"When?" Darcy asked. The question infuriated her. She wanted to ask him when did he finally find one, but thought better of it.

He shook his head and started to chuckle. "If you could only see yourself."

"My sense of humor," Darcy said under her breath, still having a hard time adjusting to his jovial attitude. "Perhaps I lost it sliding down a hill on my ass while trying to get a reading for you."

But more likely, she thought as Bonita put a sheet around her and wrapped Darcy up in it, *I probably lost my sense of humor that night in Mr. Szalwinski's office twenty-five years ago.*

A hot shower, clean sweats and a T-shirt improved Darcy's mood. Bonita gathered her muddy clothes and apologized for laughing earlier. The weather reports on TV confirmed that flash flood warnings were in effect and more rain was expected throughout the evening. Before going to bed for a few hours of sleep, Darcy called Kit to let her know she was finally home safe. Hearing Kit's voice before going to sleep was exactly what Darcy needed. Dinner with friends, rain on the roof, fresh out of the shower and an exhausting day behind her had all the makings of a good night's sleep, but she knew someone would be in to wake her up when it was time to check on the river again.

Chapter Thirty-one

Nora was pleasantly surprised about how easy it had been to get along with the usually high maintenance Dr. Sally Ortega. They had worked two shifts together recently and things had gone so well that Nora mellowed a bit whenever her name came up.

Sally had stayed at the farm with Nora and her mother both times, arriving in a rented Volvo early in the day. She drove them to work at the local county hospital, told amusing stories about old mutual friends, worked hard all night and drove them back to Opal's when their shift was over. The following day, which was a Saturday one weekend and a Sunday the next, Sally spent time with the family and offered to take everyone to breakfast. Afterward she drove back to San Antonio to drop off the rental car and catch a return flight to Dallas. The two visits had been uneventful yet fun—very much like Nora's usual dealings with her once they had decided to see other people. This was a side of Sally that Nora had seldom seen, but she reluctantly admitted that Sally's visits were a good thing.

Nora liked reflecting on reactions from her family members about Sally's whirlwind visits. All comments were positive and it was obvious that she had made a good impression. Opal adored having her there because Sally took every available opportunity to praise Opal's cooking. Sally was sincere with her remarks and enjoyed trying new and different food. Holly looked forward to Sally's visits for a different reason. She liked discussing the perils of medical school and the importance of math and science in a physician's early education. Sally's enthusiasm for Holly's upcoming involvement in science camp gave Holly a whole new respect for it. She started to look forward to attending the camp and enjoyed the attention Sally gave her when she was around. That alone made Greg like Dr. Ortega's influence on his daughter. He was there almost every weekend and added his own dynamic to the mix.

The few times Greg and Holly had gone to dinner with Nora and Sally when they were dating had not been particularly memorable, so it was interesting for Nora to see everyone together now. To round out the immediate family's approval of Nora's friend, Sally had even won Jack over on her first official visit to the area as an emergency medicine physician at the new county hospital.

Jack had cut his arm in a chainsaw mishap late one afternoon and was able to call Opal on his cell phone right after it happened. Nora and Sally had just left for the hospital to work their evening shift. When Opal and Holly found him out in the woods behind his house, he was sitting on a stump dazed and bleeding.

"Oh, lordy, young man," Opal said when she saw him. "Please tell me that arm is still attached!"

"Holy crap, Grammie!" Holly said. "Look at all the blood!"

"It looks a lot worse than it is," Jack said. His white shirt was soaked in blood and he was so pale it was a miracle that he hadn't passed out.

They got him in Opal's pickup and she sped through town with her flashers on. One of the local police officers stopped her and asked Opal where she was going in such a hurry. All she had to do was point to Jack's bloody arm and shirt.

"We need an escort to the hospital where my daughter works," Opal calmly explained.

"Yes, ma'am. Follow me."

Holly had already called Nora and told her they were on their way. Once they arrived at the hospital, Nora was there to meet them at the emergency room entrance.

"What happened to you?" Nora asked Jack as she pushed the wheelchair closer to the pickup.

"I don't need that thing," he said, nodding toward the wheelchair. "I can walk just fine."

"We don't want you getting blood all over our clean floors," Nora said, "so have a seat."

"I'll never hear the end of it if anybody I know sees me in this," he grumbled.

Sally was waiting for them inside the emergency room door. "I'm Dr. Ortega," she said as soon as Nora wheeled him in. "What happened?"

"A chainsaw whacked him!" Holly said.

Holly's choice of words made Nora smile. "Go help your Grammie park the truck, kiddo. She might not know where we are."

"Dang," Holly said. "Don't do anything to him until we get back! I wanna see what happens!" She ran out the door that opened automatically when she got close to it.

"Tell me again what happened," Nora said.

"Like Holly said. A chainsaw whacked me."

"Did the chain come off and hit you?"

"No. The whole thing sort of bounced off the limb I was cutting. The saw barely caught me, but I guess it did a good enough job anyway. Will you look at that? Ruined a perfectly good shirt, too."

Nora took a brief patient history from him and handed a clipboard to Sally when she was ready to see him. This was the most excitement they'd had since Sally had started working there.

Asthma attacks, a few nursing home patients and crying babies with a fever were about all they saw there.

Watching Sally work on a patient like Jack was always interesting for Nora when she had time to witness it. His injury needed attention, but it wasn't a real emergency. Sally explained to him what needed to be done and talked to him during the entire procedure. The nature of their surroundings and the fact that there weren't many patients there gave the small staff the luxury of time and allowed them the opportunity to add a personal touch that was often missing in a busy emergency department.

"You're a lucky man," Sally said.

Nora adjusted the light on the small table and laid out the suturing kit for her.

"I've seen chainsaws do some bad, bad things," Sally said.

"This is bad enough for me, thanks," he said. Jack glanced over at Nora and asked, "Did I get any blood on my hat?"

Nora smiled. "No. Your hat's fine."

"Okay. Good."

Sally had him relaxed and sutured in no time. Holly and Opal got to see the medical team in action and Nora was reminded about how good it felt to be able to help someone she cared about. After Opal, Holly and Jack left, Nora saw Sally in a different light. The Dr. Ortega she had known in Dallas and in a busy emergency department was a genius and a blessing to have on staff, but the Dr. Ortega Nora was beginning to see in a slower-paced emergency environment was someone she truly enjoyed being with. By the time their shifts were over and Sally had gone back home, Nora was always looking forward to her next visit. Those were new feelings for her and she was surprised at how strong they were.

Ten days later, Opal, Holly and Nora were at Jack's house for supper. After a great meal, Nora took his stitches out and liked the way he was healing.

"I'm getting better at driving a tractor with only one arm," he said.

"Put some vitamin E on that and the scar won't look so bad," Opal suggested.

They were in Jack's kitchen where the light was better and Nora was working on him in between supper and dessert. Holly had volunteered to do the dishes, but kept up with their stitch-removing progress by occasionally peeking over Nora's shoulder. With a teasing smile, Nora suggested that Opal check the back porch for more dirty dishes.

"I did those already," Jack said quickly. "I had to so we could have something to eat off of."

Opal could only watch what her daughter was doing for a few seconds before she decided that helping with the dishes was a much better idea.

"When I first saw you that day," Opal said to her nephew, "I thought for sure you'd lost an arm. I'd never seen so much blood."

"When's your doctor friend coming back?" Jack asked Nora.

"A few weeks," Nora said. She had been thinking about Sally a lot lately and wondered who she was dating now. For a fleeting moment, Nora missed living closer to her and thought about the many times they had gone out to eat after a busy shift.

"The next time she's here," Jack said, "all of you come over and I'll fix us some nice steaks." He lowered his voice so that only Nora could hear him. "I really appreciate the way she stitched me all up and then didn't charge me anything for it."

"We conveniently lost all your paperwork," Nora said. She noticed how he kept his head turned away from what she was doing. "How did that other thing turn out?" she asked. "I'm talking about the field with the padlock on it."

Jack flinched as she tugged on a suture. "I got the crop out just before the rain came."

"And?"

"I got rid of it already."

"You mean you sold it?"

"Yeah. I sold it."

Nora was disappointed that he had chosen to do that, but the two of them already had that discussion.

"There might be another little problem, though," he said. "I'm not sure how to handle it either."

"What's the problem?"

Before Jack could answer, Opal called out. "Come here and look at this!"

Nora and Jack glanced up and saw Opal standing in the back door with her hands on her hips.

"You're not supposed to be back there," Jack said.

"What is it?" Nora asked.

"Boxes and boxes of dirty dishes."

"I washed enough to get me through your visit," Jack said over their laughter.

"I bet he's waiting for another big rain, Grammie," Holly said. "Then he can just set the boxes out in the back yard and bring them in again when everything dries."

"Why don't you just throw those away and buy new ones?" Nora suggested.

"This is the best way I know of to get a serious bug problem," Opal warned.

As Holly and Opal started in on the newly discovered dirty dishes, Nora returned her attention back to removing Jack's stitches.

"Tell me about the new problem," Nora said, lowering her voice.

"The people I'm growing the weed for don't want me to stop doing it."

"So? You know you have to, right?"

"Yeah, I know, but it's not that easy."

"Well, you've already heard what I think and you know what my stipulations are. Keep it off Mom's property and when they catch you, I'll make sure my mother goes to visit you in jail."

"There won't be any jail time," Jack said, "but the people I'm in this with don't want me to stop doing it."

"You know the difference between right and wrong, Jack.

247

You've heard my spiel and I've set some boundaries. You'll either figure a way out or embrace your new life of crime. It's up to you."

"How do you do that?" he asked with a puzzled expression. "Your take on things always makes me think, Nora. It's one of my least favorite things about you."

That made them both laugh.

"What's your favorite thing about me?" she asked.

"Your brutal honesty. Even as a kid you could be counted on to tell it like it is."

Nora snipped and then tugged on another stitch.

"You've also got great taste in women," Jack said. "I don't know where you find them, but you must be doing something right."

Nora thought about Darcy then and wondered how she was doing. Thinking about the way things had ended between them made her more sad than angry now. She had worked through the initial devastation of being rejected and chalked it up to a painful life lesson. There was no way to make someone love you and Nora hoped Darcy would eventually find what she was looking for. She wondered if some day they could be friends, but the emotions were still too raw. Nora pushed Darcy Tate out of her mind—and heart—for now.

Chapter Thirty-two

They were still laughing about Jack's dirty dishes when they arrived home.

"We need to introduce that boy to paper plates and plastic ware," Nora said as she parked the truck beside her car in front of the house.

"Well, I don't know about you two," Opal said, "but I'm tired. Got the egg run in the morning. I'm going to bed."

They each had their own routine after supper that included some unwinding on the front porch with the police scanner crackling in the background. With her laptop set up in her room, Holly usually went online to talk to her friends before bed. Nora had been reading a lot in her spare time lately, but she wasn't in the mood for that now.

She gave the other two good night hugs and then sat in the swing to have some time to herself. There was a nice cool breeze blowing and somewhere off in the distance an owl made its presence known. *And hopefully eating up some mice,* she thought. On a whim she took her cell phone out of her pocket and punched a number on auto dial. Sally answered her phone on the second ring.

"Nora," she said. "What a nice surprise!"

"I hope I'm not interrupting anything." Nora had to admit that it was good to hear her voice.

"Not at all. I'm just getting home from work."

"I took Jack's stitches out earlier. He's healing well."

"Excellent. How's your mother doing? And Holly?"

"We're all fine. Everyone was asking about you earlier at supper, so I thought I'd call and see how you are."

"I have the next few days off," Sally said. "I thought I'd work on some articles that need polishing. I've been putting that off for weeks. If I get my scholarly activities out of the way for the year, that'll make the department chief happy."

Feeling an unexpected tinge of loneliness, Nora asked, "Could you do any of that from here?"

There was a slight pause before Sally asked, "Are you inviting me down for a few days?"

"Yes," Nora said, suddenly a little nervous. "Everyone enjoyed your visits so much. We wouldn't put you to work or anything. No more selling vegetables at the farmer's market. There's nothing extra left in the garden now anyway. And neither of us is scheduled for any shifts. It would just be hanging out with the Flemings."

"Hanging out with the Flemings sounds like a great way to spend some time."

Nora felt such a sense of relief at Sally's easy acceptance of the last-minute invitation.

"Let me go make a few phone calls," Sally said. "I might be able to get a flight out tonight."

"Really?" That put a spark of excitement in the air for Nora. The house was always so alive when people came to visit. Nora had never realized before what a social creature she was. "Let me know if you can make it tonight. I'll pick you up at the airport."

They hung up and ten minutes later Sally called back. She had booked a flight and would be there in two hours.

Nora knocked on her niece's bedroom door and then poked her head in to let her know she would be out for a while. Holly was still busy online with her friends and Nora was relieved that she didn't want to go with her. Nora tried not to put too much meaning into the fact that she didn't want any company on her way to the airport. She also wasn't ready to analyze why she was so eager to see Sally again this soon.

During the drive to San Antonio Nora couldn't stop herself from thinking about all the other women she had encouraged Sally to date. She wondered how many of them were still in the picture.

She arrived at the airport a little early and checked to see if Sally's flight was on time. Nora found a place to sit and passed the time reading a nearby abandoned newspaper. Before she knew it, her cell phone rang and Sally was asking where she should meet her.

"I got so much done on the plane," Sally said on the phone. A few minutes later when they finally found each other, she kissed Nora on the cheek and let her take one of her carry-ons.

"What did you get done?"

"The articles are scrubbed and polished," Sally said. "I can send them off when I get back. Your call was such a nice surprise. I'm not even sure what I packed in that suitcase. I was so excited I just started throwing things in there."

It was a short walk to the car and Nora was glad to have Sally all to herself. Trips to and from the airport might be the only time they'd be alone together while she was there.

"How are things at Parkland?" Nora asked.

"The usual. When have you ever known anything there to really change? It's not as much fun without you, but it's still too busy and the patients have long waits. What's new with you? How's that girlfriend of yours?"

The only person Nora had discussed Darcy with was her

mother. Opal had seen the sadness accompanied by random tears and wanted to know what had happened. All Nora could tell her was that it was over. She herself didn't really understand why or how it had happened. The only thing Nora knew for sure was that Darcy wanted out. However, with Sally asking questions Nora had more reason to choose her words carefully, but with her mother she could say anything. Nora wasn't sure how ready she was for complete, unabridged honesty with anyone else, though. Being dumped by Darcy was embarrassing and she felt as though she hadn't taken the time to adequately deal with any of those feelings yet.

"The girlfriend and I have gone our separate ways," she finally said. Nora unlocked the car and put the suitcase in the backseat.

"When did that happen?"

"A few weeks ago." She didn't want to talk about it. Darcy had her reasons and trying to figure it out did nothing but make Nora second guess where she went wrong along the way. She had already spent too much time doing that and it had gotten her nowhere.

"You told me once that you were in love with her," Sally said.

Nora eased into airport traffic and got in line to pay the parking fee.

"As a teenager I was in love with the sixteen-year-old Darcy Tate," Nora said. "I don't even know who the forty-five-year-old Darcy Tate is." Lowering her voice, Nora said, "We had some unfinished business to take care of and once that happened I guess she was ready to move on."

"She's the world's biggest fool," Sally said simply. "That's who she is. Only a fool would throw away a chance to be with you."

Nora didn't know what to say to that and was grateful to have something to do with her hands as she gave the airport parking attendant some money. She was glad when Sally changed the subject.

"It's nice getting away," Sally said. "Thanks for the invitation."

"This worked out well. Mom will be happy to see you in the morning."

They talked all the way to Prescott and Nora was reminded several times about how familiar and safe it felt to be with Sally. Security and a sense of belonging were two things she was learning to appreciate. They had been absent in her life for many years and it was good to have those feelings back again.

Nora drove over the cattle guard and down the driveway. She parked between her mom's trucks and noticed that the kitchen light was still on. The house looked quiet and inviting.

"Here we are," Nora said, stating the obvious. They got out of the car and each took one of Sally's bags.

"The stars are so incredible out here," Sally said.

Nora looked up at the bright moon in the sky and had to agree.

"Are you too tired to sit in the swing for a while?" Sally asked. "It's very relaxing out here. I've thought about it every day since I've been gone."

They set her luggage near the front door and then went over to the porch swing.

"I do some of my best thinking here on the porch," Nora said. *At least when I can sit here with that annoying police scanner turned off,* she thought.

"I can see why you moved back," Sally said. "Just knowing I was on my way to Prescott lifted my spirits when I was on the plane."

"This is the only real home I've ever known," Nora said. "I was meant to come back. It's where my heart is. Everything I know to be right in the world and in my life is here."

"It's interesting hearing you say that," Sally said. "That's the way I felt after you called me. While I was packing like a madwoman I had this weird feeling that I was going home. This place," she said as she glanced around the porch. "This house . . . the people in it . . . everything about you and your family is so . . . so . . . I don't know how to explain it. I know I'm not making any sense." Sally looked to her right out into the yard. Nora heard her sigh heavily. "I don't even feel this way when I go back to Ecuador every year to see my own family. That's my home, but it's foreign to me now."

253

Sally reached over and took Nora's hand. Her touch sparked an energy in Nora's stomach. "Ecuador is not where you are, Nora and Dallas isn't where you are anymore. Neither of those places seem like home to me now that you're gone."

The emotion in Sally's voice made Nora's throat swell and her heart skip a beat. She had never seen Sally cry before and it made Nora want to hold her.

"Something happened to me when you left," Sally whispered. "I think you took the best part of me with you." She let go of Nora's hand and wiped a tear away. "I knew I was losing you long before it happened, but I didn't realize how much that would hurt or how much it would mean to me. I've learned a lot about myself since you moved away."

Nora blinked back tears and knew that her voice would make it obvious that she was crying. Suddenly unafraid of expressing emotion, she said, "Tell me what you've learned." For a moment the only sound she could hear was a cricket chirping in the yard.

"I've learned what it's like to miss someone so much that my heart aches," Sally said. "I've also learned what's really important in my life." She reached for Nora's hand again and held it tightly. "I always thought that a successful career, money, investments, fast cars, boats, a house in the mountains and another one on the beach—I always thought of success in terms of things. Buying things, having things, wanting things." She looked out into the yard again and lightly squeezed Nora's hand. "I have all of those things now. I have money and the respect of my peers. But the one thing—"

Sally's voice broke and she stopped to clear her throat. When she spoke again her voice was a little stronger.

"But the one thing I discovered that I really wanted and no longer had was you." She quietly cleared her throat again and said, "I had to lose you before I realized that. So these last few weeks have been a true learning experience for me."

Nora didn't know what to say. She had never seen this side of Sally before.

"I don't expect you to understand what I'm going through or to even respond to it," Sally said.

"I'm sorry I hurt you."

"Your phone call earlier made up for that."

"You were right," Nora said. "You told me I would miss you and I did."

"Tell me about that foolish girlfriend of yours," Sally said. "What happened?"

Nora shrugged and sniffed. "I'm not really sure. There was a little fit of jealousy when she met you, but I don't understand why jealousy wouldn't fan the flames and spark some sort of passionate response. Instead she gave me a line about the possibility of her father finding out about us and . . . I don't know. She wasn't making a lot of sense to me the last time we spoke."

"Maybe she'll change her mind," Sally said.

"She also didn't like me having such attractive friends." Nora shook her head at the absurdity of such a statement.

"Which attractive friend was she referring to?" Sally asked with a smile.

Nora shook her head. "Who do you think?"

"I hope my visit the last time didn't—"

"Don't give that another thought," Nora said. "I think there's more going on with her than even she knows."

"Foolish women end up having a lot more regrets in the long run. Some day she'll be sorry for squandering this opportunity." Sally took a deep breath. "I, on the other hand, intend to maximize my potential and make the most of my opportunities here."

"Just ordinary fun with the Flemings," Nora said. "No work and lots of rest and play. That's what I promised you. On that note, are you sleepy yet?"

"Yes, I am as a matter of fact. I had a long day and a busy shift."

They got up from the swing and each took a piece of luggage to carry inside. Nora led the way to her brother's room where Sally had stayed before. As they passed by Holly's door Nora noticed that the light was off. In the next room she switched on the lamp beside Greg's empty bed and set Sally's suitcase down.

"Sleep as late as you want," Nora said. "Mom usually gets up early if she's feeling well. Make yourself at home. You should know where everything is. Let one of us know if you need anything."

Sally came over to her and gently kissed Nora on the cheek. "Thank you for the phone call," she whispered.

"I'm glad you're here," Nora said. She was no longer surprised by how much she meant it. "I'll see you in the morning."

During the time she and Sally had dated there had always been something missing for Nora. She could never figure out exactly what it was, but the "it" had been so significant that Nora was never able to really let go and sink very much of herself into the relationship. In the beginning, Nora thought over and over again how unwise it was to get involved with a coworker. Never fish in the company pond, she always told herself. She knew it was a bad idea, but there was just something about Sally that Nora found appealing, in addition to the fact that she was a beautiful, desirable woman. She couldn't explain it then and Nora was at a loss to explain it now. All she really knew was that being with Sally recently felt right . . . more right than it had in the past.

On her way down the hall toward her room, Nora touched the side of her face where Sally had kissed her. She liked having her there. This new phase of their relationship was something Nora was happy with and she was looking forward to spending more time with her.

Chapter Thirty-three

When the rooster crowed, Nora peeked at the clock on the nightstand and groaned. *The polite thing to do would be to get up and let the others know that Sally is here,* she thought, *but I'll feel a lot more polite if I could sleep just five more minutes.*

Having company in the house always brought back so many fun memories for her. As Nora dozed off again she remembered how things had been when relatives from Minnesota would come to visit when she was a little girl. The more people staying at the house, the better time they all had. As kids, when company from out of town arrived, Nora and Greg got to sleep in the same bed with their parents, which was almost as much fun as camping. Their parents' bed was always crowded on those nights, but being together in such close quarters brought out the playfulness in everyone. The four of them would finally get settled down and begin to drift off to sleep when her father would stick his cold feet against someone's bare skin and get them all giggling again.

Nora nuzzled deeper into her pillow and managed to get a little more sleep before the rooster announced the new day's arrival once more. She heard low voices in the hallway and decided it was time to get up.

"When did you get here?" she heard her mother ask Sally in the hallway.

Yup. Time to get up, Nora thought as she threw the covers off and got out of bed.

"What a nice surprise," Opal said.

Holly came out of her room with a sleepy smile. A line for the only bathroom formed in the hallway as Opal scurried in and closed the door.

"Are you two going with us on the egg run this morning?" Holly asked Nora.

"What exactly happens on an egg run?" Sally wanted to know. "I keep getting a visual of eggs with legs or something."

That comment sent the three of them off in a fit of giggles.

"It's more like my mom trades eggs for coffee, pie and gossip," Nora explained.

"Then they give her a dollar," Holly added.

"Hmm," Sally said. "Sounds interesting."

"I'm sure we can find something else to do today," Nora said with a chuckle.

"At some point while I'm here I need to go see our friend Gabe at the hospital," Sally said. "There's a payroll problem he needs to take care of for me."

"See?" Nora said to her niece. "We have something else to do already."

After breakfast Nora loaded up her mom's truck with the ice chests full of egg cartons. She and Sally got them on their way and returned to the kitchen for another cup of coffee before beginning their leisurely day of having almost nothing to do.

"I could get used to this," Sally said as she took the fresh cup of coffee Nora handed to her.

"It's really nice having Holly here in the summer," Nora said. "She keeps mom going and they stay busy doing things together."

"She's a good kid," Sally said. "And smart, too."

"My brother keeps waiting for her to reach that rebellious stage where they think they know everything. He spends a lot of time reading up on what kids are into these days. He keeps close tabs on her and her friends."

"You couldn't pay me enough to go through puberty again," Sally said with a shake of her head. Her dark hair was usually up off her neck in a braid, but she wore it loose and down past her shoulders now. It made her look younger than her thirty-seven years. "So you *know* it was bad if I can't even think of a price to put on it," she added.

They both laughed at Sally's fondness for money.

"Things are so different now for kids," Nora said. "It never crossed our minds back then that we could get killed at school, but nowadays—"

The phone on the wall by the back door rang. Nora got up to answer it. She smiled when she heard her mom's voice and was proud of the way her seventy-four-year-old mother had set her fear of "new fangled gadgets" aside and had nearly mastered the intricate workings of her cell phone.

"Can you go over and check on Jack sometime this morning?" Opal asked. "Something wasn't right when we got there a few minutes ago."

"Is he sick?"

"I don't know," Opal said. "He wouldn't come out to get his eggs like he always does. Had Holly leave 'em on the porch."

"Sure. We'll go check on him," Nora said. "I'll call you if there's a problem."

"Thanks. Something's just not right."

"We'll check it out." Nora hung up and turned around. "Do you mind a short ride over to my cousin's house?"

"I've got nothing to do," Sally said. "You mean Jack's house, right? It would be nice to see how he's healing."

"Bring your coffee if you want," Nora said as she got the keys to

259

her mother's old truck off the rack near the back door. "I hope his arm hasn't gotten worse. Everything looked fine when I saw him last night."

They got in Opal's pickup and Nora smiled as she watched Sally checking out the worn seat covers and Betty Boop floor mats. The pine air freshener hanging from the rearview mirror still had some life to it.

"This was my mom's egg-mobile for over thirty years. We just retired it recently."

"It'll probably outlive all of us," Sally said. "They don't make them like this anymore."

Nora backed up and dodged the usual bumps and holes in her mother's driveway and then did the same as she drove down Jack's toward his house. She noticed an unfamiliar car parked near his barn in the back and wondered if her mother had seen it when she was there earlier. *The only thing that would keep Jack from speaking to or coming out to greet my mother would be if he was perhaps entertaining a girlfriend or something,* she thought. But she knew that no matter who he had there, he would still have come out for a few minutes.

Nora parked the truck next to Jack's pickup and saw the carton of eggs still on the front porch. She suddenly had a bad feeling and wasn't sure what to do.

"This looks just like your mom's house," Sally said.

Nora's thoughts were racing. She knew that Jack wasn't ill. He would have called her if he hadn't been feeling well. She also knew this odd behavior of his had nothing to do with his arm since he had been fine the night before.

"You stay here," Nora said. She left the truck running and opened the door. "If I don't come back out soon, call the police."

"*Waaaaait* a minute," Sally said with a hand on Nora's arm. "The police? What's going on? If you think we might need the police, then we should just call them now."

"I can't do that yet."

260

"I'm not letting you go in there alone. Give me a two-sentence synopsis of what you think might be going on."

Nora took a deep breath and slowly looked at the house for any sign of movement inside.

"Nora?" Sally said.

Nora gave Sally's hand a squeeze for reassurance. "Jack got himself mixed up in growing marijuana. I talked him out of doing it again, but apparently whoever gets it from him is putting pressure on him to keep it up."

"Is he working for the Mexican Mafia?" Sally asked.

Just hearing the words Mexican Mafia brought a jolt to Nora's entire body. "I don't know who he's in this with," she said.

Nora suddenly had a flashback of a busy shift at Parkland one night about a year ago when Carlos Ortega, a high ranking captain in the Mexican Mafia, came in with a gunshot wound to the right shoulder. No one knew who he was at the time. Sally had been the attending physician that night and spent quite a bit of time with him. Even though their conversations had been in Spanish, it had been easy to see that the physician-patient relationship was amiable. The two of them had an ongoing joke about sharing the same last name and probably being related. Ever since that night Carlos Ortega had called on Sally to help out some of his friends with medical care when needed. She would go in on her time off to take care of them and occasionally did so while the patients were still in police custody. Now even from a prison cell, Carlos Ortega was a powerful man who never forgot those who had helped him along the way.

"But you think Jack's strange behavior today might have something to do with his involvement in drugs?" Sally asked.

"I don't know. Maybe." Nora pushed open the door to the truck. "You stay here."

"I'm not letting you go in there alone."

Nora shut the truck off, but left the keys in it. They both got out and Nora felt less nervous having Sally beside her. As they got closer to the porch, Nora saw two people inside the living room. Jack came to the door and Nora was relieved to see him.

"Nora," Jack said. "Dr. Ortega." He nodded to both of them.

Nora picked up the carton of eggs on the porch and came up the steps.

"Everything okay?" she asked.

"Everything's fine."

"You have company?" Not waiting for him to answer, Nora opened the screen door and saw Officer Stick McBroom standing to the left of the door. "Stick," Nora said. "Are we interrupting something?"

"Not really," Stick said. His police uniform was too big for him and he towered over all three of them. He looked like an outrageously tall scarecrow posing as a cop. "Just havin' a little chat with my friend Jack here."

"Excuse me, officer," Sally said. She turned to Jack, pointed to Stick and asked, "Is this the gentleman who moved into our territory?"

Nora, Jack and Officer McBroom all looked at her. Sally waited patiently for an answer, but Jack was clearly confused. Nora's didn't understand what Sally was talking about either, but she suddenly had some questions of her own to ask.

"Is this the little problem we discussed yesterday?" Nora asked her cousin as she nodded toward Stick.

Jack nodded.

No wonder he was so certain he wouldn't be going to jail over any of this, Nora thought. *He's growing pot for the local police!*

"You told her?" Stick snapped. "You dumb-ass mother—"

"Hey!" Sally yelled. "Watch your mouth!"

Stick was startled into silence by her outburst.

"I didn't tell her anything," Jack said. "She found it on her own."

"You've both got another problem," Sally said to the men. "I suggest we all sit down."

"Sorry, Jack old boy," Stick said, "but I've gotta be going."

"I said sit down," Sally repeated with enough menace in her voice to get everyone's attention. "All of you."

Everyone took a seat except for Sally. She stood in front of them with a no-nonsense expression on her beautiful face.

"Perhaps I need to introduce myself," she said. "My uncle, General Carlos Ortega, wasn't happy to learn that someone else was moving drugs through this area. He—"

"Who?" Stick asked. "General who? What the hell do we care about some—"

"She's here representing the head of the Mexican Mafia, you moron," Nora said dryly. It was all she could do to keep a straight face once she figured out what Sally was doing. *Let's see how good of an actress she really is,* Nora thought as she sat back to watch the show. If Sally was talented enough to put herself through medical school acting in commercials, she should be good enough to convince Jack and Stick McBroom of just about anything.

Wide-eyed Stick slowly said, "The Mexican—"

"Mafia," Jack finished for him.

Sally nodded and had the most adorable smirk on her face. "Do I have your attention now?" she asked Stick. "My uncle is not happy with either of you. He wants his money."

"Money?" Stick said. "What money?"

"This is his territory," Sally said. "All drugs are his. All the money is his. You don't get to be a general by letting *pendejos* like you cut into his profits. So where is his money?"

"There ain't no money," Stick said.

Sally shook her head. "My *tío* won't like hearing that."

"What if . . ." Jack said. "What if we promise not to plant any more?"

"He doesn't care what you plant or grow here," Sally said, "as long as he gets the money for it." She held out her palm and pointed her other index finger in it. "This is his *territory*! You work for *him* if you're dealing drugs!" She turned to look directly at Jack. "Where's his money?"

"It's gone," Jack said quietly.

Sally looked at Stick. "Where's his money?"

"There ain't no money," Stick said.

Sally glared at them both and then slowly took her cell phone out of her pocket. She opened it up and dialed a number. During the next two minutes, Sally rattled off Spanish so fast that Nora was only able to pick up a word here and there. Finally, Sally stopped talking and appeared to be listening.

"*Sí*," she said. "*Sí. Uno momento.*" She took the phone away from her ear and held it against her right breast so whoever she was talking to couldn't hear what she was saying.

"What's going on?" Nora asked. "Who are you talking to?"

"One of my uncle's captains. They want to come here and shoot them," Sally said, indicating Jack and Stick.

"Uh-oh," Jack said under his breath.

"Shoot us?" Stick repeated. "Maybe they don't know who I am."

"Oh, they know who you are," Sally said simply. She put the phone up to her ear again and rattled off another few sentences in Spanish.

"Hold on a minute," Stick said, waving his hands in the air. "What are you tellin' him?"

"*Uno momento,*" Sally said into the phone again. She looked over at Stick and said, "As a special favor to my friend Nora, I'm trying to talk him out of coming here and killing both of you. This is a serious offense. This is his *territory*!"

"What if," Jack said again. He sat forward in his chair and Nora could see the uneasiness in his eyes. "What if we promise not to do it again?" Jack asked.

"Yeah," Stick said. "What if we—"

"Where's the money for the drugs you had?" Sally asked.

"We told you already," Stick said. "It's gone. All of it."

Jack shook his head. "I'm not doing this again. I didn't know this was anybody's territory." He glanced over at Stick. "Did you know that? Did you know about the Mexican Mafia being around here?"

"I've heard of 'em," Stick said. "San Antonio is crawlin' with 'em."

Sally said something else into her phone and then closed it.

"What did you tell that guy?" Stick demanded.

The look Sally gave him nearly made Nora burst out laughing.

"Don't speak to me that way," Sally said.

Jack sat up a little straighter in his chair. "Is he coming out here?"

"I told him I would call back when I knew more about your intentions."

"My intentions?" Jack repeated. "My intentions include growing melons and corn from now on. I don't know what *his* intentions are," he said pointing to Stick.

Sally looked at Stick. "Your intentions are?"

Stick nodded, his long neck reminding Nora of a huge bobble head toy in a breeze. "I'll be writing a lot more tickets now, I suppose."

Sally looked at both men slowly as if sizing up their words and their character. She then turned her attention to Nora and asked, "Can either of them be trusted to do what they say?"

"Jack can," Nora said. "I'm not sure about this one, though."

"Now, Nora," Stick said. "You've known me a long time. Me and your brother go back—"

"Jack's out," Nora said to him. "He won't be planting anything else for you."

"I know! I know!" Stick said. "I'm out, too. I didn't realize this was someone else's territory. Just trying to make a few extra—"

"We don't have any money," Jack said, giving Stick a piercing look.

"Let me see what I can do," Sally said and pulled out her cell phone, dialed a number and chattered away in Spanish again.

265

Chapter Thirty-four

Nora watched Stick fidget in his seat. He eyed Sally, trying to see something new or phony about her, but she was so convincing that Jack was stunned, while Nora remained amused. Finally, Sally closed her phone again.

"I need to be goin'," Stick said, "or I'll be late to work."

"Then we have an understanding?" Sally asked.

"Oh, yes, ma'am," Stick said. "We do." He stood up. His skinny legs seemed to go on forever. "Can I have your uncle's name again?" he had the nerve to ask Sally.

"Of course. General Carlos Guadalupe Ortega," Sally said. "He's currently in Huntsville prison for drug trafficking since the murder charges couldn't be proven. You *do* know what the Mexican Mafia is, don't you? Their philosophy primarily involves ethnic solidarity and control of drug trafficking." Sally glared at Officer McBroom. "Did you hear that last part?" she asked. "The part about the control of drug trafficking?"

Nora saw Jack's involuntary shudder. She was certain that if

266

nothing else happened that day, at least they had gotten her cousin's attention.

"Your name again is?" Stick asked Sally.

Nora looked at him with a slow shake of her head. *This bozo doesn't know when to shut up.*

Sally smiled sweetly. "My name is Dr. Esperanza Carmen Ortega. My friends call me Sally. You can call me Dr. Ortega."

That made Nora chuckle.

"Would you like the name of my uncle's captain in San Antonio?" Sally asked. "I can have him come pay you a visit and reiterate everything we've discussed here."

"No, no," Stick and Jack said at the same time. "That won't be necessary," Stick added.

"When you get to your office and do some Googling," Sally said, "make sure you spell everyone's name correctly. That's Dr. Esperanza Carmen Ortega and General Carlos Guadalupe Ortega. You should have easy access to his Texas Department of Corrections number and his impressive rap sheet. I'll let him know you were interested in him."

"Oh, no need to do any of that," Stick said quickly as he did a long-legged crab walk toward the door. "I need to be going." He was out the door so fast that all Nora saw of him was a blur. He scrambled down the steps and a few seconds later his unmarked police car sped by the house and raced down the driveway.

Nora turned to find Jack sitting in his chair holding his head in his hands. Finally he said, "Oh . . . my . . . God."

Nora let him stew that way for a moment and then met Sally's eyes where she saw a twinkle of humor and mischievousness.

"You were amazing," Nora said to her. "Absolutely amazing."

"Let's hope we've heard the last of the stick officer."

"Excuse me," Jack said. "I need to go to the bathroom."

With Jack out of the room, Nora did all she could to resist hugging Sally.

"Do you think it worked?" Sally whispered.

With a smile and a shrug, Nora said, "I think it worked on Jack. He's probably losing his cookies right about now."

"If Barney Fife is as high up as this local operation goes," Sally said, "then we've probably heard the last of it."

"You think more local officers could be involved?"

"The stick officer didn't strike me as smart enough to pull this off on his own," Sally said. "Perhaps your cousin could fill us in on what he knows."

When Jack returned from the bathroom his face looked like chalk.

"Can I get either of you something to drink?" he asked. "Let's go in the kitchen. I can't think here in this room right now."

They followed him into the kitchen and sat down. Jack went to the refrigerator, got a beer, and drank most of it in one gulp. He offered them one, but they both declined.

"He was here to kick my ass," Jack said. "I only had one good arm to work with, so he might've succeeded. Then Aunt Opal and Holly showed up. That spooked him a little. He didn't want anyone to see us together, but he wouldn't let me go out to get my eggs." He drank the rest of his beer and threw the empty can away. "Jesus. What a dumb fuck."

Nora's eyes popped open. She had never heard him use the f-word before.

"Yes, he is," Sally said.

"I was talking about me," Jack said.

That made all three of them laugh and it helped break some of the tension.

"Nora, I can't have no Mexican Mafia captain coming down here to shoot me. That's not how I wanna die."

"Jack," Sally said. "I can see to it that no harm of that nature will come to you."

"But," Nora interjected, "you have to stay out of the drug business."

"That won't be a problem."

"If Stick starts harassing you in any way," Nora said, "tell me immediately."

"I have some interesting lowlife friends in high places," Sally said. "Murderers and thieves speak a language all their own."

On impulse Nora leaned over and quickly kissed Sally on the lips. Having trouble reeling in her delight in Sally's fine performance, Nora couldn't have stopped herself from expressing her gratitude even if she had wanted to.

"Oh, wow!" Jack said. "Do that again!"

Embarrassed, Nora said, "Oh, be quiet."

There was more laughter before Sally asked to see how Jack's arm was healing.

On the way back to Opal's house when Nora and Sally were finally alone, Nora asked, "Who were you talking to on the phone that whole time?"

"My cousin in El Paso," Sally said. "He's the one doing a general surgery residency there with the Army. I was lucky to find him home."

"He knew what you were doing?"

"You mean did he know I was blowing smoke up Barney Fife's butt? Yes. He knew and I would've done the same for him."

Nora parked the truck in front of her mother's house. "Well, I don't even know where to begin to thank you."

Sally smiled. "It's nice to know I could help you out in some way. Actually, it was kind of fun. Officer Barney or Stick or whatever his name is—"

"Stick McBroom," Nora said. "Even in grammar school he was taller than everyone else and skinny, skinny, skinny. His parents nicknamed him Stick and it stuck."

"Stick stuck?" Sally said.

They both giggled all the way into the house.

Nora took a shower first and then sat down in the living room to watch TV while Sally got ready. They still had to go to the hospital to check on Sally's payroll problem. Picking up the remote to turn the TV on, Nora saw that the Weather Channel was calling for a chance of showers in the area and indicated there was a little rain to the north of them. The temperatures would also be somewhat cooler than usual for late June as well.

Nora called her mother to let her know about Jack. "He's fine now," she said. "Sally checked him out."

"Okay. Good," Opal said. "I was worried. Oh, you missed a great pecan pie today. Holly had your share, too."

"We probably won't be here when you get home," Nora said. "We've got an errand to run at the hospital."

"Did I hear my name?" Sally asked as she came into the living room.

Such delightful scents mixing fragrant soap and Escape perfume drifted into the living room. Nora waved at Sally and then said good-bye to her mother on the phone.

"Wow," Nora said. "I forgot how great you always smell after a shower."

"Thank you."

"I need to dry my hair then we can go," Nora said.

She left the room and was glad for a moment alone to try and collect her thoughts. She still hadn't recovered from the ordeal at Jack's house earlier. Sally's resourcefulness on nearly all levels was almost too impressive for words. Her willingness to help Nora's family whether the problem was medical or criminal made Nora appreciate her friendship even more than she ever thought possible. Nora also realized that there were new feelings evolving for her where Sally was concerned. She tried to ignore the desire that stirred but it was getting a lot more difficult to do lately.

She finished blow drying her hair and pronounced herself ready to go. She went back into the living room and saw Sally just sitting there on the loveseat watching TV. *She's such a beautiful woman,* Nora thought as she stood there captivated by her. *And she probably saved Jack from a life of crime or worse today.*

Sally noticed her standing there and smiled. She turned off the

TV with the remote and stood up. Nora could imagine so easily walking into her arms and kissing her until their lips were numb, but for some reason she didn't have the courage.

"You ready?" Sally asked.

"Yeah."

"You look great."

"So do you," Nora replied. She found her keys, cell phone and the small backpack she usually carried with her and opened the door. She wondered how this could be happening to her as she locked the front door once they were out on the porch. A few weeks ago she thought she might be in love with someone else. And now, all Nora could think about was how good Sally smelled. She wanted so badly to kiss her.

"They say we might get some rain today," Sally commented. She looked up at the slightly overcast sky. "I doubt it, though."

"This time of year we'll settle for whatever we can get where rain is concerned," Nora said. She also looked up at the sky. "But don't hold your breath today. It looks like this every morning."

Gabe Moreno was in his office and saw them right away. He pulled out a personnel file from a cabinet behind his desk, sat down and furiously pecked on a small calculator. A few minutes later he nodded.

"I see what you mean, Dr. Ortega. It's a payroll error. I'll get it taken care of right away. You'll see the difference on your next check."

"Thank you," Sally said graciously.

"Anything else I can help you with?"

"That should do it. I appreciate your time," Sally said.

They all got up and Gabe walked out with them. When they reached the atrium near the emergency department Nora saw Kit Fleming come in the door.

"Nora!" Kit said. "Where is he?"

"Who?"

"Wyatt! He called me and said something about lightning! He was on his way here!"

Sally took off running toward the emergency department while Nora helped Kit sit down there in the waiting area in the lobby.

"You stay here," she said. "I'll see if I can find him." Nora took off in the same direction Sally had gone. *It's not fair,* she thought as she punched in the code to open the door. *This woman has been through enough already without having to worry about her son, too.*

Nora was overwhelmed with relief to see a pale and confused Wyatt Fleming leaning against the wall near the nurse's station.

"Wyatt," she said. Nora felt tears of happiness and relief at the sight of him.

He looked up, surprised to hear his name being called. He recognized her and flew into her arms.

"It's okay," she said. "Are you hurt?"

"No," he mumbled with a sniff. "Not really." Still holding onto her tightly, he finally let go after a moment.

"Your mother's here and she's worried about you. Let's go see her and you can tell us what happened."

Nora glanced around, but didn't see Sally or the physician on duty. The door to the trauma room was closed, so Nora assumed she was in there assisting.

They walked out into the atrium and Nora kept an arm around him the entire time. Kit jumped up when she saw them and ran to give her son a hug.

"Are you all right?" Kit asked through her tears.

Nora led them back to the waiting area where they all sat down.

"What happened?" Kit asked. "You scared me to death when you called."

"It wasn't raining, Mom," Wyatt said, "and there weren't even that many clouds in the sky. Darcy started to climb up the windmill and then I heard a boom and a giant flash of light."

"Darcy?" Nora said. "Darcy Tate?"

272

"Yeah, Darcy Tate," Wyatt said. "Whatever it was that hit us knocked me down. When I got up again I saw Darcy on the ground. I ran over to her and I thought she was dead. I don't even remember dragging her to the truck, but I must have. The next thing I knew I was driving toward the hospital. I found her cell phone and called nine-one-one as I was driving and then I called you," he said to his mother. "I don't even remember much about what happened once I got here."

"Was Darcy actually struck by the lightning?" Nora asked. She felt a sickening surge deep in the pit of her stomach.

"I don't know," Wyatt said. "I heard and felt the boom and I saw a flash. I don't know where it struck."

"Wait here," Nora said quietly. "I'll go see about Darcy." To Kit she said, "I'll have someone check him out soon. His memory loss could be from a head injury, so don't leave, okay?"

"All right," Kit said as she continued to hug him. They both seemed to be in shock.

Nora went back into the emergency department and then into the trauma room.

"I'm telling you the kid said there was a boom and a flash," Dr. Adler said to Sally. "We're treating a lightning strike."

He was the staff physician on duty. A short, young man with premature gray at the temples, Nora didn't particularly like working with him. He was a pompous ass most of the time, but she had to admit that he was a good doctor.

"Let's just try this," Sally said. "Her hypotensive shock might not be due to a lightning strike."

The words "hypotensive shock" sent a chill down Nora's spine. Apparently Darcy was suffering from the low blood pressure state of shock. There were too many people in the room for her to get any closer.

"The boy said boom and flash, Dr. Ortega," Adler said. "*Boom and flash.*"

"The lightning could have hit the ground and caused her to fall *off* the windmill," Sally insisted. "She doesn't have any burns. There's no real indication that lightning struck her. I think she needs an abdominal ultrasound now."

"We'll humor you, Dr. Ortega," Adler said to everyone in the trauma room. "Get Dr. Ortega the ultrasound machine."

Someone left and Nora tried to move in closer to the bed. It was the first time Sally realized she was there and put her hand on Nora's arm. Darcy looked lifeless laying there. She was breathing on her own, which was a good sign, but the uncertainty of her injuries had Nora worried.

"We're doing all we can," Sally whispered. "How's the boy?"

"He's got some memory loss," Nora said, unable to take her eyes off Darcy. "He might've hit his head on something. Can you check him over when you have a chance?"

Sally nodded. Everyone moved out of the way when the technician arrived with the ultrasound machine.

"If this isn't abdominal trauma, Dr. Ortega, you owe me dinner," Adler said.

Sally cut her eyes over at him and shook her head.

"Will you go out into the waiting area and make sure the boy isn't doing any worse?" Sally asked Nora. "Once we know more here, I'll be out to see you."

Nora looked at Darcy and felt a tear stream down her cheek. It seemed impossible that the young girl Nora had worked so hard to seduce one summer could be the same person on the bed. The thought of anything happening to her made Nora feel helpless. She went to the door and turned around one last time. Sally was watching her with concern and determination in her eyes. It was then that Nora realized why the three of them were walking this path together. Sally was there to save Darcy's life.

"Keep him awake," Nora said.

Wyatt had his head on his mother's shoulder, but Kit kept talking to him. She also filled Nora in on Wyatt's job with Darcy and about how much time the three of them had been spending together lately.

"There wasn't any rain," Wyatt kept saying over and over again. "How could there be lightning if there isn't any rain? I don't get it."

They all looked up as Sally came out the emergency department door. She wore a white lab coat, which Nora remembered seeing her in earlier, but she had no idea where she had gotten it from. She certainly hadn't been wearing one when they left the house.

"How is she?" Nora asked.

"Abdominal trauma from falling off the windmill," Sally reported. "She has a ruptured spleen and is on her way up to surgery now. She should be fine."

Wyatt and Kit hugged each other and Nora couldn't stop smiling.

"So you were right," Nora said.

"Dr. Adler learned something today."

"If we hadn't been here . . ." Nora said, letting the statement hang there in the air.

"But we were here," Sally said. "How are you feeling, young man?" she asked Wyatt. "I hear you're the one who brought Darcy in. She's very lucky you were there." To Kit Sally said, "Let's check him out and make sure he doesn't have a concussion."

Chapter Thirty-five

"What a long-ass day," Nora said as she opened the front door to the hospital for them and tried to remember where she had parked her car. Wyatt was being kept for observation and Kit stayed with him. Darcy was out of surgery already and doing well.

"Yes, it has been a long day," Sally agreed.

"We went from impersonating the Mexican Mafia to dealing with lightning," Nora said.

"With all that lying I did at your cousin's house, perhaps there was some confusion up there," Sally said, looking at the sky. "Lightning might've struck near the wrong lesbian."

"He or She doesn't make those kinds of mistakes," Nora assured her with a smile. "I don't know how to thank you for what you did today."

Sally shrugged. "You could buy me dinner, but your mother probably has something better cooking right now than we could get anywhere else in this part of the world."

On the drive back to Prescott, Sally talked about her experiences with patients who had actually been struck by lightning. She had even written a case study and two articles on the subject.

"Your girlfriend should have a full recovery," Sally concluded.

Nora could tell she enjoyed referring to Darcy as "your girlfriend," but Nora let it go by without comment. She drove over the cattle guard and down the driveway that led to her mother's house. She saw Jack's truck parked next to her mom's pickup. It felt good to be home.

"Why didn't you answer your cell phone?" Opal asked as soon as Nora went into the kitchen. Holly was helping her grandmother cook supper while Jack sat at the kitchen table watching them.

"I didn't hear it ringing," Nora said in her own defense.

"How many messages did we leave?" Opal asked her granddaughter. "Five? Thirty?"

Everyone including Opal laughed. Nora dug around in her backpack and found her cell phone. She checked to see if she had any messages and announced, "Seven."

"We had the police scanner on and heard about someone getting struck by lightning," Holly said. "Then they mentioned something about a windmill so we started calling around thinking you might be at the hospital."

"I was wondering about Darcy," Opal said, "but they also mentioned there was a boy with her and she doesn't have any kids. Answer your phone next time when we want to know something about other people's business!"

After the chuckles died down, Nora told them what happened and let them know the young man who got Darcy to the hospital was Wyatt.

"Oh my gosh!" Holly said. "That's right! He has a job now helping someone fix windmills. I forgot all about that!"

"The best part just happens to be—" Nora said as she looked across the table at Sally. Their eyes met and Nora suddenly lost all train of thought.

"What's the best part?" Jack asked. He leaned closer to Nora and whispered, "Let me know if you two are gonna kiss again. I don't wanna miss that."

"Oh, shut up!" Nora said with an elbow to his ribs.

"So what's the best part?" Holly asked.

"The best part is," Nora said, "our Dr. Ortega saved Darcy's life today."

"We don't know that Dr. Adler wouldn't have eventually come up with the correct diagnosis," Sally said.

"That's not what I heard from the support staff," Nora said. "He even nibbled a little crow afterward."

"Way to go, Sally," Holly said with a high five.

All through supper there were conversations about the egg run earlier in the day and the phenomena of a lightning strike without any sign of bad weather. Nora noticed how quiet Jack was during supper, but mostly attributed that to his appreciation for his Aunt Opal's cooking. Afterward, Nora and Holly did the dishes while the other three settled on the front porch to enjoy the evening and listen to the police scanner.

"She really saved your friend's life today?" Holly asked as she handed Nora a plate to dry.

"That's what I heard," Nora said.

"I'd like to be a doctor some day."

"You could probably be just about anything you set your mind to."

Holly handed her another hot, wet plate. "Is Sally your girlfriend?"

"She used to be."

"I know, but what about now?"

"No," Nora said. "She's not now."

"Does she have another girlfriend?"

"I don't think so."

Holly dunked the skillet into soapy water. "Grammie and I really like her."

"Good. I like her, too."

"But you don't like her the way you used to?"

"Did I say that?" Nora dried a glass and set it in the cupboard. "Why all the questions?"

"We think you're lonely."

Nora reached for the silverware Holly was rinsing. "We who?"

"Grammie and me."

"I'm fine. Don't worry about me. Besides, there are a lot worse things in life than being lonely."

They finished the dishes and joined everyone on the front porch. Nora noticed that Sally sat alone in the porch swing. That spot usually belonged to Nora and her mother every evening. Sally patted the place beside her and Nora obliged.

"What a day," Opal said from her wooden rocker.

"No kidding," Jack mumbled.

"If Wyatt's still in the hospital tomorrow, can I go see him?" Holly asked.

"We'll all go see him if he's still there," Opal said. "He's a brave boy. I'm not sure I could've gotten an unconscious Darcy Tate in a truck the way he did."

"It's amazing what we can do when we have to," Sally said. "The human mind and body are incredible. I never get tired of hearing stories like Wyatt's."

The police scanner crackled into the evening air like the abrupt interruption that it was. Nora still jumped each time it came on.

"Was that Officer Stick?" Sally asked, referring to the dispatcher's voice on the scanner.

"Stick McBroom," Holly said. "What were his parents thinking?"

Jack and Holly had dessert on the front porch while the other three listened to the low rumble of thunder in the distance. Nora couldn't stop thinking about Sally and how she had played such a big role in helping the Flemings and their friends that day. Listening to her easy laughter, feeling her arm pressed against Nora's as they sat together in the swing and an occasional whiff of her perfume when the breeze was just right made Nora want to be even closer to her. Holly's questions in the kitchen earlier had started Nora thinking about Sally in several ways. It had been a long time since intimacy was an issue for them, but Nora couldn't help but go back to the early days of their relationship.

"I heard about a farmer who won the lottery," Jack said. "Someone asked him what he was gonna do with all that money and he said, 'I guess I'll keep farmin' until it's all gone.'"

For Nora it was good to see Jack chisel out a little humor from his situation, but she could still see the weariness in his eyes.

"I'm gonna head on home," he said. "Another wonderful supper, Aunt Opal. Why don't the three of you come over to my place tomorrow evening? I'll throw some steaks on the grill."

"He must need more dishes washed, Grammie," Holly said teasing him.

"Oh, that's cold, young lady," he said with a smile. Jack stood up and came over to the swing and got down on one knee. He looked at Sally and Nora and said, "Thank you for what you did this morning. I'll make you proud of me yet, Nora." He stood up again and kissed Opal on the cheek. "See you tomorrow." At the bottom of the porch steps he turned and said, "You'll see. There won't be *any* dirty dishes when you get there tomorrow."

"Anyone here believe that?" Holly called out to him.

"You'll see!"

Opal was off to bed and Holly went to her room to chat with her friends online. Nora requested that the scanner be turned off so they could have some peace and quiet on the porch for a change. Thunder occasionally rumbled in the distance and oddly, it gave Nora such a nice, warm feeling.

"Are you tired?" Sally asked.

"Not really."

"Me neither. I guess I'm still all wound up from today's events."

"Did I thank you for everything you did?"

"Only about six times already," Sally said. "You're quite welcome. So when are you going to tell Jack I'm not really related to anyone in the Mexican Mafia?"

"Never."

"Ha-ha. Never?"

"Fear's good for him," Nora said. "He obviously has too much time on his hands. I want him looking over his shoulder for a while yet. I still haven't forgiven him for planting marijuana on my mother's property. Oh, don't get me started on that. I'll be too pissed off to sleep later."

"Ah. So that's what he did," Sally said. "Then I don't blame you. Keep him on the hook a while longer."

Without thinking, Nora reached over and took Sally's hand. It felt soft and familiar. She liked touching her.

"Can I ask you something?"

"Sure," Sally said.

"In your opinion, what do you think went wrong with us?"

"I was too demanding," Sally said without even having to think about it. "And perhaps a bit arrogant in some of my beliefs."

"Demanding, huh?"

"Am I right about that?"

"Maybe," Nora said.

"Tell me what you think happened."

Nora shrugged. "I never felt like you were serious about anything but your work. You were more interested in having someone to sleep with and go out for dinner occasionally. More like a friend with benefits, as they say. I guess I felt like you wanted to be entertained more than anything else."

Sally squeezed her hand. "I guess that's a fair assessment of what was going on. I can see now that I never took the time to tell you what I was feeling then. I just assumed you knew."

"We never really talked much about anything when we were together," Nora said.

"All that wild monkey sex," Sally said quietly. "I used to love hearing you call it that."

281

"There's more to a good relationship than wild monkey sex," Nora noted.

"I would do things a little differently now."

"Oh? How would it be different?"

"I'd make sure you knew every day how much I love you," Sally said quietly. "Every single day."

Nora felt a huge sense of relief rush into a tiny twinge of hope in her heart.

"When you had quit your job without telling me, it was an instant wake-up call," Sally continued. "Then when I realized you had moved without telling me I knew I had screwed up *really* bad. I never want to experience either of those things again in my lifetime."

Sally leaned closer and kissed her. Their lips lightly touched just moments before Nora reached up to put her hand on the back of Sally's head.

The kiss easily became a sweet mixture of heat and passion. Nora remembered nights of wanting this woman's touch and aching for her in a way that only Sally could satisfy. Making love with her had always been like magic for Nora and she had to admit that she missed it.

"Every single day," Sally whispered.

Nora kissed her again as the low sound of thunder accompanied the beating of her heart. *Even if this is a mistake*, Nora thought, *I want it.*

"I love you," Sally whispered.

Reaching for her breast and pushing her hand up under Sally's shirt, Nora said, "Come to bed with me. Please."

Nora switched on the lamp by her bed. Turning around she saw Sally leaning with her back against the closed bedroom door. Sally seemed to be watching her with acute but loving anxiety. The thrill of anticipation touched Nora's heart at the prospect of making love with her again. It seemed as though they had been moving toward this moment for weeks now.

"What's the matter, baby?" Nora asked as she moved across the room toward her. The silence loomed between them and Sally closed her eyes and took a deep breath. After a moment the tension was gone from her face when she opened her eyes.

"Talk to me," Nora whispered. "What's the matter?"

She felt a tight knot in her stomach at the possibility that Sally had changed her mind. The anxious expression on her face was something Nora had never seen before. With her heart thumping madly, Nora didn't know what to do. As casually as she could manage, she asked, "Have you changed your mind?"

When Sally tried to speak, her voice wavered. Awkwardly, she cleared her throat and tried to manage a feeble answer. In a hushed whisper she said, "I don't want this just for now . . . or just for tonight."

Her brown eyes were full of life—and pain. Nora felt a warm glow seep through her. She pressed her body against Sally's and kissed her with such passion that she suddenly felt weak. Sally's lips seared a path down her neck and shoulder before recapturing her mouth.

"I want this forever," Sally whispered before kissing Nora again. "Forever."

Somehow they ended up on Nora's bed with their clothes strewn about the room. She had no recollection of how they got to the bed and didn't really *care* how they got there. All Nora could think about right then was how perfect their bodies fit together and what a great kisser Sally was. Then Sally did something that Nora had forgotten about . . . something that never failed to light a fever of passion. Sally whispered something to her in Spanish, lightly touching Nora's ear with her lips. Nora had no idea what she said, but the rhythm and cadence of the words set her off into emphatic currents of desire. Her emotions whirled and skidded and Nora's senses reeled as if something had short-circuited. Blood pounded in her brain, leapt from her heart and made her tremble all over. How could she ever think of leaving this woman again?

How could she have so easily forgotten how good things were between them?

Nora surrendered to Sally's insistent need to please her. Nora's breasts surged at the intimacy of Sally's touch and craved the attention of her eager mouth. As Sally's fingers and tongue danced over Nora's hot, tight nipples she could hear the faint rhythmic whispers of Spanish. Instinctively, Nora's body arched toward her, wanting her lover to take more of her breast into her mouth. After taking her sweet time adoring Nora's body, Sally's lips traced a sensuous path down her pulsating flesh.

Nora moaned softly and surrendered to Sally's exploration of her body. Reaching down and filling her hands with Sally's dark, thick hair, Nora shamelessly opened her legs in a bold, blatant invitation.

"Oh, God," Sally said, her voice filled with emotion. "I love it when you do that."

Caught up in a net of growing arousal, Nora made a mental effort to keep from coming too soon. She wanted to prolong this pure and explosive pleasure, but she gasped as waves of ecstasy throbbed through her as Sally teased her with her tongue. Passion and exquisite sweetness pounded the blood through her heart, chest and head. Nora gripped Sally's hair and pulled her closer until every fleeting ripple of pleasure had subsided.

Love flowed in her like warm honey. Nora felt her defenses weakening as Sally kissed the inside of her thighs before lying down beside her. Contentment and peace slowly inched their way through Nora's brain with more of Sally's kisses. Tasting herself on Sally's lips awoke something new in Nora. She rolled Sally over on her back . . . warm flesh against flesh . . . woman against woman . . . as they melted against each other while desire coursed through their veins.

Nora woke up several hours later to the sound of rain. She covered them up with a sheet and kissed Sally's back and pressed her breasts against her warm skin. It seemed like the most natural way in the world to fall back to sleep. Sally stirred and wiggled her butt against Nora's belly.

"Mmm," she murmured sleepily.

Nora moved her hand up and found one of Sally's nipples. Lightly caressing it as she closed her eyes, they both drifted off to sleep again.

The first time Nora heard the rooster crow she got up, put on a robe and went to the bathroom. No one else was up yet. When she came out of the bathroom Nora found a sleepy Sally in the hallway waiting for her turn.

"I'll meet you back in bed," Nora whispered on her way by. She kissed Sally lightly on the lips and returned to her room. A few minutes later she heard her mother's voice in the hallway. Nora was disappointed when Sally didn't come back to bed with her.

She got up, put her robe on again and made the bed. There were so many things she would've liked to talk to Sally about. *A little cuddling session would've been nice this morning*, she thought. Tightening the sash on her robe, she went into the kitchen and found her mother with a can full of chicken scratch for her girls and Sally holding two cups of coffee.

"I was just on my way to see you," Sally said. Her hair had that "I haven't been up that long" look that Nora always thought was so adorable on her.

"You were?" Nora said, pleasantly surprised. "Then let me go back to my room." She turned and left the kitchen. A short time later Sally came in holding the two coffee cups and gently closed the door with her foot. She sat down on the bed beside Nora and handed her one of the cups.

"This is nice," Nora said. "Thank you."

"It didn't seem right to sneak back into your room with your mother up puttering around."

Nora smiled. "She doesn't care about things like that."

Sally took a cautious sip of her coffee. Nora sipped hers too and then set both cups on the nightstand.

"There's something I want to tell you," Nora said. She already knew that Sally was in love with her and during their evening of passion Nora had tried to show Sally how much she meant to her. Nora remembered saying once as they were falling asleep that she loved her, but Nora couldn't be sure that Sally had heard anything. She wanted there to be no doubts where feelings were concerned. If nothing else, being with Darcy Tate had taught Nora the importance of communication.

Sally sat on the edge of the bed with her arms crossed hugging her body. "You're scaring me," she said quietly.

"What?"

"If you're about to tell me that last night was . . . was . . ." She sniffed and Nora saw a tear roll down her cheek.

"You're crying!" Nora put her arm around her and pulled Sally close. Kissing the top of her head, Nora felt tears of her own stinging her eyes. "I was about to tell you again how much I love you," she whispered. "This has taken us full circle. I've gone from avoiding you to craving you. I don't know how it happened or why it happened. All I know is I want to be with you. It's like you're the missing piece in my life now."

Sally crumbled into her arms and sobbed, holding onto her tightly. Nora kissed her hair and whispered, "It's okay, baby." Nora sniffed too. "I think we both realize that we've got a lot more going on here than wild monkey sex."

Through their tears and laughter they kissed again. Nora stopped trying to analyze it. The only thing that made sense to her now was how Sally made her feel. In her heart Nora knew this was the person she was supposed to be with.

Epilogue

Ten Months Later

Darcy felt a huge sense of relief when the first rush of water came out of the Franken-mill. Wyatt's enthusiasm made them all laugh as they watched his Fleming Feed and Seed cap sail through the air.

"We did it!" he shouted. "We've got water!"

"Hey, you had doubts?" Darcy asked.

"I didn't think so while we were putting it together," he said, "but then maybe I did since I'm so happy to see it really working now."

Darcy reached down and picked up his cap and stuck it on his head.

"How many windmills have you set up from scratch?" Kit asked her.

Darcy looked at the windmill with a new sense of pride and

accomplishment. Putting one together from spare parts and using her welding skills to firm up a few pieces here and there had been fun and challenging.

"Actually, this is my first one going solo," Darcy said, "and I have to admit it looks pretty good."

Kit smiled. "It's pumping water so that's all I care about."

Since her recovery from the accident, Darcy had learned several things while her injuries healed, the most important being the value of friendship. She would forever be grateful to Wyatt for his courage and resourcefulness in a life and death situation. His sense of urgency and quick thinking no doubt had saved her life. It also didn't take long for Darcy to remember how fast news traveled in a small town. She had received cards, flowers and phone calls from customers and neighbors while she was still in the hospital. And Wyatt and Kit were there every day to visit. The Hometown News also covered the accident and followed her progress until she was on her feet again. Darcy even got a nice long visit from Opal and Nora just before she was released from the hospital.

"Can you stay for supper?" Kit asked. Her smile warmed Darcy's heart. She adored this woman and was glad to finally get the windmill project completed for her.

"What are we having?" Wyatt asked.

"Sloppy Joes."

"Mmm. My favorite," he said. Wyatt went over to the windmill and filled his hands with water before looking up at the spinning blades. "We did it, Darcy. We got it going from old boneyard parts."

Kit leaned against Darcy and gave her a nudge with her shoulder. "He's sure proud of that Franken-mill."

"He should be," Darcy said. "I couldn't have done it without him." She liked the way Kit had been touching her lately, a hand on the shoulder or sweeping a wayward lock of hair from Darcy's brow. Since the accident they had grown closer and Darcy was enjoying getting to know her better.

"So can you stay for supper?" Kit asked her again.

"Sure," Darcy said. She smiled and was looking forward to spending the evening with them.

Nora, Sally, Opal, Greg and Holly all gathered around the kitchen table one Saturday evening in April. Nora handed a sheet of paper to each of them.

"This is what we came up with," she said. Holding up her piece of paper, Nora pointed to the far left on the diagram. "We build a large master bedroom here with its own full bath. That'll be our room," she said, indicating her and Sally. "Then we'll put in another bathroom here just because." Nora pointed even further to the left. "Building out this way shouldn't disturb the girls at all."

"Two more bathrooms?" Greg asked. "If the new master bedroom has its own bathroom, why would we need another one?"

Opal nodded. "That's what I was wondering, too."

"Wouldn't it be nice to have a bathroom that you could turn the light on at night if you wanted to?" Nora asked with a teasing smile.

Greg scratched his head. "Wouldn't it be a lot cheaper to just relocate that rooster somewhere else?"

"Actually," Nora said ignoring him, "the extra bathroom will be totally handicapped accessible. No one's getting any younger around here. That was Sally's idea. All the new additions will be handicapped accessible."

"Hmm," Greg said. "I think that's a good idea."

"These plans look fine to me," Opal said.

Nora sighed heavily. "Good. Then we'll get on it right away. Hopefully the new additions will be done by the time Greg and Holly move to San Antonio this summer."

Opal held her copy of the paper in both hands and looked at the drawing of her house. She smiled and set the diagram down. "Having my kids so close to home again has been a dream of mine for many, many years." She reached over and gave Sally's hand a pat. "You're like one of my kids, too."

Nora saw the tears well up in Sally's eyes. Things had been so good between them since Sally had moved to Prescott that Nora couldn't imagine being any happier. They still worked part time together at the county hospital a few shifts a month and Sally had gotten a fulltime position at University Hospital in San Antonio making an outrageous amount of money.

Greg picked up the diagram that was in front of him and studied it again for a moment. "It would still be a lot cheaper to just move that rooster somewhere else."

Nora took the piece of paper out of his hand and set it on the table. "And that's why you're not in charge of any of this."

As the chuckles went around the table and Greg made a face and stuck his tongue out at her, Nora felt the warmth and love spread through her body as she looked at each of them. She was home with her family and nothing meant more to her than being there with them. Sally's smile was contagious as she winked at Nora across the table.

"If we took that rooster over to Jack's house," Greg said, "it would save about—"

"It's like Nora said," Opal interrupted as she held the diagram firmly and looked over the top of it at her son. "That's why you're not in charge of any of this."